D1053136

Also by William Wharton

BIRDY

DAD

THESE ARE BORZOI BOOKS
PUBLISHED IN NEW YORK
BY ALFRED A. KNOPF

A Midnight Clear

A
MIDNIGHT
CLEAR

William Wharton

ALFRED A. KNOPF   NEW YORK   1982

THIS IS A BORZOI BOOK
PUBLISHED BY ALFRED A. KNOPF, INC.

Grateful acknowledgment is made to Lewis Music
Publishing Company, Inc., for permission to reprint from
the lyrics of "The Jersey Bounce," words and music by
Feyne, Plater, Bradshaw, and Johnson. © 1941 Lewis
Music Publishing Co., Inc., Carlstadt, N.J. Copyright
Renewed. Used by permission.

Library of Congress Cataloging in Publication Data
Wharton, William. A midnight clear.
I. Title.
PS3573.H32M5   813'.54   81-20897
ISBN 0-394-51967-1   AACR2

Manufactured in the United States of America
First Edition

To those ASTPRers who never
reached majority

...We need you now.

FEAR

I gasp in the still of one breath;
A wisp of bird feathers burning,
The smell of death in a flower.

Nothing to see and nothing to say;
Afraid to look, I can't turn away;
My blink of emptiness pearling gray.

I watch myself watching me watching me.

The names in this
wintry Christmas tale
have been changed to
protect the guilty. . . .

—W.W.

A Midnight Clear

1
Briefing

"Holy God, Mother! What's the matter?"

He pushes me back hard against my shelter half. He struggles, elbows, presses himself to his feet, boots sinking ankle deep in mud and melted snow at the bottom of our dent. He stands there, looming over me, staggering, slipping, not saying anything; staring into the sky.

Then he unslings his M1, grabs it in his right hand, arches his lean body into a tight spring and tosses that rifle, like a javelin, out of our hole, in a long, twisting arc at least a hundred feet downhill. He throws so hard his metal-rimmed GI glasses fly off his face, bounce against my chest and slide slowly into mud and water. They're going to get smashed for sure.

He doesn't look at me. Without his glasses, Mother's face seems empty; he probably couldn't see me anyhow, even if he did look.

We've been squatting in what could be a leftover one-man trench from World War I, but is probably only a root hole from a rotted, blown-down tree.

Over the past two and a half hours we haven't said much. We're on for four. Sometimes I think Mother might be crying but I don't look; I'm so close to it myself, I don't want to start anything. Mother's scrambling now, rifleless, up onto the edge of our hole. He's pulling at his webbing equipment, trying to unhook it.

Normally, the band would be standing this perimeter guard, but they're in town with the officers entertaining Red Cross ladies. The Red Cross battled its way up to our regiment yesterday and sold us doughnuts, ten cents apiece, two lines, enlisted men and officers. I didn't peek to see if officers paid. I bought one and shat it half an hour later.

Squatting there with Mother, I'd been watching one of those little buzzing L5 artillery observation planes circling over us. The motor has a peaceful sound like an airplane on a summer day at the shore dragging an advertisement saying

P E P S I - C O L A

in the sky. Only now it's winter and it isn't peaceful.

I lean down, carefully pick up Mother's glasses, then shove myself off from the bottom of our hole, pushing against my muddy shelter half. The frame's twisted but nothing's broken; the lenses are thick as milk-bottle bottoms; they'd be hard to break. But they're slippery, gritty, wet and smeared with mud.

Mother's up on the lip of the hole. Now he's crying hard but isn't making much noise. I start scrabbling my way out; I want to pull him back down before someone sees us.

We're on the side of a hill at the edge of a forest. In fact, we're surrounded by hilly forests. It's snowed a few times but green's showing through today and mostly everything's either thin hard-crusted snow or mud. I know it's somewhere around mid-December, but that's about all. Even though we're in reserve here, for some reason neither mail nor *Stars & Stripes* has been getting through.

Now Mother takes off. He's gotten himself unhooked and slings his ammo belt, his pack, entrenching tool, bayonet, canteen; the whole kit and caboodle, looping, twisting through the air, downhill. Just before he disappears into the trees, he flips his helmet, discus-style, off in the direction of his rifle. He acts as if he really *is* quitting the war!

I'm torn between running after him and not deserting the post. After all, I am sergeant of the guard; can you believe that? I don't.

First, I run down to get the rifle, helmet and webbing equipment. Then I run after Mother, picking up his things as I go. When I reach down to snatch up his field jacket, I peer back; nobody's watching. Everybody with any sense is sleeping, taking advantage of all those missing officers. I know both Ware, that's our platoon leader, and Major Love, our S2, are off playing "hero" for the ladies. We still don't have a new platoon sergeant, either.

I prop my rifle against the first tree, with Mother's things, and run after him. He's speeding like the wind, not looking back. Without his glasses he's liable to smash into a tree. There's no use hollering, so I squeeze tight and keep on. Who knows, maybe he'll run us both right on out of the war, through division, corps, army, the whole rear guard. Maybe we'll find a French family with a lovely daughter and they'll hide us. If we get caught, I can always say I was only trying to catch Mother, trying to salvage government equipment, picking up Mother's clothes.

The trouble is we're going the wrong way. He's headed south; all we'll do is run into the perimeter guard for some *other* tired, mixed-up regiment. We're all so scared we'll shoot at anything, especially some bare-assed, bare-eyed skeleton in boots.

From what I've scooped up so far, Mother is down to boots and socks. I almost caught him while he pulled off his pants, but when I stopped to pick them up, he scooted away again. We're playing a unique version of *Hänsel and Gretel* with strip poker overtones; or maybe something of Atalanta's race.

Because of the exertion, I'm having my usual problem; the stomach's turning upside down; soundless, burning squirts are slipping out. I'll smell like a portable latrine when I catch up with Mother. Big headlines: POISON GAS USED IN ARDENNES!

Mother's definitely outdistancing me. I determine to grit it hard for another burst of two hundred yards, then I'll have to give up. Christ, what'll I tell Ware?

The next time I look, I don't see Mother anywhere. We're still in forest but we've gone down a steep hill. Then I spot him. He's flopped into a streambed and is digging in it, throwing rocks left and right like a dog searching a bone. I slow down, stunned, and stop, staring, while I catch my breath.

I start moving slowly downhill toward him, wondering what's next. What happens now? What sergeant-like thing am I supposed to do? I'm sliding and slipping on a combination of iced snow and pine needles. My entire body's shaking. These days, I'm so shaky most of the time I need to wait for a good quiet moment to draw or even write a letter. I've taken to printing in capital letters, short quick strokes; not much chance for a wild, erratic, uncontrolled twitch to give me away.

I squat at the edge of the stream beside Mother. That water's got to be ice cold but he's kneeling in it on naked, white legs. I know I'm thin, what with my GIs and all, but Mother's so skinny it's hard to believe he's even alive.

I stay there quietly, watching him toss stones, concentrating between his knees. I've got to do something.

"Here, Mother, I have your glasses. You forgot them up there in our dent."

He turns and stares blankly at me, stops digging, kneeling in that fast-running, cold, clear stream. I hold the glasses out. Slowly he crawls toward me, takes hold and slips the glasses across his eyes, carefully hooking behind his ears. He'd stopped crying but now he starts again. I help pull him out of the creek and we don't say anything. I can't think of a single word I can possibly say to make any sense and I'm not sure Mother could talk if he wanted to.

Piece by piece, I hand him his clothes and he puts them on. He dresses slowly, taking deep breaths, as if he's in a barracks on a Sunday morning. His boots and socks are soaking wet, but after he buttons his field jacket, he looks almost normal; except for his blue-white face and the crying.

"Mother, I've got your rifle, helmet and webbing stuff back there at the edge of the forest. How are you feeling?"

Mother looks into my eyes for the first time since he started running. Snot and tears are smeared across his face. God, it's so weird seeing *our* Mother Wilkins like this.

We call him Mother Hen Wilkins because he's always hounding *us* for being sloppy, bugging us about leaving things around or not cleaning out mess kits and canteen cups. Once Fred Brandt complained how Wilkins would sneak up on everyone after breakfast and give the sniff test to see if we'd brushed our teeth.

Mother's one of the oldest in our squad and he's married. He had his twenty-sixth birthday two days before his baby was born dead. Mundy told me that. Some birthday present!

Mother's still staring at me through his fogged-up glasses. He's leaning slightly forward with his arms dangling in front of him, a puppet waiting to be used. He starts talking in his slow, careful way, thinking out each word, every phrase, sentence, as if it's going to be engraved on platinum.

"You know, Wont, I don't know if I have combat fatigue or not. One whole part of me knows everything I just did, from tossing my M1 to scratching in this frozen creek. One part of me knew and wanted to stop, but another part kept going, wanted to keep running, throwing off things, doing any kind of crazy business it could think of. That part was definitely bucking for Section Eight. That part, the deepest inside part of me, will do anything to get out of all this and go home with Linda."

"Want me to turn you in, Vance? I could write up the most beautiful Section Eight certification evidence anybody ever heard of. Between the actual wild things you just did and the stuff I'd make up, you'd at least get back to some psychiatrist in a hospital."

Mother lowers himself cross-legged onto the ground. He props his head in his frozen hands, his elbows on his knees. He's thinking about it all right.

"No, I'd never make it. I'm still not scared enough. I'm too scared of them and not scared enough of myself. I couldn't fool anybody. Part of what let me go through all this shit was it was only you there and it didn't really count."

"You sure fooled me, Mother; I'll tell you that. You also broke a squad rule."

He lifts his head off his hands, straightens up.

"What rule? What squad rule did I break?"

"You said 'shit.' What would Father say? Don't let them

get to you, Mother. No matter what happens, don't let them get you."

There are many peculiar things about our squad. I'll start out with a few. First, we almost never call the Germans KRAUT or JERRY or HUN or NAZIS, any of the usual army names. At the most, they're "the enemy." Only Stan Shutzer, our professional Jew, calls them anything he wants. Father Paul Mundy gave him a special dispensation. Yes, we have a squad father, too; Mother Wilkins, Father Mundy. But that isn't the second squad's second peculiarity, it's only an accident.

Father Mundy invented our squad "no obscenity" rule. We want to make it clear we are not actually part of this army. We're princely orphans left on the wrong doorstep, maybe bastards of the blood. It helps. This might well be one of Father's greatest coups. For a guy who acts so dumb sometimes, he can be shrewd. Mundy's twenty-six, a dropout —but not fallen—almost priest. He and Mother are the old men in the squad now, the rest of us are under twenty.

We pick up our equipment at the edge of the forest and are back in our dirt dent before the next guard comes on. Mother's got himself fairly well in hand. It'll be Bud Miller, our mechanical genius, crossword-puzzle inventor and child poet, along with Stan Shutzer, Jewish avenger and aspiring millionaire advertising executive. Both Bud and Stan have jewelers for fathers, but I think it's about the only thing they have in common, except being smart and at the same time dumb enough to be in an infantry I and R squad. They're on the next four, from two to six. Edwards's squad's got the night part but then there're twelve of them so they can keep it two hours each, and it shouldn't be bad. After the ball is over, the musicians will take their usual guard duty again.

Mother and I straggle back to our bivouac. He and I are tenting together now. Before the Saar, he was with Jim Freize. Jim was definitely a close second to Mother in the neatness competition. They'd fuss around getting their area cleaned up, everything neatly packed away; then they'd meander down to the motor pool to wipe and shine their jeep. Neither of them knew the first thing about how to keep a jeep running, but theirs was always spic and span, even in the damned Metz mud. Miller, the mad mechanic, won't let the motor pool jocks near any of our squad jeeps, but he'd only laugh at Jim and Mother puttering around.

I crawl into my sloppy side of our tent and pull out the book we're reading right now. It's called *A Farewell to Arms*. I have pages 215 to 310. Wilkins is ahead of me and Shutzer behind. Shutzer's been hounding me all day to hurry it up; Wilkins finished last night. It's just my luck being caught between two of the fastest readers on our side of the Siegfried Line. We rip books apart so we can read them together.

The book before this was *All Quiet on the Western Front*. We talked it over and voted as a squad to quit the war first chance we got. We were still together then, outside Saarbrücken. Father Mundy didn't realize, until we told him, the characters in the book were German. But he might have gotten skipped over with some pages. We usually leave Father until last; he reads each word as if he's licking it.

I finish my pages and put them at the opening of our tent for Shutzer.

This chapter is called briefing. There is a typical military briefing coming up soon but I think I should give our real briefing here while I'm supposed to be drifting off to sleep.

Briefing, in the army, means explaining. The army mind wants everything short and simple, except wars. Maybe that's why they call it briefing. But sometimes it's hard to be short and simple. Probably, in a certain way, this whole book, not just this chapter, is a briefing; but I'm not quite sure for or about what.

Our squad is half of the I and R platoon, the second half. The I is for intelligence, the R for reconnaissance. The I and R platoon is part of the regimental headquarters company of the Umpty-eleventh Regiment, of the Eighty-tenth Infantry Division. A regimental headquarters company is basically a lot of nothing.

To give an idea. We have a bird colonel, his adjutant and assistant; all and each with orderlies. There's the S_1, S_2, S_3, S_4, S_5 and so on, each a major, each with an assistant, all with orderlies. An orderly in the army is a low-paid military servant.

Then, we have cooks, cooks' helpers, cooks' assistants, permanent KPs, supply clerks, mail clerks, file clerks, typists, messengers; a plethora of personnel people, plus the motor pool crowd. The motor pool is where they park the vehicles, almost exclusively jeeps, staff cars or two-and-a-half-ton trucks; nothing very warlike. Actually these vehicles mostly only carry people and their junk from one place to another. The drivers of this hauling fleet are T_4s and T_5s; that is, sergeants and corporals who aren't expected to shoot anybody on purpose.

We've also got the regimental band: thirty of the most unlikely soldiers to be found on the wrong side of division. As I said, they usually stand perimeter guard for the company. I've never heard them play, but then there haven't been many parades. We liberated a violin at Rouen and Mel Gordon wanted a tryout but was told there's no room for violins in a military band. But wouldn't it be great, hearing taps or reveille—better yet, retreat—played on a violin?

Last and least comes the I and R platoon. There are twelve in a squad; squad leader's buck sergeant, assistant corporal; no orderlies. Our squad is down to six. Mel Gordon became corporal to our squad the same time I made sergeant. It wasn't for much we did except stay alive. He hasn't sewn on his stripes yet, either.

I and R is the eyes and ears for S2. S2 is regimental intelligence. Our S2 is Major Love, both name and job gruesomely inappropriate. Love was a mortician in civilian life. He's "eyes and ears" to Colonel Douglas Sugger, regimental commander, usually referred to as "the Dug Sucker." The Dug's a past master at war costumes and heroic jaw thrusting. Major Love has a slight talent for jaw thrusting, too.

Love's main passion is generating business for his professional colleagues, the grave registrars. His most available target has been the I and R platoon, with which he has had some sporadic but notable success. Whistle Tompkins always claimed that any living, moving human body was an insult to Love's sense of propriety.

It's thanks to Love and his military-mortuary skills I've made my recent headlong leap to three stripes. We lost half our squad in the Saar, attempting one of his map-inspired, ill-conceived, so-called "recon" patrols. You can't imagine how meaningless and stupid this was. It's so bad I won't tell about it; I hope.

When I say *lost*, I mean killed. Nobody in the army ever admits someone on *our* side is killed. They're either lost, like Christopher Robin; hit, as in batter *hit* by a pitched ball, take your base, or they get "it," as in hide-and-seek, or, maybe, "get it," as with an ambiguous joke.

Our squad leader was Max Lewis, twenty. His assistant, Louis Corrollo, nineteen. We called them "the Louie [like *Louie, Louie, You Gotta Go*] twins." The other four of us who got "it" that day were Morrie Margolis, Whistle Tompkins, Fred Brandt and Jim Freize.

Morrie was my tentmate. We shared shelter halfs, buttoned them together to make a pup tent, shared other things, too. Not one of those six had an AGCT (AGCT is another inbuilt military paradox, an *army* intelligence test) score of under 150; each, intellectually, one in ten thousand. But that's all another story, a story even more stupid than Love's patrol. I'm liable to tell that one.

I have a penchant for telling true stories no one can believe.

My being squad leader is also another story. It's another story the way *Peter Rabbit* is another story from *Crime and Punishment*.

Our division took a mauling outside Saarbrücken. We gained a few miles of European real estate and lost the beginnings to untolled (much more than untold) generations of very bright people. I think the U.S. Army considered this a good deal.

So now we've been moved north into the Ardennes Forest to rest and wait replacements. This is supposed to be a sector where nothing's ever happened and nothing is ever going to happen, a kind of high-class halfway house; a front-line position for adjusting makeup, straightening out nerves and general refurbishing.

I'm not sure if I myself am recuperable. I'm scared all the time and can't sleep, not even on a long guard. I've already had two crying fits but nobody saw me and I gave them every chance. I hung around Mel Gordon, our unofficial squad doctor and psychiatrist, moaning, but he didn't even notice. Nobody wants to look.

My biggest immediate trouble is an absolutely historic case of GIs. Thank God for olive drab underwear.

The medics here have marked me down as a paregoric addict and won't give me any more. Yesterday I walked to my old company, Company L, and begged two doses from Brenner, third platoon medic.

I shat five times going and only three coming back so it must've helped. I'm eating K ration biscuits and K lunch cheese almost exclusively; but I'm too gut scared for processing food. Making me squad (try squat) leader might be one of the greatest impractical jokes of the war.

With this jolly thought, I end our briefing and drift off into what passes for sleep these days; Mother is snoring beside me.

In the morning, Lieutenant Ware pulls open our tent flap; the pages are gone; Shutzer got them, I hope.

"Sergeant Knott, Major Love wants us at the S2 tent. You chow up, then I'll come by at o-*nine*-hundred."

He waits to make sure I'm awake, then he's gone. I lie back and try to think of some appropriate non-obscene word to express my feelings. I'm not awake enough. "Shit!" is all that comes. Father says we are succumbing internally if we think in their terms. I admit it; inside, I've succumbed. Maybe *that's* why they made me squad leader. Maybe that's why I have the GIs, too; I'm polluted.

But it's better this morning. I can even lean over to lace my boots without feeling I'm squeezing a balloon filled with sewer water in my stomach.

While I'm getting dressed, wriggling in a pup tent, trying not to wake Wilkins, I should explain something about my name; more briefing. Our family name is Knott. My parents wanted to call me Bill or Billy, but because there's no Saint Bill or Billy, I was named William. They insist no joke was intended.

By third grade at school, I was Will Knott. I learned to live with it, my private martyrdom. So I was more or less prepared to grit it out again in the army, Willingly or Knott (Ha!). What I wasn't ready for was the conglomeration of certified wise guys and punsters called the I and R platoon. They decided my nickname must be Wont or Won't; only the spelling was contended.

All through basic, the controversy raged. Max Lewis was leader of the apostrophe group, claiming I'm a natural radical, troublemaker and guardhouse lawyer who *Won't* do anything I'm told. Mel Gordon headed the no-apostrophe crowd, insisting I'm too nice, and *Wont* to do anything I'm asked.

They called themselves "the apostates" and "the anti-apostates." Father Mundy says it's all in the mind of the beholder.

So everybody calls me Won't or Wont and it's up to me. That is, all except Max, who called me W-O-N-apostrophe-T right up till he got IT.

I'm dressed now and sliding out of the tent, mess kit and cup in hand. I see Mother Wilkins has cleaned out the bottom of my cup again. I wonder what he leaves for his wife to do at home?

I mention all the above nonsense about my name to give some idea of the wheel spinning that can go on when you have too much brain power concentrated in too small a place. Our squad has one hell of a lot of intelligence but not much reconnaissance. We're a covey of nit-picking Talmudic Jesuit Sophists continuously elaborating one unending bead game.

. . .

I decide to take the big risk and eat some regular, scrambled hot eggs and one sausage. I know better than to try coffee. Coffee works like castor oil on me. I'm not sure if it's coffee itself or all the coffee I've drunk scared; but the smell, the taste, the *feel* of coffee makes me jumpy, shattery, scared shitless, to be precise. It still does today.

I take my mess kit and climb into one of the communications trucks, slink down and try to eat carefully, quietly, in peace, chewing each mouthful twenty times and swallowing slowly.

I'm almost finished when Lieutenant Ware finds me. He's standing looking over the tailgate, his helmet pushed back on his head. He's Van Heflin playing Van Johnson in a war movie with Marlene Dietrich as the Nazi spy.

A word here about Ware while I'm trying to get down the last two forkfuls and mediating my stomach into some kind of operational order.

Ware was in the Aleutian campaign. After that, he was reassigned to the Eighty-tenth Infantry Division, and more or less retired from the army. As Mel Gordon puts it, "He says he'll do anything and then does nothing he says." Stan claims that when he starts his Shutzer Surefire Advertising Agency after the war, he's going to hire Ware; talent like his shouldn't be wasted.

Colonel Sugger brought Ware into headquarters company to form the I and R platoon. Ware caught the I part. He had the regimental records sifted until he came up with the twenty-four people in the regiment with the highest AGCT scores. This was a wild idea in itself, but what made it even more bizarre is the way this goofy division was put together in the first place.

Two years ago, that original National Guard division Love worked out with between funerals, was spruced up and prepared for combat. But before it was shipped overseas, a maneuver with two similar divisions was held across the states of Mississippi, Tennessee and Louisiana. This was an overwhelming catastrophe. How can all three divisions lose in a war game? They did.

In the aftermath, someone realized that somehow the average AGCT for these particular divisions was in the mid-eighties. When it came to brains, they were on the down side of the second standard deviation to the left. Everybody with ability had been picked off by the air corps, the signal corps, the tank people, artillery and so forth. This was the sludge.

The military solution was shipping off to the South Pacific, as replacements, all the privates in these three divisions. This left cadres of not very bright officers and noncoms.

Meanwhile, back in civilization, another scenario was being played out. In the year 1943, most U.S. male graduating-high-school seniors were tested for entrance into what were called the A12 and V12 programs. Those selected would be sent to universities and trained in engineering or medicine. A12 was army. Their idea was to train us and rebuild our world after the nasty war.

Several thousand were selected and, upon duly enlisting, sent to universities. Since many of us had in the course of our scholastic careers been double promoted once or twice, we were too young for enlisting. At that time, the accepted age limit for being allowed to kill or be killed in a war was eighteen. So we were placed in the ASTPR, or Army Specialized Training Program Reserve. We were sent directly to universities, and were to be given our basic training when we came of age, then sent back to the university. It was sort of an early kindergarten arrangement.

However, while we were in infantry basic training at Fort Benning, Georgia, the ASTPR and most of the ASTP were disbanded; taken off the drawing boards by the powers that be. We were sent to various infantry divisions to play at being real soldiers. It was like being super promoted from nursery school to grad school.

We ASTPRers have many outrageous theories about what actually happened. We're strong on suspicion. The theories go all the way from selective genocide (to make the mediocre feel superior) to the idea that the whole ploy was a rather clever recruiting device.

Many of us were plugged in as replacements for those privates of the National Guard divisions who had been sent off to die in the South Pacific. This *did* boost the average AGCT and so solved that slight quantitative problem.

A large group of very young, arrogant almost soldiers unwillingly joined the Eighty-tenth Division in Camp Shelby, Mississippi, to help form a strange topsy-turvy organization: moron officers and noncoms trying to lead a disgruntled group of smart-ass privates. In retrospect, it wasn't actually such an unusual situation.

So when Lieutenant Ware pulled us from the regimental records, he was wittingly, or unwittingly (if he had a whit of wit), tiptoeing through the tulips, culling the called, the chosen. Except for Father Mundy and Mother Wilkins, all our squad is, or was, ex-ASTPR, all with impressive AGCT scores.

ASTP is an unpronounceable acronym. However, Whistle Tompkins insisted it was easily pronounced; that the TP was a Babylonian diphthong pronounced as "S." Shutzer counterclaimed that the TP went with the AS for wiping purposes.

That's a lot to squeeze around two bites and some stomach settling, with Ware standing there tilt-hatted, watching me. I either chew exceptionally slowly, or I think very fast.

"Come on, let's go, Knott! Love's waiting."

He looks at his watch.

Everything in the army is run by the clock, o-five-hundred and all, but they don't issue watches. In our squad there are now three watches; there were once five. I don't have one myself. In the world I come from, having a watch or a telephone is a privilege of the upper classes.

We move off toward the S2 tent. I do the usual thing, like an old-time Japanese wife, or a dog well-trained to heel, walk beside and about a step behind Ware; it's part of the conditioning. He stops and looks around at me.

"Jesus Christ, Knott! Haven't you gotten those fucking stripes sewn on yet?"

"The supply sergeant says he doesn't have any buck stripes in right now, sir. They're waiting for a new shipment."

"Hell, get some staff stripes and cut off the rocker."

"That'd be destruction of government property, sir. I suggested it to Sergeant Lucas."

I'm hoping that's ambiguous enough. What happened was Lucas tried to push off staff stripes on me to be cut up and I suggested it would be destroying government property and we'd need to make out a Statement of Charges. This scared Lucas; he's from the original division and somewhat slow.

"Well, I just hope to hell that son of a bitch Love doesn't notice."

You'd be surprised how much profanity goes on in the army when you're tuned to hear it. At first, stopping cold was like going on a crash diet. For a while there, Father Mundy was running his private Profanity Anonymous Therapy Clinic.

At the S2 tent Ware goes in first. Just inside the flap, we snap to attention. It's the usual setup. In the center, by the tent post, is a field table with a map covered in celluloid. At the rear tent wall is an extra-large cot and a down sleeping bag, already neatly arranged by one of Love's orderlies.

On the left wall of the tent, Major Love is shaving in front of his portable sink and portable mirror. He's wearing his tailored trousers (no other kind, even his fatigues) and a tailored OD undershirt.

We stand there at attention; I know he knows we're there. Pfc. Tucker, his first orderly, is playing altar boy, standing beside him, holding out towels and a soaping dish. Tucker tailors his uniforms, too; he does this on his own and gets away with it, thanks to Love.

Finally, after we've watched some rigorous efforts to get a few last hairs from under the nostrils, Love glances at us, first using the mirror, then turning his head.

"At ease, men."

Ware and I slouch, giving correct submission signals. Tucker hands Love a steaming towel from a bowl. Love sinks his face in it, rubbing strenuously. He continues to the top of his head, massaging with even greater vigor, then hands the towel to Tucker and takes a fresh, dry one. All our towels are army OD, so you can never tell if they're filthy or clean, except by the smell; but these look fresh off supply.

Next, we have the privilege of watching Major Love comb his hair. First, he rubs in a few drops of Vaseline hair tonic. He has the kind of hair in which the mark from each tooth in the comb is left like a plowed clay field.

I think of the latest Squad Spoonerism Award. Gordon took it. Question: What's the Bible? Answer: A fine couth tome. How in Saint's name am I ever going to make it as sergeant with a mind that's scattering all over the landscape like this? I've got to concentrate!

Now Love slips his fresh, orderly-ironed, tailored shirt over his sagging shoulders and turns to face us in his combat pose, shined combat boots about two feet apart, rocking slightly on his toes and buttoning. The tucking of shirttails is a prolonged ritual.

Lord, he's got on his "recon patrol" face. We're going into combat, yes, sir, stand up to the Huns. My slouch gets easier to hold. I can feel that sausage where my heart's supposed to be.

Love walks around behind the map and leans on it. It's angled slightly toward him. He looks up at us and smiles. Here it comes. Three of us on a tiger patrol sneak behind the Siegfried Line and take a prisoner—preferably an officer of staff rank, one who speaks English.

Love picks up a marking pencil and points at the map.

We are in for one of *Love*'s briefings. It's usually a rehash of what's been funneled down from division which some creative soul dreamed up at G2 or army intelligence from aerial photos taken fifteen months ago. I must admit, though, Love has the dramatic flair; probably comes from selling all those expensive coffins to grief-stricken little old ladies.

"Lieutenant Ware, Sergeant Knott, as you know, here in this sector of the Ardennes, we have a fluid and, at the same time, static front."

He looks to see if we're comprehending the big words.

"It's fluid because of these large forest tracts, virtually without roads."

He circles some fuzzy parts of the map with his pencil.

"It's static because nothing has happened here for several months.

"We're here. And they're there."

Again some pencil twirling to show the lines.

"Neither side wants to set up a line without clear fields of fire, and nobody's moving."

He snaps off another of his Robert Taylor glances up from under the eyebrows. By God, that's it! I knew Love looked familiar; he's a sort of faggy Robert Taylor. I need to check this with the squad; it could be only personal prejudice.

"Right here is a five-hundred-acre forest."

He traces, again on the celluloid, the forest. This time he makes real marks, so we're getting serious. My eggs have put themselves back together and are a whole egg, shell and all, just behind my belly button.

"There's an intersection of two tertiary roads, not paved, almost in the center of the forest. At the intersection is a château.

"At the eastern end, here, is a hunting lodge."

He gives us another conspiratorial—up from under eyebrows—steely glance.

"We strongly suspect Jerry has an observation post or outpost there."

Oh boy, the plot sickens. Just snuggle up behind those guys and capture a few. I think I'll faint here in the S2 tent. Or maybe I'll dash over and tear at Tucker's fly, while working up a proper drool. Sorry, Father Mundy, I know not what I do; just testing out a possible quick Section Eight.

"Sergeant Knott, I want you to move into that château with your reduced squad. Take two jeeps, one with the fifty caliber mounted; also a week's rations. Take a 506 radio and keep in contact with us here at regiment."

Is this it? Is Love telling me we're going to live in a château? I wait.

"Lieutenant Ware, you maintain radio contact with Sergeant Knott. We'll hold the other recon squad here at regiment for any additional patrol work.

"Sergeant Knott, your squad will either be relieved by the end of the week or additional rations will be sent out, according to operational conditions."

Ware sort of halfway pulls himself to attention.

"When do you want these men sent out, sir?"

"Tomorrow morning at o-eight-hundred. They're to keep an eye on any enemy outposts in the area and man posts to surveil the bridge and road going past the château."

Love turns to me.

"Well, Sergeant Knott, your squad can't complain about this one. The Whiz Kids can live like kings."

"Yes, sir. Sir, is there any evidence of occupation at the château?"

"That's one of the things you're to find out, Sergeant. Here's a chance to use our 'intelligence' in a little 'reconnaissance' for a change."

He smiles his undertaker's smile, ghoulish anticipation.

"Yes, sir."

Always a hooker. Six guys in two jeeps rolling up to a château in the middle of somebody's (nobody's sure whose) forest and inviting themselves in. We can always dog it if things look bad. Most of us have wagging tails, floppy ears and the mange from dogging it during times like this. We are *not* the best choice for I and R work.

Love's finished with his after-toilet before-breakfast military operation. We go through the whole saluting dismissal routine and I break clear of Ware fast. I need advice from the squad. Maybe this might be the chance we need to quit the war. A whole week with nobody looking.

That's rot! We'll do it. For sure, we'll baby-sit Love's château in the middle of a frozen forest filled with people trying to kill us.

I don't know what makes us think we're so smart. Just because we can take tests, do crossword puzzles, play bridge, chess and other games; just because we read too damned much, we think we're something special. Shits like Love or Ware are the real smart ones if you look at it objectively. They stay alive. That's intelligence!

2
The Longest Night

It snowed during the night, but lightly; temperature's dropped at least ten degrees. The first snow fell in the Saar for my nineteenth birthday.

I was on a full-day artillery observation post with the squad twenty-power scope. I'd spent the morning peering through drifting whiteness, trying to keep from breathing on the lenses. It was beautiful, even the black blossoms of mortar; they were far enough away. I'd pick a spot and wait till it happened; you can do this when you get to know the patterns. Now, when I look at the Brueghels in Vienna, I remember my nineteenth birthday.

Here, this morning, going out, there are frozen leaves and pinecones on the ground when we pass through K Company and drive into the forest. The road's just two hard ruts; the light, new snow's blown into them. No sign of other traffic; rough riding, slippery, cold. Miller's driving our jeep; Wilkins and I, in back, take turns on the fifty caliber. I'm up; it's miserably cold sitting there in the icy wind.

As we go deeper into the forest, huge pines loom dark on both sides. Some light is coming into the sky. We drive along not saying much; absolutely beautiful sniper targets.

Gordon's driving the other jeep, with Father Mundy and Shutzer; I look back to see if they're still with us.

Wilkins taps me and I slide down. He uses the handhold to climb up and crouch behind the sights. Wilkins looks scared, but we're all looking scared most of the time. We haven't said anything about our cross-country jaunt through the woods. Maybe it's because we can't figure out who won. Wilkins is acting as if it didn't happen. That's OK; just thinking about something like that scares me.

Mother has a piece of blanket cut into a long scarf; he's tucked it under his helmet like a burnous, then wrapped it around his neck and stuffed it inside his field jacket. It gives him a sad Lawrence of Arabia look. Thank God Sergeant Hunt isn't around for this.

Mother's glasses have slipped to the end of his nose. I'm not sure if he can actually see anything through those sights, anyway. His nose is long, bright red against his face, but he looks all right: maybe it was only a bad moment, something to forget.

"I'll tell you, Wont. I feel exactly like a target being towed across a firing range."

"Don't sweat it, Mother; pretend we're going for a winter Christmas stay at the family château. Imagine yourself a member of the old European élite."

I look ahead, over Miller's shoulder. The road's tough, twisting, narrow. We're winding along switchbacks now, working our way deeper into the forest.

I'm just checking the map again to see if we're on the right road, going the right way, when the world seems to explode. The jeep jumps so only Miller could've kept it from turning over. I think at first we've hit a mine but then realize it's Mother firing off a long burst. He's shooting past Miller's left ear at something on that side of the road, so the jeep's reared up on its two right wheels. I'm already clambering out before it gets settled back on four. Miller cuts the motor, grabs his M1 and dives, crawling under the jeep. Half our junk we'd piled in back, behind the gun, is spread along the road. I'm hunched in the middle of it.

Jumping out, I banged a knee on that damned handhold and my stupid mind is more wrapped around this pain than on keeping me alive.

Wilkins is still up behind the gun. He's not firing but continues sighting down the barrel. I can barely get my voice together for a whisper. I've crept behind the right rear wheel, away from the direction Mother fired.

"What is it, Wilkins? What'd you see?"

There's a moment before he answers. He stands up from his crouch behind the gun. He pushes his glasses farther up his nose and leans forward.

"There was a German soldier standing behind a tree— there. I think I got him; he's lying on the ground. I don't see any others."

"You're sure, Mother? And you can still see him?"

Mother takes off his glasses, wipes the lenses with the leather fronts of his woolknit gloves and peers again.

"Yeah, he's there. You can see him yourself if you stand up."

This is not the kind of thing anybody who likes being alive does. But if it's an ambush why aren't they shooting Mother off the jeep?

Bolstered by this slight bit of hasty logic, I scurry into

trees beside the road. I look back and see everybody's dispersed from the other jeep; the motor back there's still running.

God, I'm scared, I'm expecting the BBBrrrRRRppppPP of a burp gun any minute. I sling my rifle and take a grenade off my jacket. Anything close, I'm better off with a grenade than a rifle. I slide my finger in the ring and move up two, then three trees. It's a German all right and he's sure enough dead.

About one minute later, after I've carefully snuck up in good infantry manual procedure on our "dead German," I look down on something I've seen in dreams at least a thousand times during the past thirty-seven years.

He's been dead a while and is frozen with one arm over his head and the other twisted across his stomach. He's lying on his back but he died on his stomach with his head turned. One side of his face is iced and flaked so pieces of frozen flesh hang from the bones; this flesh is bluish green and there's no sign of blood. I see where one of Mother's fifty-caliber bullets went through his neck just below the chin, a perfect unbleeding fifty-caliber hole.

I've seen the dead and the dying but I've never seen anyone dead, shot. They call a sharpshooter a dead shot, but this is a real one, shot while dead. It seems to me, then, like the final violation.

Miller comes beside me.

"Jammed dog tails! What happened?"

"Somebody must've stood him against that tree, Bud. They hauled him from somewhere and propped him there."

I reach down and pick up a typical German bolt-action Mauser balanced beside him. There's also a piece of white paper with holes in it, no writing or printing.

"They maybe even had this rifle balanced on his hands,

sticking out, leaning against the tree. That's what Mother saw."

Except for Wilkins, the rest of the squad's drifting over now. Boy, am I ever the great leader. "Come on, everybody, let's bunch together so we can be mowed down easily." Wow!

Father Mundy kneels by the German. He tries closing the one open eye with his thumb like a real priest, but it's frozen open. The other eye is only goo, frozen goo. Father pulls off his glove, jams his thumb into the bolt of his M1 and rubs it around. Then he makes little crosses on what's left of the German's face: his forehead, his eye, his ear and his lips, then the backs of the stiff decaying hands. He's mumbling prayers to himself in Latin. I kneel down on one knee beside him, as much to keep from keeling over as anything.

"That isn't Extreme Unction you're doing there, is it, Mundy? I thought you had to be alive to get it and a priest to give it."

Mundy stands up slowly, still praying. He's functioning, but he's in almost as much shock as I am.

"Right, Wont. But those were the best prayers I could think of. I asked the angels to help and the devils to leave. What else?"

He pulls off his helmet and his head's sweaty. We start moving back to the jeeps. Mother Wilkins, like the only good soldier in the pack, is still sitting up there behind the fifty caliber covering us. Mundy reaches into his helmet liner and pulls out a wad of toilet paper.

"Is it all right, Wont, if I go off into the bushes for a minute? Something like this turns my insides out."

I wave everybody our private "piss call" sign, and Father Mundy goes deeper into the woods. I move back to the jeep. Miller's sitting in the driver's seat, his legs hanging over the sides. He has his helmet off, and is pounding on his ears.

"Look, Mother, could you give me just one second's notice before you start that thing up again? I have a flock of mockingbirds doing a duet with a squeaking oil well in the middle of my head."

Miller turns to me.

"Won't, is it OK if I take a smoke while we're waiting for Mundy?"

"Sure, but I don't approve. I have to live with Gordon, too, you know."

I look down the road at the other jeep; Shutzer and Gordon are leaning against it.

Melvin Gordon is squad health nut; he intends to become a doctor if he lives through the war. (He actually does; both those things.) He's taken on the personal responsibility (unasked) for the state of our bodies. Mundy works on our souls. In today's terms, I guess Mother's our ecologist, Miller's our mechanic and poet, I'm the artist and Shutzer's our business manager.

Gordon has gotten all of us who smoked to stop, at least in front of him. It can be an enormous nuisance. Miller resists Gordon most, the way Shutzer resists Mundy.

About then, Father Mundy comes dashing from the forest at half mast. He still has the toilet paper in one hand flapping along after him and he's holding on to the belt of his pants with the other. His rifle has slipped down to the crook of his elbow so it's swung in front and is thumping against his knees with every step.

"Mother of God, save me!"

He looks back over his shoulder. He feels for his head with his toilet paper hand and realizes he doesn't have his helmet. He stops dead in his tracks.

"No, Lord! Don't make me go back!"

Father Mundy's trying to buckle and put himself together. He keeps tangling in the toilet paper. We've all sprawled in the snow again except Wilkins, who's swung that fifty caliber so it's aimed just over Father's head.

"What in the name of heaven is it, Mundy?"

Mundy shambles over and flops beside me. He's about six three and better than two hundred pounds; on the edge of being soft. His usually white skin is even whiter and his Irish upper lip is covered with beads of sweat; quivering.

"You won't believe it, Wont."

The rest of the squad has scrambled, sprinted or crawled over to us. Maybe nobody could ever lead this bunch of gregarious genii. The trouble is they always want to *know*. Wilkins leans down from beside the gun.

"What was it, Mundy? What's in there? Is there a German patrol?"

"It's OK, Vance. Only I wasn't expecting it. I don't know what's going on, but you all ought to go look. I'm not exactly sure what I saw. I was so scared I took off without looking much."

Shutzer pushes himself up, wiping the frost and dirt from his knees and elbows.

"What'd you see, Father, a little grotto with a mysterious light coming out of it and this lady dressed all in shining blue and white who talked to you? Come on, tell us!"

Mundy gives Shutzer one of his "forgive them, Father" looks.

"OK, wise guy, what would you think of a German and an American soldier dancing together in the woods there; without music yet?"

Shutzer's climbing up to take Wilkins's place behind the fifty caliber. He should really be squad leader. That's the kind of thing you're supposed to think of. He slips into place while Mother Wilkins lets himself slide off the side of the jeep. He must be frozen. Gordon shakes some snow out of his glove.

"What's this? Father Mundy bucking for Section Eight? Well, fan my jawbone. A little counseling might help, Father; my office hours are two till five. I think I can squeeze you in."

It's time to play sergeant.

"OK, Mundy, let's see whatever it is. Shutzer, you stay here and cover. Miller, you give us cross fire from behind the other jeep."

I figure Miller can get his smoke in up there while we're gone.

We start into the woods, rifles at the ready. We get to the spot; Mundy picks up his helmet and points to the left.

I'm almost ready to believe anything; but I have a hard time with this. They look like a statue. They've been standing long enough so the last snows have sprinkled helmets and shoulders like powdered sugar. We advance slowly, Gordon in the lead.

Somebody's propped an American and a German soldier against each other in the final of final embraces. Their arms and legs are cocked so they look like waltzers, or ice skaters about to move off into some intricate figure. I stop; I don't want to look. Mundy and Gordon go on, with Mother behind them; then Mother turns around and comes back.

"I don't understand, Wont. What's going on? Who's standing up these corpses? It's crazy! This whole war's gone off the track somehow!"

I shake my head. I'm afraid if I talk I'll start bawling. It's not so much I'm scared; more confused, disgusted, discouraged. I stand there, rifle at the ready, pretending I'm doing something military, while Mundy and Gordon untangle the bodies and lower them to the ground. Mundy does his ersatz

Extreme Unction thing, Gordon hovering over the bodies.

I have time to pull myself together. Gordon and Mundy come back and we move toward the jeeps without saying anything. Even for a bunch of self-proclaimed smart asses with a wisecrack for almost anything, there isn't much to say.

Shutzer and Miller won't believe it when we tell them. They've got to go in and see for themselves. We tell them they aren't "dancing" anymore, how Mundy and Gordon let them down, but they want to check. Faith is going out of style, even in our squad, despite Mundy's heroic last-ditch efforts.

We get the rations, grenades, camouflage suits and other junk, including twelve mini chess sets, packed tight in the jeep; Mother climbs in with me behind the fifty. Gordon starts the other jeep and rolls close behind ours.

When Shutzer and Miller come back, Shutzer's like a lunatic.

"Those filthy, Nazi, Kraut-headed, super-Aryan, mother-fucking bastards. Only pigs would even think of a thing like that. That whole Goddamned country doesn't deserve to live with human beings. We should shove them in their gas ovens and wipe them all out. I personally would be glad to supervise the entire operation.

"And don't give me any crap, Mundy! You tell me why anybody'd do something like that to anybody else! What kind of God lets things like that happen?"

Mundy's sitting in the other jeep. He's quiet. Then he looks at Shutzer climbing in beside him.

"Yes, it's a terrible thing, Stan, a horrible way to treat the temple of the Holy Ghost, even if the immortal soul has departed. But we don't know for sure the Germans did that."

Miller turns over our jeep and guns the motor so I just pick up what Shutzer says.

"For Chrissake; who else, Mundy, gremlins?"

We go along slowly, twisting, turning; up and down hills, around cuts in mountains, under snow-covered trees. I stay behind the fifty, head ducked tight into my shoulders, trying to follow on the map where we're going. It's a small sector map of the one Love had, a contour job, an inch to a thousand feet, so it should be reasonably accurate. But we're making more twists and turns than are shown.

"What's the mileage, Bud?"

He looks down at the odometer.

"We've come about six and two-tenths so far, since K Company."

We go through a narrow defile and suddenly there's a bridge over a small stream, the bridge I've been looking for, the one we're supposed to watch.

Up a steep road from this bridge is the château. I mean it's really a château, not just a fancy house. It isn't all that big, but this is something from a French fairy tale.

Miller glides to a stop; I hand-signal back to Gordon. We turn off both motors and listen. It's quiet except for winter birds, running water and the sound of wind through pines. Slopes of forest come down behind, close to the château. Looking at the bridge, I can see there's no vehicle or foot traffic marks. It appears the place really might be deserted.

We scramble out of our jeeps. Gordon takes the scope and inches forward to a tree nearest the château with a good view and some cover. He leans the scope against this tree and scans everything for maybe five minutes.

Nobody's saying anything. All of us are staring at that château. It's built in pinkish-gray stone with a blue-gray slate roof and white shutters. All the shutters are closed. It's three stories tall and has a mansard roof. It doesn't look real.

Gordon comes back.

"I don't see anything, Wont: no smoke, no movement, no tracks. The windows and doors are all closed; there are no vehicles and no smells."

"What do you think, Mel? Send in a two-man patrol or just charge up that hill with the jeeps?"

"I thought Shutzer and I could ford the creek downstream a ways and approach from that side. We can look around back, then come on down the road in front to the bridge and check for mines. How's that sound?"

"We'll spread out and cover for you."

If Mel hadn't gotten trench foot in the mud at Metz, he'd sure as hell be squad leader and that's the way it should be. Or maybe he'd be dead.

He and Shutzer start down through the trees. I pass the word for everybody to spread out and be ready to give covering fire if they need it. I slide down to Gordon's tree, where there's a good field of fire.

I watch as they ford the narrow stream on some rocks. Shutzer slips and dunks one foot up over his boot top. They clamber uphill on the château's left, keeping the hill between themselves and the windows.

It's like watching a war or cowboy movie, actually more a cowboy movie with the good guys sneaking up on the shack where the cavalry colonel's beautiful blonde daughter, in total décolletage, is being held by a bunch of wild-eyed bandits who sweat a lot, wear black hats and two-day beards.

Then they disappear. I figure they're behind the château. I wait. Waiting is 99 percent of soldiering. Sometimes it's only waiting for chow, sometimes it's waiting like this; but definitely too much waiting.

Then Shutzer comes around the other side of the château. He leans forward and peers through one of the shutters. Gordon slinks along behind him and is swinging his head back and forth like some bird dog trying to pick up a scent.

Gordon and Fred Brandt both claimed they had the best schnozzolas in the world. They insisted they could pick up smells other people don't even dream about. Once at Shelby, out on the firing range, we had a smelling contest using a pair of Jim Freize's socks as bait. Freize could stink up a pair of socks in two days so they stood by themselves. His feet were like a dog's tongue; it was the only part of him that sweated. And some sweat.

It was a treasure hunt. I went into the woods and hid a pair of Jim's socks; then Gordon and Brandt had to search them out by scent alone. Both of them were remarkable. They'd find those socks faster than it took me to hide them. Fred won in a best of ten series but it was close. I think the difference was mostly a matter of luck with the wind.

Now Mel has it to himself. We called him Mel the Smell for a while there, but he objected to the double meaning. Actually, Mel's on the neat side, not in a class with Wilkins, but way ahead of me or most of the squad, even Morrie.

Gordon and Shutzer start down the hill. They both take a side and are peering carefully at the steep road. Once Shutzer leans and carefully scratches at a spot with the tip of his bayonet. They cross the bridge, then the road on our side of the bridge, and come up toward us. I step out from behind my tree.

"How'd it go?"

Shutzer sits on the ground beside me.

"Nobody home. Looks like nobody's been there for a while, either."

Gordon hands me back the scope. I should've asked for it before they left. Chalk off another two points.

"Can't see what's inside. There are curtains or drapes inside the shutters. I checked the doors and there're no signs of boobytraps. It looks as if we've got ourselves a château."

Of course everybody's dribbled in from the spots I put them and are gathered around. Shutzer's pulled off his boot and is wringing out his sock.

"Well, it isn't the good old University of Florida with fifteen hundred acres of orange trees growing under Spanish-moss-covered oaks around an Olympic-size swimming pool, but it's a step in the right direction, I'll say that."

When Shutzer gets his boot back on, we climb into the jeeps and roll uphill to the château; no mines, no machine-gun bursts, no snipers, nothing.

We force a front shutter and window with a bayonet. It's a French window-door and, as Gordon predicted, no boobytrap. We sidle in the door and stand just inside, letting our eyes get used to the dark after all the glare outside.

My God! What a room. It looks like a ballroom or a very fancy small gym. There are parquet floors and on one end is a gigantic fireplace, big enough to walk into. Long golden damask curtains go from floor to ceiling over the windows. The windows must be fifteen feet high.

Everybody files in so we're all standing there staring. None of us has ever seen anything like this before. And what makes it so eerie is there isn't one piece of furniture in the room.

I know it's time to play sergeant again; somebody has to. We need to unload all the rations and crap from the jeeps and set ourselves up. But we only stand there, overwhelmed.

I'm definitely feeling like Cinderella who was *not* invited to the prince's ball. I feel very disinvited. Shutzer's the first one who moves; he sashays out to the center of the floor. Shutzer's about five six, round but not fat. He's loaded down with all the military furbelows: bulging field jacket, two bandoliers around his neck, ammo belt filled with M_1 cartridges, bayonet, aid kit and canteen. He wears camouflage netting over his helmet, the only one in the squad. Gordon says it makes Shutzer look like an escapee from the South Pacific. Shutzer claims he wears it so he'll recognize his hat; helmets are too much all alike.

Shutzer's OD pants are stiff with greasy dirt; we're all the same, even Wilkins; there's no way to wash them and no others to change into. The wool soaks up grease and gets darker until the fronts are stiff and almost black.

Shutzer steps out onto the floor and gazes around; then he starts singing, grunting, humming "The Jersey Bounce," and breaks into a jitterbug routine by himself in the middle of that huge room.

> *They call it the Jersey bounce,*
> *The rhythm that really counts,*
> *The temperature always mounts*
> *Whenever they play ...*

"Come on, Mel, let's show 'em how we did it at the old USO."

Gordon comes out, rifle slung on his shoulder. He starts dancing with Shutzer. The two of them, bayonets clanking, canteens bouncing, bandoliers swinging, try some of the classic hand-over-head jitterbug maneuvers but their rifles get in the way. I watch those crazies, working it out in the middle of the Ardennes, and I remember Shelby.

In those last days, when we finally believed they really were going to ship the Eighty-tenth Division overseas, we went into a mild state of panic. Shutzer insisted this was proof that, despite all the propaganda, we were losing the war. Sending *this* outfit to fight *anybody* must be a desperate last resort.

But the thing bothering us most is that in our squad, with the exception of Wilkins, we're all virgins, eleven unwilling, unready to die, virgins. I don't know if all this virginity was only a normal factor of the times or if there is some negative correlation between sexual precocity and what we call intelligence. Maybe it was only an accident of space and time. Who knows.

We'd spend evenings trying to coax details out of Wilkins. His wife was in town and he'd do anything to make sure he got his weekend pass. If his KP or guard duty happened to fall on a Saturday or Sunday, we were all willing to jump in and sub for him, a vicarious pleasure. None of us ever met Linda, but we all knew her. In a sick, sex-hungry, Biblical sense, we all knew her.

Of course, Mother was very reluctant. He wasn't about to satisfy our puerile salaciousness. To all our entreaties, questions about how often and how much, his only reply was a sly smile and bashful "Oh, it isn't like that at all," or "You guys are sex maniacs."

So, it got to be less than three weeks before shipping out. I think it was Morrie who came up with the idea, or maybe it was Shutzer. Four of us managed a weekend pass and headed into town to hunt a nice, complaisant whore who could put us out of our misery, initiate us into the rites of manhood, emancipate us from the lonely compassion of our five-fingered widows.

All together we had fifty dollars. Ten was for a room at the Jefferson Hotel. This was for two but we knew a back way to sneak in the others. It was Gordon, Shutzer, Morrie and I. We figured any more would be some kind of gang bang and we had more romantic aspirations. The rest of our money was to go into the "investment" and a bottle of bourbon. Forty dollars was a lot of money in those days.

There was much speculation and discussion on the kind of woman. I think each of us was scared we'd get involved with a real woman and wouldn't be able to manage it. We agreed pure chance, not game skills, would decide the "pecker order," so we matched coins. Morrie won, Shutzer second, me for sloppy thirds and Gordon on the tail end. (Think of that, a quadruple pun!)

We settled into the hotel. Gordon and Shutzer had been nominated for the search, the recon part. We knew better than to hustle girls at the USO. We'd all tried that at one time or another, but the forces of morality were greater than our tactical skills. The B-girls in the bars were generally too much for us. None of us could make the grade with a genuine soldier-town whore, and none of us was willing to get a case of clap or syph. We were well-conditioned by the U.S. Army VD films. These films of festering mouth and cock sores were usually shown just before chow. Thank God they were in black and white. Morrie was convinced they showed them when the quartermasters were running short on chow allotment. Jim Freize insisted it was only *a priori* population control. The war was, by common consent, *ex post facto* birth control.

Probably what we wanted was some girl who would resemble the girl we took, or wished we'd taken, to our high-school prom. Morrie and I knew we could never make any kind of approach under any conditions. I personally had decided to sacrifice my contribution to the cause if it looked impossible. I don't know what I actually thought could bring together my absurd romantic notions with, what seemed then, my pressing physical demand.

Gordon and Shutzer left the hotel all slicked up. They were wearing fresh underwear, had rubbed in enough Mum to make a smeary mess in their armpit hairs, splashed themselves with after-shave lotion. It was early summer, and muggy hot in Mississippi.

Morrie and I had decided to enjoy the privacy of the room. We each had a book from the post library. We stripped to our skivvies and jumped into the beds. We luxuriated in the quiet; it was accented by the sound of a huge long-bladed wooden fan hung from the ceiling rotating slowly. In turn, and on schedule, we took baths, timing ourselves as the water heater recuperated. It was a fine evening and great contrast to the streets outside roiling with other soldiers, MPs on the prowl and glaring townspeople. The feeling of civilians in Shelby seemed to be "What the hell are you doing here when you should be out there fighting Nazis and Japs?"

It's past midnight when Shutzer and Gordon come back. I'm asleep; I'm sure Morrie is, too. After the baths and the quiet reading, I'm not even nervous anymore. I'm convinced Shutzer and Gordon aren't going to find anybody, anyway.

But they have; they sneak into the room and a young girl comes in with them. I can't believe it. I sit up in bed and look over at Morrie. He's sitting up, too, his OD undershirt dark olive drab against the sheets.

This girl fulfills my wildest dreams. She can't be much more than twenty and she's beautiful. Shutzer and Gordon are giggling nervously. It must have been some fun smuggling this girl through town and up these hotel back stairs at this time of night. After the last bus has gone back to camp, the whole area swarms with MPs.

The girl's standing just inside the door, smiling at us. I know right then I won't be able to go through with it. I'm glad I'm third down the line.

It doesn't seem possible it's happening but it is. It's about here I realize Shutzer and Gordon have been drinking, probably trying to boost their flagging nerve. Gordon has a bottle in a paper bag; it turns out our bottle of bourbon is almost a third down already. None of us is much at drinking; in fact, we class drinking, along with cussing, as army pseudo heroics, to be avoided.

With nothing said, I slip from my bed. I'm embarrassed wearing only GI underwear, large unbuttoned slit in front, like the back of a hospital gown. I scurry into the bathroom. Gordon and Shutzer come in after me. Shutzer's picked up the pillows from one bed on his way in; he locks the door behind him.

"We might's well make ourselves comfortable; never know how long a guy like Morrie's going to take."

Shutzer's playing big shot but his hands are shaking and he's sweat through his suntans under the arms and in the small of his back.

Gordon sits on the toilet with the seat down; he slides one pillow under him. I climb into the bathtub and tuck a pillow behind my neck. The tub's ice cold and hard; I get out and start filling it. Who knows when I'll have a real bathtub to use again; besides, if I'm going to be awake at one o'clock in the morning, I might's well be doing something; I've finished my book.

Shutzer looks at his watch, pulls out a cigar and tries to light up. Gordon glances at him disgustedly. Shutzer starts undoing the buttons on his shirt.

"You know, she says she's doing this for nothing; 'anything for the boys overseas,' or almost overseas, anyhow."

He pulls off his sweaty shirt.

"Won't, you wouldn't believe it. We went into every bar and joint, up and down every creepy dark street, arguing all the way. When we'd finally agree on one, the price'd be something astronomical like twenty bucks a throw, no cut rate for groups."

He drops his shirt on the floor and looks into the mirror over the sink. He squeezes a pimple under his ear. He tries to light his cigar again. He doesn't even know enough about cigars to trim it.

"Ya mind gettin' off the toilet a minute, Gordon; I gotta take a piss."

Mel stands with his pillow clutched against his chest. Shutzer lifts the lid, pulls out but can't do anything. He stands there, looking down, puffing on his uncut cigar trying to keep it lit. We're quiet; we can hear Morrie and the girl talking in the other room but can't hear what they're saying. Shutzer buttons up and looks at his watch again. He undoes his pants and slips them off.

"Might's well be ready; never know how long ol' Morrie Margolis is gonna take; might come right off without knowing it. No sense wasting time."

He sniffs his armpits, then takes some after-shave lotion from his toilet kit and rubs it in. I try the water in my tub; too hot. I turn on some cold.

"We'd just bought the bourbon and had almost given up when we found this girl. We were all the way down by the Greyhound Depot. She was in there sitting on one of the wooden benches. Gordon here goes over and starts talking to her. Before we know it, we're telling her about what we've been doing all night; how we're looking for a whore to defoliate four overripe virgins. We're laughing and then, right there, out of the blue she volunteers to come back with us. God, you never know! I thought she was kidding, but she's serious and it isn't costing us a dime."

Gordon sits down on the toilet seat again. The tub's full to overflow so I turn off the water, ease myself in.

"Stan, I have a rubber and a pro kit you can use if you want."

"I have my own. Don't worry me, Won't; you're getting bad as Wilkins."

He searches the pack out of his pants on the floor.

I'm glad I said it. Shutzer starts pacing; that is, if you can really pace in a hotel bathroom with two other people. He's wearing his shoes, socks and underwear; the cigar's clenched in his teeth and he's clutching a packet of three rubbers in one hand. He's balanced his pro kit on the edge of the sink. He looks at his watch.

"Should've known Margolis would take forever."

"Ever try one of those pros, Stan? I did once just as an experiment. It doesn't hurt but feels peculiar, like rubber snakes squeezing up the end of your prick. Just relax."

"Don't worry, I'll figure it. What the fuck could they be doing in there?"

"Watch the language, Stan, we have gentlemen in the gents' room. What would Father Mundy think?"

"Fuck Father Mundy!"

Gordon shakes his head, puts my pillow on his lap along with his own and lowers his head onto it. Shutzer looks at his watch again; he leans against the door to the bedroom.

"Hey, Morrie, how's it goin' in there, huh?"

No answer. Shutzer puts his ear against the door.

"Maybe she rolled him and slipped out, knockout drops or a blackjack. Could be anything."

Shutzer knocks on the door, first soft, then hard.

"Hey, Margolis, give us other guys a chance, huh? At least say something."

Still nothing. Shutzer slowly, quietly, unlocks, then opens the door, peeks, goes in. He closes the door behind him.

I stand up in the tub and dry myself off. Shutzer doesn't come back. Gordon and I look at each other. I slip on my skivvies and we go in after Shutzer.

The three of them are sitting cross-legged on the bed. Shutzer and Morrie are still dressed, that is, if army OD underwear can be classified as dressed. The girl's in a slip and crying. Gordon and I stand at the edge of the bed and listen. I'll give a quick version of the story. It's not what this book's about anyway, or maybe it is.

Her name is Janice. She was engaged to a boy named Matt. Matt was killed in the Sicilian invasion. Janice only heard a week ago. She came down to see all the last places Matt had been in his short military life. She's a junior at Penn State but isn't going back to school. She's twenty. She came down here to kill herself but didn't have enough nerve; all she has now is a ticket back on the bus.

So what do you believe?

She and Morrie got to talking because they were embarrassed. They began kissing; then she was crying and that's how it came out.

We wind up pushing the beds together into one big bed and start drinking the rest of our bourbon in the paper bag.

Five people on two-thirds of a fifth. There might be some mathematical sense there, but it would be the only logical part of that night. It was like an X-rated version of a classic unmade war film starring Shirley Temple with Audie Murphy.

Janice has only made love with one person, Matt, just before he left. Now she's volunteering herself to all of us. She's insisting it's what she wants to do.

Of course, this brings out the contemplative, cantankerous, contentious ASTPR in each of us. We're also guilty, scared. This idea, this simple, lovely idea, must be subjected to every kind of spurious rationale. We wind down before dawn and sleep; tired, medium drunk, intimately wedded in our double-double bed. As the springing light of the new day grays the room, Janice comes, quietly, privately, half in our dreams, to each of us: Santa Claus, the Easter Bunny. We cry and giggle, passing through the mythical barrier between boys and men, men and death.

Janice takes us with her.

At ten o'clock, after a luxurious mass breakfast in bed, Mel escorts Janice to the bus station. We don't talk about what happened. I don't think any of us can put it together with anything we've known.

I personally have always had an eerie feeling about my first sexual experience, masquerading as a dead boy named Matt. And I still, to this day, have the lingering sensation that any woman with whom I make love has some other ideal person in her heart and mind.

Once more we're up against my weakness for the true but unbelievable. Mel and Janice correspond through the war. Mel goes back home and they marry. They have three children and are divorced after fifteen years. Perhaps because it was a mixed marriage, or maybe only an ordinary marriage, subject to the pressures of our times. Perhaps Matt could always have been there.

Shutzer and Gordon finish dancing. We haul in the rest of our supplies. I have Miller back our jeep with the fifty caliber up against one side of the château so its barrel can traverse the entire road along with the bridge. Our other jeep we bring around behind the château. I drag in the snowsuits, the whitening, a box of grenades and the 506 radio. Mother helps me with all the schlepping. I also break out the field telephones. Miller begins untangling them. I struggle out our two big reels of wire for the phones. They're still caked with mud from when we pulled them up in the Saar.

When I'm finished, I stop to get my breath and look over the situation. From in front of the château, we look down across a series of terraced fountains almost to the stream. This is the stream under the bridge we drove over up to the château. There are statues of dolphins and different fish in the fountains, with verdigrised copper piping coming from fish mouths for spurting water. The statues look like cast cement: spotted black, green and yellow with clots of hardened moss. The basins of the fountains are filled with frozen leaves.

I decide I'll set up two guard posts; one downhill on the other side of the fountains, behind a retainer wall to the right of the bridge; the other up on the side of the hill behind the château, just higher than the roofline. I scramble uphill to locate a spot where we'll have a good overall view of the road, both directions, and still cover the lower guard post.

I can't think of any way to protect this higher post from infiltration behind. Still, someone climbing on this steep slope in frozen leaves and dead branches isn't going to have much luck sneaking up on anybody. It'd have to be a good-sized attack patrol charging in, and if anything like that happens we're goners anyway.

I find just the right position and clear a space with my foot. I break off a branch from a tree and jam it in the cleared space. My innards seem to be behaving themselves, even after the climb uphill. Maybe just getting away from Ware, Love and all the chickenshit will help.

I slide downhill to the château and pick up one of the wire reels. I unhook the tie and knock off more mud.

The guard's going to be a drag. Days, it'll be one in a hole; that's two on and four off. Nights will be tough. We'll need two in each hole so that'll be four on and only two off. We'll have to do our sleeping daytimes. But I don't see any other way. I could try it with only one guard post, up on the hill; it could cover everything. Maybe after the first few days, if nothing happens, that's what we'll do. Or maybe just one post down by the bridge. We'll figure something; the squad will have ideas.

Mel comes out and helps me carry the reel of wire downhill to the bridge. I explain my idea for posts and he agrees. We find a perfect place about twenty yards right of the bridge. The retainer wall is shoulder high and makes an ideal firing parapet. With cover from the other post, it should be safe. That is, if anything is safe in a wood, in a war, with other people trying to kill you.

I tie the wire to a ring set in the wall and begin backing uphill to the château. Gordon says he'll take the first guard and stays down there.

I struggle uphill, laying wire alongside the road and looking out at the hills around. I could be under observation by somebody out there. Some guy in field green could be sitting with a gun and a scope watching me.

I turn my head to see how much farther there's still to go

and start hurrying the wire, dropping it off in loops. I'm already shaking; laying wire isn't all that hard; my nerves are just shot. When I get to the château, I run the wire through a window to the fireplace.

Mother is arranging rations and equipment. He's started his homemaking routine already and this is some home he's got to play with. I'm sure we're all going to get lectures on the statues, the architecture, the wood walls, the fireplace; the whole thing. Wilkins can't help but turn any place into a nest, and here he's got a palace. He seems to be making it fine; just a little too tense, too conscientious.

Once, on a sixty-hour nonstop convoy from Rouen to Metz, Mother rigged a sleeping hammock in the back of his jeep. That was the jeep he and Jim Freize shared. It was named Linda, of course. I painted the name on it with a picture of a rabbit. Mother calls Linda Bunny sometimes. Nothing seems to embarrass Mother; it's as if he's immune to all the things he should be embarrassed about.

Mother also had a sort of altar along the front of that jeep next to the instrument panel. There was a picture of Linda and cutout phrases from some of her letters glued around it. Sometimes I used to think Jim was as in love with Linda as Mother was. He'd better have been, because with Mother that's all you get to talk about.

When Hunt saw this whole affair, he blew his top and made them rip everything out. Hunt got "it" near Ohmsdorf, under a cross by the side of the road. It was just into Germany; we had the distinction of being the first American troops to penetrate into what the Germans called German territory at that time. This lasted all of three days and we were pushed back. I tried smuggling a message home to tell where we were. I asked Joan, my sister, to give my love to

Gertrude, Moe and Jack. I knew she'd figure it out and she did. I also knew Glendon, the assistant S2 who censored our mail, wouldn't catch it, and he didn't!

Hunt picked that cross for the platoon CP. Hunt was a noncom from the original Umpty-eleventh Regiment, and not very bright. Gordon insists guys like Hunt, Ware and Love are the real enemy; that is, if there is an enemy.

Inside the château I check how Miller's doing with the phones. He has them untangled and we tie in the wire I've pulled through the window.

"Would you check out the 506, too, Bud? I'll roll wire up to the other post. Gordon's taking first guard by the bridge."

Shutzer and Mundy meander over.

"Stan, would you take one of these phones down to Gordon and tell him to hook it in? Then bring this other phone up to me at the post behind the château? You'll have the first two hours on, so bring your rifle and a couple grenades."

"OK, Sarge."

I look quick to see if he's kidding, rubbing it in; but it came naturally. I'll never get used to it.

I tie wire to the handle of the window-door with enough slack to reach the central phone, then start rolling it up the hill. The smart way would be to unroll wire from the top down but I'm not thinking well. I struggle up the slippery hill with the wire reel, holding on to trees to keep from sliding on down into the back of the château. I finally work myself to where I've marked the spot, and stop for breath.

Below Stan and Mel are hooking up the other phone. While I'm watching, Mel cranks the handle and puts the receiver to his ear; it must be OK because Stan starts climbing uphill toward me without heading to the château.

I tie my wire to a tree; sit down and wait for him. I pull

the twenty-power scope from my field jacket pocket and scan
the hills around for a quick look. I don't see anything particularly suspicious: no smoke, no sign of movement or glints on
metal. Stan comes puffing up beside me.

"Phone's working fine down there. Miller says he's got the
radio tuned in and warming up, too."

We hunt for a good place to dig the hole. We want a spot
showing the fewest roots. But with pines all around like this,
there'll be roots, no matter what. Stan isn't enthusiastic about
digging but I stick it out. I'm not thinking so much about
protection from bullets or shrapnel as from wind and cold. At
night, two guys can keep warmer in a hole. One can sit down
in while the other watches. Nights here are ungodly long this
time of year.

I leave the scope with Shutzer and tell him to take a look
around every fifteen minutes or so; give him a rest from digging. I scramble on down the hill.

Miller's started hooking the wire to the other phone while
I begin the crappy army call business on the radio. "Able one
to Able four, over." I get Leary, one of the few radio people
at regiment who're even half human. I forgot communications
when I listed the nothings in regimental headquarters company. They're so nothing they're easy to forget.

Leary says he'll get our message to Ware. I say we've
occupied the château and are digging in posts. That sounds
military enough. I also schedule a call back at twenty-two-
hundred; that's ten in the evening, army talk.

Mother says he's ready to cook lunch if we'll go hunt
wood. He wants to light the fireplace, warm up the room and
cook over it. We have two primus stoves with us but Mother
is wound up to make a real cooking scene. There's a kitchen

opening onto the back wall along with a pantry, but it's cold and there are no pots or pans. Wilkins says it'll be better cooking out here in front where we'll sleep.

I don't know what to say. If we have a fire with smoke coming out the high chimney over the château, it'll be no secret we're here. At that point we're distinctly not a recon patrol; we're some kind of occupying force. Then again, we'll freeze our asses off at night if we don't have heat.

Father Mundy and I go around in back of the château. In the space between the château walls and the hill there's a woodshed and a stable for two or three horses. We break open the door to the woodshed but there's no wood. We go into the stable. There are some armfuls of dry hay still in the loft and we pry loose a few good-sized, worn boards from the stalls. If we do run a fire, wood's going to be a problem. The trees and everything on the ground around here are wet and impossible to burn. Even if we could burn it, there'd be regular clouds of smoke. The Germans will think we've got Indians out here making signals.

When we get back, Mother has a little flame going from D ration boxes. We add the hay and some smaller pieces of wood. But the fireplace isn't drawing; the smoke's pouring into the room and drifting to the ceiling. Miller looks up the flue and finds it's been plastered closed. He uses the butt of his rifle and knocks out some plaster; a few bricks fall, then the smoke starts going up fine. I go outside to see how much comes out. There's a twisting snake of pale blue. It's bad but not bad as I expected. It's a chance we'll take.

D rations have assorted goodies such as number ten cans of jam or fruit cocktail, so Mother whips up a tasty lunch. We finish off with coffee and I'm praying my stomach will handle it. For some reason, I'm not scared as I should be; maybe having a fire burning and being inside help.

Mundy finds a hand-pumped well beside the château; he and Miller prime it. They bring water back in worn wooden buckets and it looks clear. We might even be able to keep our mess kits clean for a change. This could help my insides stay where they belong.

I'm trying to work out a fair guard schedule. Gordon, Shutzer, Miller and Mundy will want time off together in the daytime so they can play their crazy, four-man, cardless duplicate bridge. Also, I don't want anybody getting stuck with straight-six overlapping day and night shifts. It's almost as complicated's making their handmade bridge hands; that's another thing needs doing before tomorrow. Maybe Mother will help; he's better at it than I am anyway and it'll take his mind off things.

Shutzer and Gordon come in. Mother's kept chow hot, dishes them out some, then leaves for the bridge post while Father Mundy pulls the one up top. This squad practically runs itself; anybody trying to lead it only gets in the way. I probably don't even need to make any guard schedule.

Miller's also found some empty wine bottles and is cutting up feed sacks from the stable into strips with his bayonet. He's making flambeaux, using gasoline from a jerry can on his jeep. That way, we'll have light tonight.

It'll get dark before five, so there'll be one more turn before night double guard starts. We'll stick it out for now; then tomorrow, if nothing's happened, we'll drop to one post. Nobody said we have to *defend* this place, just keep an eye on the road and bridge.

I crack out new grenades and issue two extras all around; we're each carrying bandoliers, plus the clips on our belts. Our fifty caliber is loaded with armor piercing, every sixth shell tracer. We can't do anything against a tank, even with AP, but maybe it'll slow down a weapons or troop carrier.

Hell, nobody'll be rolling through here with anything like that; I should relax.

Miller comes in with a ring of rusty keys. He found them hanging on a hook inside the well when he took off the cover checking to see if it looked polluted. There're about twenty keys, all huge and ornate.

Gordon lights one of the flambeaux. He, Shutzer, Miller and I go on an exploration. We're finally doing some recon; Major Love would be proud of us.

We find stairs to the cellar outside on the back wall and work our way down winding eroded steps to a dirt floor. It's warmer here but humid. The ceilings are arched in stone and festooned with dirt-heavy cobwebs. If it gets really cold, we could live down here, but we've had enough sleeping in cellars.

I'm looking for another entrance from inside to use in case somebody comes charging through the front door upstairs, but there are only three small rooms, a dead end, and nothing but the outside stairwell we came down.

Miller's working out the permutations and probabilities for twenty keys and three doors; finally he gets them open. In one, there're eight bottles of wine. From the straw and empty racks it looks as if somebody's already ransacked most of it. In another cellar there are two crates of canned sardines. The last cellar is empty except for rusty old tools and some broken chairs.

We gather up the wine and sardines; they'll give some zest to the D rations. Miller hauls along three of the broken chairs for burning. We stash the cans of sardines and bottles of wine beside the hearth; Miller cracks the chairs and throws some rungs on our fire.

Next we climb a stairway on the far wall from our fire-place. It curves upward to a landing, then turns back along the rear wall. We open a tall, wooden door onto a hall running the length of the château, almost like a hotel hallway. Miller's fooling with his keys again. He's marked off the cellar keys so he's down to seventeen. It turns out one key opens all hall doors.

The first room has three walls lined with books, including a recessed spot for a globe of the world. Most of Europe on it is German. The floor is carpeted and there's oak wainscoting up about three feet. I pull aside the curtains on the fourth wall, open a window and push out the shutter. I'm looking down from the front of our château and see Mother by the bridge.

Maybe I should make the upper guard post in here; be a hell of a lot more comfortable. But somehow it seems wrong, turning a beautiful room like this into a guard post. Wilkins probably wouldn't let me anyway. Also, if anything happened, whoever was up here would be trapped.

I go around looking at the books. They're all French or German, no English. I'm not exactly sure which country we're in; could be Belgium, Luxembourg, France or even Germany; we're at a place where they more or less come together. I don't know what time it is, what day or what country. I'm not even sure of my own name. Next thing they'll be making me a general.

The other rooms are bedrooms, five of them. There are furniture marks on the floors but the rooms are empty. The biggest room has full-length mirrors along one wall, the wall away from the windows. God, we're ugly; dirty, gangling, baggy; shuffling in a hunching crouch like animals. We're walking, talking Bill Mauldin cartoons or van Gogh potato eaters. We look as if we're holding things in, at the same time, keeping things out; a permanent state of negative expectation.

I stop in front of one mirror, straighten, try to recognize myself; who is this, who am I?

Gordon's up close to another mirror, inspecting his teeth. Miller and Shutzer are laughing, posing; pointing at each other. Shutzer gives himself the finger. I don't think we've been seeing ourselves the way we look in these mirrors; it's hard to accept. *We* look like the enemy.

At the end of the hallway are two doors. One opens onto a gigantic bathroom with more mirrors along the walls. In the center of the room is a strange-looking copper bathtub shaped like a giant shoe. It looks something like the house for *the old lady who didn't know what to do*. It also looks like the kind of bathtub Claudette Colbert would use to take a bath with lots of bubbles, steam and Clark Gable. She knew what to do.

Miller wants to make a bucket chain, haul water from the well and take a bath. But it's so cold there's frost on the insides of windows and the mirrors are steaming up with our breath and the heat of our bodies. There are closets behind the mirrors, all empty; and in one corner is a sink without water. There's also something like a footbath, which I now know was a bidet.

We go out and open the other door in the hall. It leads onto a narrow turning staircase. We tromp up in a row. At top is a small door; Miller gets it third try.

The attic's divided into small rooms and these rooms are stuffed full with furniture. Things are piled King Tut tomb-style, helter-skelter. It's fantastic: musical instruments, rugs, satin-covered chairs, beds, paintings in big gilt frames. We poke our way around. Wilkins is going to go ape exploring all this. He'll probably be cataloguing the whole shootin' match before he's finished.

But we have some needs right now. We carry down four mattresses and satin quilted covers. The second squad of the regimental I and R platoon, Umpty-eleventh Infantry, Eighty-tenth Division, will be living in luxury for a few days.

Downstairs, we square our mattresses around the fire and spread the quilts over them. We put fart sacks on top. We'll always have at least two on guard so this should work fine. I spread out on one and enjoy the softness; it's been a long time since I've slept in an honest-to-God bed.

Shutzer, our kosher gourmet, hungering for the smell of fish, opens a sardine can with his bayonet. Miller, the man who has everything, even a corkscrew, works the cork from a bottle of wine. This could well be the coup de grâce for my stomach, perhaps my entire digestive system, top to bottom. We pass the wine and sardines around; wine's sour but cold, sardines float in thick oil; some writing on the can's in German. Maybe this is the German secret weapon; maybe we'll all wind up in some nice American field hospital with a gaggle of Purple Hearts, victimized by the terrible Huns and their secret weapon, poisoned sardines.

I sit there trying to work out bridge hands for the maniacs. Soon as I'm on duty, it'll be Gordon, Shutzer, Wilkins and Mundy locked in mortal combat. Concocting hands is more fun than playing. Sometimes I watch and count tricks. For me the game is guessing what the contract will be and if the hands will make. Each day, I'm getting better at playing this inside-out, bass-ackwards kind of bridge. The secret is making the hands as Machiavellian as possible.

Before that Saar patrol, the squad usually played ordinary duplicate bridge. Once a week at Shelby, we'd nominate a team to play against the first squad, Edwards's squad. We always won. If you don't count Wilkins, Morrie and

Gordon were our best players. At Shelby, Wilkins would never play; now he only plays once in a while to make an emergency foursome. Morrie, Fred and Jim were regulars, too. Max Lewis would play sometimes. Now, when the maniacs want a really good game, they beg Wilkins to sit in; but poor Mundy's stuck with it most of the time. He never played before he joined the squad and he'll never be any good. He's not devious at all, and doesn't care enough about winning. It drives Shutzer mad.

When we lost half the squad, we also lost our only decks of cards. They were on Morrie, and he was back with the medics before he could pass them to any of us. We weren't thinking much about bridge right then.

He died in the field hospital. With his right hand gone and his face the way it was, I don't think he tried hard to stay on. I wouldn't. Gordon and I wrapped him; it looked as if his eyes were empty; the side of his head was spongy soft.

We're continually writing home for playing cards, candles, pencils and dictionaries but not one of us has gotten any. We get warm, hand-knit socks, too thick for our boots, or boxes of cookies mashed into crumbs. Corrollo used to get hot Italian peperone sausages and hard Italian cookies uncrushed. Corrollo also would steal sausage off dead Germans. He said it was good but not so good as he got from home.

Father Mundy's mother packs each of her cookies in a separate wrapping of waxed paper, then stuffs shredded newspaper tight around them. She's been sending packages to relatives in Ireland for years, so she knows how.

Father considers those cookies an act of love. They are. He's the one guy we never hound for seconds but he passes them out anyway. It's almost as if he's giving communion;

one at a time, carefully unwrapped and handed to you directly. They're usually tollhouse, with lumps of real chocolate and deep in butter. One of Mundy's mom's cookies is something to be eaten slowly with much concentration, almost worth reconverting for.

Maybe the folks back home *are* actually sending us dictionaries, pencils, candles and cards. Maybe the military considers these subversive objects and confiscates them. It could be Love has a whole duffel bag filled with bridge decks, dictionaries, pencils, pens, thesauri and bundles of candles, even blessed ones for Mundy.

I work out four hands in standard bridge annotation on separate cards. I make these cards from the turned edges of my K ration boxes when I cut them off with my bayonet. We thought of making a deck with these pieces but Miller calculated fifty-two of them would be over three inches thick and they'd get battered in no time. I put the finished hands face down on top of the phone battery box; they'll find them. It'll be Gordon-Mundy versus Shutzer and an unwilling Wilkins, so I don't have to think much; with that set of baroque minds, any distribution of cards becomes a drama. They can stretch out a single three no-trump bid to over half an hour.

We've been playing this new way three weeks now; sometimes it seems like three years. Gordon invented the game; it's titled "compact, cardless, replay duplicate bridge." They'll each choose a chunk of K box and that's their hand. I've asked to assign hands but they don't trust my impartiality. As Shutzer put it:

"For Christ's sake, Won't, you're already playing God; what else do you want!?"

When playing a hand, they draw a line under each card as it's played. Mel insists they all go through the motions of placing the phantom cards empty-handed on the table, dirt, blanket, mud or wherever they're playing, calling out which card is being played. Miller complains this is one more stupid atavism, but goes along. What else? If Mel doesn't play; no bridge, everybody down. By the way, Miller is one reason we need a dictionary. He also creates crossword puzzles which make *The New York Times* Sunday puzzles seem simple as tic-tac-toe.

When a hand's finally played out, the cards are given to me. At my discretion, I then, in the future (of which there sometimes doesn't seem to be much), give back the cards with clockwise rotation for replay. My upper-left field jacket pocket is stuffed to bulging like Mae West on one side with these sets of bridge hands. Maybe someday a piece of shrapnel will bury itself in there and save my life the way Bibles always seem to save the lives of religious Protestants. I'll be saved by bridge hands rather than the hand of God.

Pencils are pure gold in our squad. If one pencil has arrived for each pleading request, Love must have enough to start a stationery store after the war, no one duffel bag could possibly hold them all.

I cherish my trusty 2B and a 4B, wide lead, carpenter's pencil. I bought the 4B in a hardware store at Shelby and have carried it all the way. It's more than half worn down. It's a race to see which ends first, my 4B, the war or me. Pencils like that are ruined if you drop them, because they break inside the wood; I keep it wrapped in toilet paper and tucked under the bandage in my aid kit. I use those pencils exclusively for drawing. That 4B might be the one thing that's holding me together. I won't lend either pencil to anybody for anything; some things are private even when you've just been kicked up to sergeant.

I don't even use them to make up bridge hands; I use an ordinary 2HB for that. I'm the only one in the squad with three pencils. I'd rather leave off a bandolier than be without them.

Most times I draw on the inside of torn open K ration boxes; the whole squad saves these K boxes for me. I can't carry the drawings with me, so I roll and bury them ten at a time. I have a list of burial places. It's in my duffel bag on the kitchen truck. I also have ten or twenty of the best drawings in that bag.

I'm thinking then how maybe after the war I'll come back, use my maps and dig the drawings up. I didn't think they'd rot; I hoped not; K ration boxes are waxed on the outside.

I draw everything. I have good drawings I did of Morrie and Max, Jim and Fred, Whistle and Louis. I draw our equipment and different places we've been. I draw trees and pinecones, farmhouses, scenes, mess cups, bottles; anything. It makes things more real; at the same time, not *so* real.

Actually, my duffel bag with maps and drawings—everything I owned—got lost when I was wounded on the Moselle. Even so, twenty years later, I did go back with my wife and kids. I didn't find anything; it'd all changed so much and I couldn't remember any exact places.

It's getting to be four o'clock. Miller and I are on from four to eight. I'm counting it a day guard with only one of us in each hole but most of it will be dark. I put myself up on the hill to have a good look at things. I'll especially be watching for smoke or fires. Maybe I can catch them cooking dinner, figure out where they are; if there *is* somebody; there must be.

On the way out, I ask Bud to listen for any vehicle traffic

while he's down there. Hell, I should tell him. I crank up
the phones to let Mundy and Wilkins know we're coming. I
have a horror of being shot by somebody on guard when I'm
coming out as relief. It's the way I'm liable to go, a friendly
useless casualty.

Miller and I check rifles, hook grenades in our pockets.
I'm hoping the damned hole is finished up there. With both
Shutzer and Mundy digging over the past four hours, it should
be. Digging at dusk through roots is miserable. You get yourself sweaty, then have to sit out in wet cold as the dark comes
on.

Going uphill, I can feel the temperature dropping. The
sky's an even, low white; if it drops a few degrees more, we
could have snow; that's all we need. I go back for my shelter
half. If it snows, I'll need to work out a less visible path for
climbing to this post.

Father's about frozen. He's standing up out of the hole
stamping his feet. The hole's finished but the dirt's still in a
pile. Shutzer and Mundy should know better.

"Wow, Wont, is it ever getting cold up here."

"Yeah, well it's warm inside. Bud put some hot water on
the primus before we came out; there's even a fire and comfortable beds, with quilted silk covers."

"Aw, come on, Wont. Don't kid me."

"No kidding; you'll see for yourself."

He slings his rifle on his shoulder, takes off his helmet. I
sit on the pile of dirt.

"By the way, Father, I forgot to give the password. Tell
them it's 'cold—witch.' Have Gordon phone it out to Miller."

I'm wondering if Mundy will catch on. He was already in
junior seminary at thirteen, so things like that can pass right
over his head. Normally we get our password from division

but they can't give it on the radio so we'll make up our own.

"Don't forget, Father; 'cold—witch.' "

He's started down the hill.

"Yeah, I got it, 'cold—witch.' "

I watch him pick his way downhill, his shoulders hunched, his woolknit cap on his head, his helmet hanging in the crook of his arm, rifle sliding off his other shoulder. Mundy hates wearing a helmet more than anybody I know. He might also be prime contender as squad's sloppiest soldier.

Then I'm alone. I sit there on the pile of dirt; I'll spread it in a few minutes. The scope's on a bed of leaves beside the hole. I tuck it into my belt inside my field jacket; it's best to keep a scope warm; then the lens doesn't fog up next to your eye.

Father's not careful enough; he isn't as afraid of dying as the rest of us. If I could believe the same things he does, or says he does, I wouldn't be afraid to die either; I'd walk around playing hero, bucking for paradise. It worries me he'll make some dumb mistake from not thinking and get himself killed.

I shovel all the dirt back under pine trees and pile pine needles on top. I crank the phone and tell Shutzer I'll phone on the hour; I've borrowed his watch. I can tell the game's already started: Stan talks to me as if I'm interrupting; I'm only the war now, getting in the way.

It's beginning to fall dark fast; the reddish parts of deciduous trees are drifting toward purple; shadows under the pines are almost blue black.

I pull out my scope and scan the opposite hill. Near the

bottom I pick up a fast-running stream. There's a flat, gray rock above, with water fanning lightly over it. Just below, between the rock and stream, I spot movement!

The light reduction in the glasses is tremendous and I've started shaking so it's hard to hold still. I slide down into the hole and brace my elbows on the parapet.

There're three small deer browsing on moss at the base of that overhanging rock. One looks straight at me, long ears twisting to pick up sound. It can't possibly see this far and there's not enough light to glint on the lens.

I tuck the scope back in my belt and pull out my 2B pencil along with an opened, trimmed, flat K box.

I try to sketch what I've seen, the magic moment, but can't make it. My memory isn't strong enough and trying to put all that on a small gray surface is beyond me. It's partly because it's so far away, so much sky, mountain, forest; partly because I'd been expecting something else. It's hard to transmit the joy of peace, even with a drawing.

I pull out my scope again and continue scanning the hill, trying to imagine I'm actually walking over there. I traverse the road but it's getting so dark I can't see much. I can just pick out Miller down by the bridge. He's smoking and there's a glow when he takes a drag. It looks as if he's writing. Maybe we're in for another puzzle, or, better yet, one of his poems. He writes poetry about all kinds of things but mostly about machinery. Words like camshaft, universal joint, differential, drive shaft, overhead shims, dual carburetor or even piston displacement are music to Miller.

I search out a little K ration four-pack from my field jacket pocket, duck down in the hole and light up. I'm down to only three a day but when I'm cold and scared it's hard resisting. The cigarette companies thought up a sharp deal giving cigarettes to young soldiers. They'll have us all as lifetime customers when the war's over. (That is, if any of us are alive.) It's one of Gordon's best arguments.

I take a deep drag; it makes the stomach feel warmer and smooths out jitters. My stomach's acting up a bit from the shoveling. One little shot of paregoric would help; maybe I *am* becoming an addict.

It's much darker now. There's only a blue glow against the tops of trees and a thin haze of light on the hills behind me. There's no sense thinking about time; I'll be finished soon enough. I'm not going anyplace, just working my way through a short-sighted war on one more short-lighted day.

I climb out of the hole and go back for a piss. God, it's cold and now there's a wind springing up. We probably should've packed overcoats. I come back and wrap myself in the shelter half. The trouble with overcoats is they're so heavy, take up so much room. They make you feel clumsy, tied in, tight and not really warm. They're like the stupid galoshes we wore in the mud over combat boots at Metz. They jingled with every step and were perfect for producing trench foot. Gordon screamed all night till he just couldn't take it anymore. Morrie, Shutzer and I traded boots for socks, wore socks inside galoshes, three pairs; our arches almost broke down but we didn't get trench foot. Then good ol' Sergeant Hunt was going to court-martial us for losing the boots, even passed out Statement of Charges forms.

Terrible way he died, guts slipping between his fingers into the mud; stupid to the end, rocking there on his hands and knees. When he fell forward, dirt was ground into everything; nothing we could do.

I phone in. Gordon answers this time.

"Were you drunk when you made this deal, Wont? West sat on a fistful of spades and still killed a perfect four-heart bid. Goddamned Wilkins did it again. You didn't tell him, did you?"

"Hurts to lose, huh, Mel? Maybe you should stick to medicine and music, stop trying to be the ASTPR Renaissance man."

"Look, all I ask is next time, just try to randomize the cards; no tricks, no traps. I'm convinced Vance has you figured, can read your mind."

"OK, Mel, I promise. I'll make my mind a bland blank."

"That should be easy. Try not to concentrate, or even think, OK?"

"I told you, Mel, I promise, but it's hard shutting down a fine-tooled, high-power thinking machine like my brain. You've got to appreciate that."

"Horsepiss! Now to serious things. Mother's brewing some hash, also pork and beans. Which of our entrées would you prefer, sir?"

I choose the hash. I'm not sure I'll be able to eat it but anything's better than beans.

"We're also opening up the fruit cocktail. If you're reasonable with the next deal, we'll save you some; we'll even save a bit for Miller."

"I promise; for Miller's sake."

I hang up. It seems even darker, lonelier, quieter. It's always weird, cranking up and talking on a field phone at the bottom of a hole. In my mind I can see them down there around the fire, eating. I really should trade my fruit cocktail share for that lousy lunch cheese.

I keep watching for a flash of light or fire, but there's nothing. The only thing I see is Miller lighting up, then the glow each time he takes a puff. God, I hope he *is* working up a crossword mind breaker; get the bridge fanatics off my back for a while.

I'm tempted to have another cigarette myself, but don't.

Mel's convinced me. I should stop; it's stupid to smoke, sucking on burning dead weeds.

The wind's whistling in the highest branches; tree trunks sway, rubbing against each other, creaking like masts on a boat. There's the rattling noise of frozen leaves blowing along the hard ground. I don't know if I could hear anybody sneaking up or not. I look over my shoulder to make sure. The pines here were planted; there are long lines of them at almost any angle.

I call in again. I tell Wilkins to make it hash for sure. I'd fart all night with beans. I ask him to save some wine and forget the coffee. Wilkins asks if I'd like one or two scoops of the chocolate ice cream. Classic Wilkins humor; he must be OK.

"Skip the ice cream, Mother. But could you save me two cherries in the fruit cocktail?"

So now I'm committed. What the hell, maybe I can work up a real dysentery and be sent back. Whistle got a whole week in a field hospital that way once; said he slept all the time he wasn't eating.

It doesn't seem much later when I hear a noise beside me. I could've been half asleep, it came on so fast. It's Shutzer and Mundy.

"Holy cow, you guys scared the snot out of me."

Shutzer slides into the hole.

"Thought this place was further up the hill. Fine feathered fingers but it's dark out here."

I boost myself out with my arms. My legs are stiff and numb. I really could've been asleep.

"You'll get used to it; nothing to see anyway. Gordon and Wilkins go down to relieve Miller?"

"Yeah, came out with us. Gordon's so pissed about the

game he's hardly talking to anybody. That hand you set up was just the kind of thing he can't play. It's hard for him, laying back and waiting. Mother mousetrapped him; you know, that Wilkins is incredible."

"How's Mother doing?"

"Seems fine to me. You can't play Grand Master bridge like that and have much wrong with you. Stop worrying, Won't. It doesn't make sense mother-henning a mother hen."

I peer down the hill. I can see Miller trudging up past the fountains; Wilkins and Gordon are black forms against the wall. I decide again not to say anything about Mother's run through the trees.

"You give them the password, Mundy?"

"Yeah, 'cold—witch'; you dirty-minded army sod."

"Here's the scope, Stan, keep it in your pocket or tucked down inside the belt of your pants. Pass it on to the next guys."

"What's good's a scope? I can't see anything with my bare eyes even."

"You never know, Stan. Mostly watch those two guys down there. Look for anything moving up behind them.

"Miller will be out in two hours to relieve you, Mundy; after he eats and warms up. Stan, I know four hours is a long time in the night, but if we keep two posts there's no other way."

"Yeah, I know."

Shutzer sniffs the air.

"Smells like snow coming, too."

I gather up my shelter half. They've both brought along theirs. Then I realize I'll have no use for it inside.

"Here's one more shelter half; if it snows, you can spread it over top. Phone down on the half hour. You have your watch, Father?"

He nods. I start down the hill, then stop.

"When Miller comes, he'll give the password from right here. OK?"

"Right, Sarge. Could you please stop it, huh? Relax. The chow's warm and there's almost half a bottle of wine beside the fire. There's hot coffee in Miller's cup."

"Thanks."

I go down the way they came up, but I'm looking for another way we can get to the post without walking straight across the face of this hill. About halfway down, I see a light leak where the curtain isn't tight enough. Inside, I go over and pull it closed. I slip the grenades off my pockets, pile them in a corner with my bandolier. I stand my rifle beside the fireplace. I keep it loaded with one in the chamber, and locked. Miller's already there, has his boots half off and is sitting on one of the beds eating. I'm more tired than hungry myself but I know I ought to eat.

Miller passes me the bottle of wine.

"Sumps but it's cold in that streambed. There's a miserable damp wind blowing right through there. I was sure my flinchin' feet were going to freeze right off me. I *still* can't feel them."

"Be careful lighting cigarettes, will you, Bud? I could read your dog tags from up top. Some German eager beaver might crawl up behind and put one in your ear while you're formulating immortal verse."

"And here I am, trying to share the crankcase drain sensation just behind my nose when I'm scared: something of the smell in burning chicken feathers and tar."

"This war's totally out of control, Bud. Be careful."

The hash is good. I swallow slowly, chewing carefully. I alternate bites with K ration biscuits and wash it down in wine. I had decided to skip the coffee even though it might help keep me awake.

. . .

I'm deep asleep when the phone rings. Miller's on so he gets it; he's still playing with his poem by the light of our fire. Gordon reports in; everything fine. Shutzer calls in next and that's OK, too. Chess moves are passed on all around. Miller pulls out his boards, moves his pieces, stares at them. Everybody in the squad, except Wilkins and me, packs three miniature fold-up chessboards. Some games go on for days. The squad rule is, when you're in a hole, you can only pass on your play at regular call-in time. Given a chance, they'd run the phone battery right down dead in a day.

Mother is, by far, the squad chess champ, but most times won't play. He'll play bridge once in a while if he has to, but insists he doesn't enjoy chess at all.

I get up, wash Gordon's cup out in one bucket and fill it from the other. I do the same thing for Shutzer. Sloppy Shutzer put his cup away dirty and there's sugar like candy coated brown all over the bottom and up one side. Honest to Pete, I don't think he ever washes his stuff; never has the shits either; must have a cast-iron stomach.

I put the cups close to the fire. They can heat up in a hurry on the primus when they come in.

I go upstairs to the toilet. This was another of our great discoveries. It doesn't flush because we haven't figured how to turn on the water but it doesn't have a bowl like American toilets, so the crap drops straight down a hole. This is what I call luxury, not having to dig a latrine. Digging the regimental headquarters company latrine is, for some reason, an I and R preserve.

I'm still loose and crampy but it's much better. Maybe some château living will fix me up. I come down, fill two flambeaux, move the phone, then crawl into my sack and wait. I see from Miller's watch it's only five minutes till the next calls but I fall asleep again anyway. I wake up scared. It must be the second or third ring I catch. It's Gordon.

"Wilkins says he saw something on the hill across from us!"

I sit up in my sack.

"Let me talk to Mother."

I try to control my breathing. It comes in staggered stutters. So fast, I was so deep asleep! Wilkins comes on.

"What'd you see, Vance?"

"I'm not sure, Wont, but something moved up on the hill where the big rock is. There's moonlight shining on that rock and I saw something."

"Could be some deer I saw earlier, Mother."

"Yeah, could be only that; but I saw something."

"Give me back Mel."

The phone scrapes and rattles in my ear. Gordon comes on.

"Mel, one of you keep your eyes on that area and the other scan the road. The guys on top will watch in back of you. Challenge anybody who comes close. You guys got grenades?"

"Yeah."

"OK, I'll call Shutzer."

I get Mundy.

"Father, Mother thinks he might've seen something up on the opposite hill beside the big rock. You see anything from there?"

"No, nothing here. That Wilkins must have eyes like an owl. I can hardly see my own hand in front of my face."

"Could be he's only jumpy. I saw some deer up there earlier. You guys keep an eye left, right and in back of them, OK?"

"Got it."

"No smoking or talking till the next call-in and watch for anything coming down behind you. Call in if you hear anything suspicious. You both have grenades?"

"Yeah. Right."

I hang up and lie back. Probably nothing. Wilkins is only nervous. Maybe I should tell the squad about our weird dash through the bushes. The news of his baby being dead did him in for sure. I graze my mind over some of it, trying to decide what I should do.

The whole of Wilkins's life at Shelby was only empty space between weekends. When we aren't in the field, he's spending all his time making sure his gear's in order, his rifle's clean, his webbing scrubbed; all that crap. His wife has moved down into town and has a job as a waitress; all Mother cares about is getting his weekend pass.

Since he's terribly nearsighted, he carries his head pushed forward on slumped shoulders as if peering through a haze. He doesn't exactly look like an induction poster for the perfect infantryman, and has a miserable time with the field exercises. He barely gets his marksman medal with the M1, and he was trying.

Hunt finds out about Wilkins's wife being in town and makes it tough for him. He calls Wilkins "the perfesser" and rides him unmercifully. Wilkins only presses harder so he'll get his pass; Hunt was one son of a bitch; big guy, over six feet with a red face and beer belly. His favorite threat was how he's "gonna stomp the pissin' outen us."

One Saturday morning, after inspection, after Ware has done his thing, Hunt comes back, calls us together and gives a speech about how he "ain't satisfied with the way we're shaping up." He's gonna "turn us into sojurs for our own sakes"; there's too much mollycoddlin' going on, and so forth; a typical Hunt speech. Wilkins'd already taken down his overnight bag. He'd put it on his bunk just when Hunt came in. Hunt walks down the barracks to Wilkins.

"And this here's the worst Goddamned goldbrickin' fuckoff in the whole fuckin' outfit."

He looks at the bag on Wilkins's bunk.

"Just where in fuck you think you're goin', perfesser?"

Mother stands at the foot of his bunk looking straight ahead in his hunchbacked version of attention. He doesn't say anything.

"Well, you ain't goin' nowheres. Your fuckin' ass's confined to quarters this weekend. This is one Saterday night you'll have to live *without* your cunt."

It's dead quiet.

"She's my wife, Sergeant Hunt."

Mother's face is whiter than his glasses and his lips are tight, thin, blue.

"She's just cunt like the rest of 'em, Wilkins; all cunt wants is reg'lar fuckin', that's all. She ain't no different'n the rest."

He's turned his back and is walking through the barracks when Mother lands on him. Hunt goes down under the impact. He had no idea, none of us had. Lewis reaches back and pushes shut the barracks' door to the stairs.

Hunt's on his stomach but struggles to his knees. He grunts and roars. Mother has his long legs wrapped around Hunt from the back and his heels hooked into Hunt's crotch. He has an arm scissor hold around Hunt's neck. Hunt reaches up to pull Wilkins's forearm from his throat. Mother jams down hard and Hunt falls forward on his face again. Mother's glasses are hanging from one ear. Lewis goes over, untangles them, folds them and puts them on Wilkins's bunk. By now, except for heavy breathing and scuffling of boots against the wooden floor, there's no sound. Hunt tries standing up again. He gets to his feet but, with a backward lurch,

Mother pulls him over so he crashes against a bunk and Hunt rolls onto his stomach. Hunt tries again but his arms and legs are quivering; he slides flat onto his stomach.

We all stand watching; it can't be more than three minutes since Mother pounced. Corrollo goes over and kneels beside them. They're half jammed under a bunk. It's like the last part of a desperate dog or cat fight; nothing seems to be happening anymore. Hunt's eyes are open and his face is blue-purple.

"For Chrissake, Mother, you'll kill him."

"Not yet; I've let up some."

Mother speaks in short breaths, low rasping; hard to hear. It's deathly quiet. Hunt's face turns red again, his eyes move. Mother's voice is low pitched, edge of hysteria; he's crying; his face is covered with sweat.

"Listen, Hunt. I could kill you now; you know it. With these witnesses, I'd get off with ten years at most. I'd miss the war."

Mother's humped himself down so he can talk into Hunt's ear. Five seconds go by, five blank seconds.

"Hunt, you don't deserve to live; you're the scum of this earth. I can't think of anything to stop me."

It seems forever with just the hard breathing; Hunt tries to struggle once more but Mother puts pressure on and he stops.

"Do you want to live, Hunt? If you do, kick your left foot on the floor."

We watch. The foot lifts, kicks the floor.

"To live you need to do just three things. First, apologize about my wife; next, leave me alone from now on."

We wait. Mother pauses for breath.

"And now, you go to the orderly room. In half an hour I'll be there for my pass. You understand?"

Mother's been putting on more pressure as he talks.

Hunt's face is purple again, his eyes watering, his fingers digging into Mother's arm. A thin line of blood is oozing from his nose. His foot lifts and kicks hard against the floor three, four times.

Mother lets go and stands up. Hunt doesn't move. Nobody goes to help him. Mother stands over him shaking, the buttons torn from his shirtfront, his whole uniform soaked through with sweat. He stares down at Hunt several seconds, then turns away and lies out on his bunk.

Finally, Hunt sits up. He wipes his nose with the back of his hand and looks at the blood. Then he turns over on his hands and knees; he vomits. He struggles slowly to his feet, bent forward, his arms splattered with the vomit. He looks around. His voice is a harsh whisper.

"He jumped me from the back, you guys saw it."

Nobody says anything. The smell of vomit is beginning to spread. It's early May and warm. It could go any way from here.

"Listen, you bastards, I apologize for what I said about Wilkins's wife."

Still nobody says anything. Hunt staggers toward the door. Corrollo opens it and Hunt walks down the stairs out of the barracks.

We're all in a state of shock. Mother sits up on his bunk, removes his sweaty clothes. He goes down and showers. When he comes back, he dresses slowly and takes out his sewing kit. He sews back the buttons that got torn off, then hangs his sweat-soaked suntans on a hanger. We're half expecting a troop of MPs to come charging into the barracks but Wilkins doesn't seem excited at all. His face is still red and his glass frames are slightly bent so they sit on his face wrong, crooked; one side half an inch higher than the other.

Without saying anything to anybody, he picks up his

overnight bag from the bunk where it's been all this time and goes down the stairs.

He never would tell what happened in the orderly room but that was it. Until we shipped out, Hunt never bothered him, and Wilkins had his weekend passes right to the end.

A week after the Olsheim crossroads, Mother got the letter from his wife about the baby. We didn't even know she was pregnant. Mother told Father Mundy the baby was born dead, but he still hasn't said anything to the rest of us.

After that, Mother's seemed to lose the delusion of his immortality. I think that's what it is, anyway. Without it, nobody could do the things we all do.

It must be fifteen minutes later when the phone rings again. It's Shutzer.

"Won't, what's the chance of there being wolves around here?"

"I don't know, Stan, could be. These are real forests, the kind Little Red Riding Hood walked through."

"Mundy thinks they're owls. Can you hear them down there?"

"Haven't heard a thing; I've been half asleep and not listening."

"Hot pistols! There they go again! Did you hear them that time?"

"Nothing here. Where they coming from?"

"Sounds like up on the hill behind us and then across the hills on the other side. It's hard to tell, like echoes or they're talking to each other."

"Let me call Gordon."

Soon as I put the phone down, it rings.

"Suckin' ants, Wont! We've got Indians or something down here. Mother thinks it's Germans signaling back and forth. I can't figure it!"

"Hold on, Mel, I'll be right down!"

I hang up, shake Miller.

"Bud, there's something funny going on out there: voices or animal noises. I'm going down to the bridge; you sit on the phone. Call Shutzer and tell him what's up. Then call Gordon and Wilkins, remind them not to shoot me."

"OK. Probably only some animal; must be all kinds of night hunting going on in a forest like this."

"I hope so."

I pick up grenades and bandoliers. I take two extra grenades from the box. It's too dark for much shooting. I edge down along the side of the road where I ran our wire; they challenge me at about ten yards. I hurry and lean against the wall with them. They're tense; we whisper.

"Hear anything more?"

"Not since the last one."

We wait there in the dark; maybe five minutes. Then it comes. It does sound like an Indian, a bad imitation of an Indian imitating a wolf. But it's human all right; I begin to get scared. Wilkins looks at me.

"Closer that time!"

We wait in the dark some more. I'm trying to decide if it's better for Wilkins, Gordon and me to stay together, or spread out. I decide we'll stick it here. This is not so much a decision as what I want to do anyway. I pick up the phone and call Miller.

"Bud, you stay there on the phone."

"Sure, what's up?"

"I think we've got a German patrol sneaking around us!"

"Jesus! OK, I'll ring Shutzer and Mundy again. Anything else?"

"Yeah, tell them to be careful, but keep us covered and make sure nobody sneaks up behind them."

"Right."

"And, Bud, if anybody comes charging into the château, give up, surrender. Got it?"

"Sure, yes, sir, just end the ever-lovin' war."

"That's it. No nonsense, no blue-eyed Aryan poetic hero stuff."

I don't hang up. There's only more quiet. I take off my helmet to hear better. We wait, silent, tense, another five minutes; then there's some caterwauling up on the hill. It's almost like laughing, a hyena laugh, or the mad mechanical laugh from the fun house at a carnival. Then, not a minute later, we hear a voice close on the other side of the road.

"Heh, *ami!*"

We freeze. I look out the corners of my eyes but can't see anything. Next, there's another voice about thirty yards to the right.

"Heh, *ami!* Schnapps? Zig-zig?"

There's the distinct sound of hard laughing. We wait. I take off a grenade, pull the pin and hold down the handle. I expect every minute something's going to come in on us, most likely one of those masher grenades. They've got to know just about where we are; we should've spread out.

There's nothing I can think to do. I switch the lock off the M1 with my left thumb; Gordon and Wilkins unlock, too; makes an awful racket in the quiet. The phone is still off the hook, exhaling into the night. But if I hang up, Miller is liable to ring us, so I leave it. My legs have started their own private dance and my whole body's vibrating.

"*Ami! Schlaf gut, ja!*"

This comes from the same place; then I think I hear movement but still can't see anything. We wait some more in the dark; there's the crashing of brush going uphill and away. Miller's whistling over the phone trying to get us. I pick it up and stoop close.

"Miller?!"

"Hey, what's going on? I've been trying to get you!"

"Anything happening up top?"

"Nothing."

"They've been talking to us down here."

"Holy bells!"

"I'll call in ten minutes. Don't call here."

"Right."

I ease the phone back on its hook. I've been holding the grenade in my right hand with the pin and ring on a finger of my left. I work the pin back through its handle and let up lightly till it catches. It holds fine. I'm shivering so I could easily just have dropped the damned thing. We squat there, crouched, waiting, ready to run, ready to shoot, not ready to die. After another five-minute year, I motion Gordon close.

"Mel, you go left and I'll go right. We'll close in on the other side of the road. I'm fairly sure they took off but we'd better make sure. Wilkins, you cover us. Whatever we do, let's *not* shoot each other."

Gordon edges along our wall to the other side of the bridge; I slink along to where it curves. I wait till Gordon starts across the road, then we sprint over at the same time. Nothing happens. We slowly, noisily, close in through the trees till we see each other; no grenade traps, nothing. We wave, then both dash back across the road and jump down the bank beside Wilkins. We're out of breath, more from fear than anything. Mother looks at me.

"Nothing out there now, Vance, and I'm not exactly complaining."

"Yeah, I watched you both all the way; nothing moved, I could see."

I pick up the phone and crank.

"Bud, everything OK here; think they took off. How're things on the hill?"

"Mundy says somebody up behind them was laughing and they could hear what Shutzer claims is Kraut talk, but that's all."

"It's enough. But they're OK?"

"Sure, I just talked to them."

"It's quarter to ten; tell those guys you'll be up there in about ten minutes. I think we've had our show for the night."

"You mean I don't get to end the war?"

"Not this time."

I hang up. We look at each other. Somehow, now it seems halfway funny; at least we're smiling.

"Mel, I'm going inside to get warm again and I'll be right back. If anything else happens, call. Keep me covered on the way up that hill."

There're flakes of snow coming down as I start trudging up to the château. I was so busy being scared I didn't notice the beginnings. The ground's hard and the snow isn't melting when it lands. When I come in, Miller's heating water in both our canteen cups. He's also heating some for Gordon and Mundy. We break in a couple Nescafe packets and sugar, then sit on the beds watching our fire. The damned fire's eating wood like mad. The phone rings and my heart jumps. It's Shutzer from the upper hole.

"Hey, Won't, what the hell's been going on down there?"

"Stan, I think maybe the German Army is cracking up. There's some good news for you."

"Miller says they were talking *to* you. What'd they actually say?"

"First it was 'Hey, *ami*,' and 'schnapps and zig-zig'; everything prisoners say except '*Kamerad*.' Then it sounded as if they were threatening us; something like 'slap good.' That's what they said just before they left."

"Say that again!?"

"Maybe it was 'slaf good,' didn't make sense."

"Hey, Won't. That's Yiddish! My grandmother always said it when we went to bed. It's '*Schlaf gut*,' means 'Sleep well.'"

"Wait a minute, Shutzer. Are you telling me all this creeping around in the cold, scared, with snow coming down, was only some crazy sauerkraut slurpers making a bed check? I'll tell you, Stan, if that's it, they've been in this cockeyed war too long."

"I'll bet that's what it was, though, Won't. I'll bet pickles to bagels that's just what it was. Lousy, hot shit Nazis laughing at us, softening us up for the kill."

At five before ten, I slide down to the bridge and Miller goes up the hill. The snow's getting thick. They challenge me just where I told them to. Gordon starts up trying not to slip on the snow-covered pine needles. We're all slightly punch drunk.

Wilkins and I sit quietly watching the snow fall. There's something relaxing about the constancy of snow coming down. Could be all the good memories of sledding and ice-skating when I was a kid. God, somewhere inside, I'm *still* a kid; what happened? One day I was seventeen and in high school, then suddenly I'm nineteen and here.

"What do you think this is all about, Wont? It sounded as if there were more of them than there are of us. What if they make some kind of charge? We wouldn't have a chance."

"I don't think anybody's going to charge anybody, Mother. They were probably only trying to find out if we're here and how many of us there are. They saw our smoke and checked us out, that's all."

To keep Mother's mind off what's going on, I ask him to help make up some new bridge hands. Here we are, two hands down by the bridge making bridge hands. We'll need to stock up for the fanatics. When they're nervous or bored, they play more than usual. They'll probably even start with PANTRANT again; that's Shutzer's screwball game of "dictionary," only without a dictionary. The scoring on that one's gotten so complicated you need a mathematical wizard or a Monroe calculator to know who's winning.

I pull my sets of once played bridge deals from my pocket. There are seven. The most aged, the vintage deal, is only five days old. I might be able to slip that one in on them but I need new hands. I keep the bidding, contract and results from the first play; also, who was North-South, East-West. They sign and date the card they've played. It's a regular four-dimensional merry-go-round. I'm half squad leader, half bookkeeper.

So Mother and I stand in the snow leaning against the wall, writing in the dark on my little bits from tab edges of K ration boxes. Shutzer once traded off a German bayonet to one of the typists in personnel for some three-by-five cards but they were mostly used up before we lost the decks on Morrie. Shutzer even got a pack of rubber bands in the trade. I use those to keep each deal separate; I also use them to keep my drawings together. Shutzer's our best squad trader and negotiator as well as squad "Why We Fight" cheerleader. Maybe I can get him to work up a trade for the P38 pistol I took from an SS officer at Metz; maybe a pack of typing paper. I can work tears up thinking of crisp white bond paper.

Mother is absolutely diabolical when he concocts hands. He says it's like writing a mystery story; you start with what you know is the right ending, knowing who's the murderer and who the victims are, then work backwards, throwing in as many false leads and confusing directions as possible. Mother's idea for the consummate deal is for both sides to feel cocksure of a cold slam but with in-built boobytraps guaranteeing failure either way.

I keep peeking around as he figures out his complicated maneuvers. I'm mostly only writing down what Wilkins tells me. I can assure Mel I'm *not* thinking; my mind *is* a blank. I'm not much at bridge but I know enough to recognize these deals Mother's coming up with could turn any serious bridge player into a staggering paranoid. Who'd believe holding all forty points with four-four fit and going down fourteen hundred points? There've been times when I've been convinced Miller, Shutzer or Gordon was going to murder Wilkins. Father never gets that excited about things. I think all he wants to do is get through the games without making any serious mistakes. The only comment I've ever heard him make was one time he said that if the devil could play God for a while, it would be like Wilkins making up bridge hands.

Shutzer spends hours trying to teach Mundy the subtle art of bidding. Gordon and Miller are convinced Shutzer's training Mundy in inflected bidding and is desecrating our only holy one by turning him into a bridge cheater, a dastardly type, destined for the lowest level of the inferno.

Wilkins doesn't want to play because he says he can't forget a hand once it's played, no matter how many days or games are stuck between. At first, everybody laughed, but now they're convinced. They like having Wilkins play because he's so good, but he and his partner, even if it's Mundy or me, will always win the second time around. Mother claims he can't help himself; he tries to forget but can't. For him a bridge hand is like a face, something you remember as a sort of gestalt, without any real effort to memorize cards or plays. Bud is sure Mother's an idiot savant of some kind. Idiot he isn't by any count, savant yes.

I call in regularly as the first two hours pass. Wilkins comes up with four deals to ruin their lives. We're liable to roll out of this château with *true* idiots, blithering idiots, slobbering at the mouth, muttering "Chinese finesse" or "Yarborough." It could happen; you can only push the human mind so far.

Toward the end, Mother is deeply cold. He's so thin, as well as tall, that despite all the bits of cut-up blanket he has wrapped around his chest or pinned to the inside of his pants, or wrapped around his head and neck under his helmet, he gets miserable. I hate to think what'll happen when the winter really comes on; after all, it isn't even Christmas yet.

We still don't talk about what happened on the hill two days ago. I'm not going to mention it unless he wants to.

A quarter hour before Wilkins's time is up, Father Mundy comes clumping down the hill. He tramps along as if he's walking across a golf course following a tee shot. He has his head tucked in and doesn't look up; he forgets to stop and give the password. But he's there and he's there early; there's nothing you can say against Mundy. Mother looks at Mundy's watch.

"Come on, Paul, I still have almost fifteen minutes."

"I got tired listening to Gordon snore. He makes more noise than a screaming meemie! Maybe we should aim him at the Germans and destroy them by sound waves. He could be the squad's private secret weapon. Go on up and you'll hear what I mean, Vance. But put your fingers in your ears as you go through the door or you'll wind up with broken eardrums."

Wilkins stamps his feet and shakes off some of the snow. I tuck away the cards we've been working on.

"You're sure it's OK? You'll take over now?"

"Sure, just plug your ears. I'm fine."

"Thanks. I'm about frozen."

He starts up the hill, leaning forward, dragging his feet. Father slides his rifle off his shoulder and jams the butt plate in the snow. There's about half an inch over everything already. My eyes are wanting to close and the slow-falling snow doesn't help. I'm also having a reaction from being scared.

The snow is like somebody waving a wand in front of my eyes. If I concentrate on the near flakes, I feel my eyes turning up into my head. If I look out through them, the whiteness fuzzes and I start fixating.

"OK if I light up, Sarge?"

"That's between you, God and Gordon, Father; or maybe that's 'amongst.' Only duck down when you light, and keep it covered. I don't think anybody can see much through all this white stuff, but be careful."

Mundy bends over like a bear and smothers most of the flare. He comes up puffing his cigarette between the fingers of his glove. I fumble out one more from my four-pack and light on him. It'll help keep me awake.

I left my shelter half up in the other hole and Father didn't bring his down either. It's going to be a cold two hours and there's a long way to go. I try using my personal con game of telling myself it's time passing and the more time goes by, the closer we get to the end of the war and going home, so enjoy it; stop waiting. But I'm too tired.

Father and I stand there smoking, staring out through the snow, hoping not to see anything. It's even more complicated than that. We're desperately wanting to see anything there is to see, but praying there's nothing there. It can twist the brain. Mundy's leaning his elbows on the wall looking over it and I have my back against the wall looking up toward the château. I can feel it coming on. Father Mundy, professional Catholic, has some time alone with a lost soul and he's going to try reconverting me again.

"Look, Wont; could you explain one more time why you left the church?"

"Come off it, Mundy, I haven't left any church. I haven't written to the Pope and asked for excommunication; you're just making this whole thing up."

"But you don't go to mass."

Father's from Boston and his accent is exaggerated by a thick-tongued, slow enunciation. It's fun talking with him; like playing tennis against a wall, you always know where the ball's going to bounce. It's not that he's dumb; except for Wilkins, he could be the smartest one in our squad. He's just simple. Morrie always insisted Mundy might be the world's best slow thinker.

"For me, Mundy, going to mass is hypocrisy. When I watch all the hoopla, I automatically turn sacrilegious inside, like cream turning sour, or jelly jelling. Any halfway sensitive priest would exorcise me right out of church before he'd say a proper mass."

"Aw, you're not so bad, Wont. Pray for faith and it'll come; you know that."

He looks straight into my eyes, he's so Goddamned sincere. I should shut up.

"Praying itself takes faith, Father; and I'm not sure I ever had it; I don't think I even want it. It's like singing, flying, dancing or writing poetry; some do and some don't, some can and some can't."

I take another quick peek around. We can't actually see

more than ten feet. With the dark, the snow falling and now the snow muffling every sound, anybody could creep up and we'd have no idea. If you get to thinking about all the things that might happen, you could go psycho in no time.

"When I was twelve, Father, the Jesuits offered me the whole bag: free school, university, study in Rome. I didn't sign up."

"You never told me that. The Jesuits, boy, they're the tops. What happened?"

"I just said no. Now, if you really believe, Mundy, have faith, it's dumb not to be a priest. What's a lousy fifty or sixty years compared to eternity? Well, I didn't do it, I'm not stupid, therefore, *ipso facto*, I didn't truly believe, no faith. I thought my mom and dad would never speak to me again."

The snow seems to be falling even harder. I promised myself I wouldn't get into any more of these conversations. Mundy's never going to convince me with the same old arguments and what do I want to do, ruin *his* life? Deep inside me, maybe I do want to be convinced. I could use something, that's for sure. Father's quiet. We reverse positions in the hole. He stares up at the château; I turn and try to peer through the trees into the forest. My feet are going numb. I knock off some snow from my shoulders. I don't feel cold in the chest or stomach and I'm not particularly scared. My stomach isn't rumbling and I don't feel desperately tired. It's only my eyes keep wanting to close.

"You mean, that's how you lost your faith, because they wanted you to be a priest?"

"What's a twelve-year-old kid know about faith? I'd just finished having faith in Santa Claus and the Easter Bunny. I wasn't even sure there wasn't a real Jack Armstrong and Daddy Warbucks. I was at a place where I could believe anything or nothing."

"Then how does somebody know if he has faith? What is it?"

"That's your bag, Father. You're the specialist; you tell me."

He's quiet about three minutes. It's as if I've lobbed one against the wall.

"Then how come you're fighting this war? Hitler's Nazis are saying the same kind of atheist things you're saying. Maybe you're on the wrong side."

"Cut it out, Mundy. You've seen it, German GIs with rosary beads, missals, holy cards; they're the ones with *Gott mit uns* on their belts. German priests're telling them *they're* fighting a holy war against us. We're busy making martyrs of each other, fighting Godlessness. Same religions sending us all to the same heaven. We won't be able to turn around up there. All young guys, no girls, no women, no old people, no priests."

I'm awake now. Amazing how arguing can even make your feet warm. I only have one more cigarette for the day. I'll light up when I feel cold again. Snow's made everything softly quiet; there's no wind right now. I look at Mundy's watch; almost one. I'll make it.

"Besides, Father, I don't have to worry. I've made the nine First Fridays three times. I'm guaranteed 'The Grace of a Happy Death.' I'll spill my guts at that last minute and sneak right through them pearly gates."

"You've got to make them in good faith or they don't count."

"Jesus, Mary and Joseph, did I ever make them in good faith. I'd be there in church at six o'clock mass, freezing my butt, praying my ears off. Sometimes it'd just be the nuns and me. We're in there gilding our halos, burnishing the silver stars in our crowns. Man, you're looking at an old burned-out true believer here, that's all."

I pull up Father's sleeve and look at his watch. Time is creeping by. If one were on night guard in the snow all the time, a life would seem about five hundred years. Mundy's watch is a Benrus, his family gave it to him when he went to seminary school. His father's a bus driver and his family's even poorer than mine, so they put out to buy that watch. About once a day, Mundy mentions his genuine Benrus watch. Sometimes he sounds like an ad.

"You know, Wont, I never made it. Twice I got to seven. Once I broke my fast taking a drink from the fountain right in front of church. Honest to God, sometimes it's as if the devil himself is after me."

"Probably is."

"Don't say things like that."

"If I were the devil, I'd go after a big prize like you; I'd never waste two seconds on some flawed bit of flesh like me. I'm already in the bag, anyway."

I forgot to make the one o'clock call-in. It's almost ten after. I crank up and it takes two rings. I get Shutzer.

"Everything OK down here, Stan. How're things on top?"

"Fine, they've already called in. We began to worry about you two; thought you might've taken the chance to run across the woods and do a little parlaying with our distinguished enemy, like WE GIVE UP!"

"Sorry, no guts. Father's converting me again. If we work something out, we'll fly up there on angel wings. Don't get confused and shoot us down."

Mundy's got his head against mine so he can listen in. Shutzer whispers into the phone.

"How about taking on one li'l' ol' slightly circumcised angel; nobody'll notice; I'll wear a fig leaf."

"We'll consider it. Wait a minute; we have a pronouncement ex cathedra from Father Mundy himself. Here it is. He says if goldbricks like us get to heaven, he's taking his chances with the devil. Unquote. You know, Stan, I think the devil's got a thing for Mundy."

"You bet your life, Won't; big, soft, white Irish ass like that should be just the thing for Old Nick."

"You sound hot for him yourself, there, Shutzer. What're you doing, working it up as squad fairy?"

"If it moves and squeaks, I'll take it. By the way, we're almost out of wood again."

"I'll knock down a few more slats from the stable on my way in."

"I was about to rip off some of these wooden walls here, but Mother went into a screaming panic, claims they're genuine seventeenth-century 'boiserie' and part of our cultural heritage."

"OK, Stan, don't take any wooden walls, and *Schlaf gut.*"

I hang up. Now it's snowing like mad; if you hold your face up, you can scarcely breathe. I stay down with the phone and sit against the wall. Mundy slides down and joins me. There just can't be anybody out there at this time of night in the snow and I'm not caring enough.

"You know what, Father; I'll make a deal with you."

"What kind of deal you gonna make? You want to show me one of those hands we'll be playing so I can fake the pants off Shutzer one time?"

"No, listen to this. We're dealing in futures, eternities. You see, I've got more First Fridays than I can use. Two sets ought to be plenty even for a big sinner like me. I'll trade you one."

"You and your big deals."

"No kidding, Father; seriously; you never know, right? You absolutely sure you're in a state of grace?"

Mundy turns his head and stares at me, then shakes it slowly in disgust. I just can't resist.

"Look at it this way. If I can pray for your soul and have

novenas said, or masses, *after* you're dead, why can't I do you a little favor while you're still alive?"

"That's sacrilegious. Cut it out."

There's still no wind but the temperature's dropping fast. It's not crisp cold, just the thick, fat, air-filling kind.

"Besides, Wont, if you say a novena for somebody, you're not trading; it's a free offering. It's not the same. You can't trade or buy or sell things like First Fridays."

"Come off it, Mundy. Wars were fought over this; millions of people killed and tortured, torn in half, boiled in oil; kings made and broken. What do you think old Luther was pounding nails into church doors about anyway?"

"Aw, them was the olden days. So the church made a few mistakes. That doesn't mean the church is wrong; it only made some mistakes."

"OK, whatever you say. But, if your mother sends some more of those tollhouse cookies, you give me nine of them and I'll sign over a full set of First Fridays."

"Yeah, and I'll buy Park Place."

I look around; nothing. We sit and don't talk for a while. I decide not to light up my last cigarette. Time's going fast and soon I'll be inside for two hours. I hate to think of going into that dark stable for wood. I look over at Mundy.

He has his helmet on his lap so it's getting filled with snow; his woolknit cap is pulled over his ears. Snow's sticking to the cap and he's sitting there, elbows on his knees and thumbs hooked over the swivel of his M1. There's snow piling up on his knees. The bottom of one pants leg has come out of the boot. Snow's sticking on his shoulders and even on the grenades hooked to his pockets. He's like a statue inside himself, but awake. I don't know it but I'm absorbing the main picture I'll have for all my life, of Mundy. As an artist now, sometimes I try to register an image in my memory bank and can't; then other times, when I'm unaware, unprepared, something will sneak in intact. I don't have enough control of my mind.

"You know, Wont; if we didn't trade, it might be all right. If you *give* me those First Fridays as a free offering, as a Christian gift to my soul, it'd probably be all right."

"OK, Father, put them in the golden book; they're yours. *Et cum spiritu tuo.*"

Mundy fumbles in his pockets and lights another cigarette; then he lights a second one on his. He gives it to me.

"Don't tell Gordon."

He's quiet again. I'm thinking at first he means don't tell Gordon about the First Fridays; but he means the cigarette. He takes a deep drag and exhales slowly.

"In fact, the whole box is yours, but we're not trading."

I pull one in myself; the smoke goes all the way down to my lungs and I hold it, some warmth to keep out the cold. It's almost one-thirty and I crank up the phone again. The line's busy, so I hang up. I'm feeling better, no cramps since I took the crap. I crank up again, get Wilkins this time.

"Things OK here, Mother. How're things on top?"

"Fine. Gordon says he and Miller are playing 'paper, rock, scissors'; his arm's so sore he can't lift his M1. Says after the war he's taking Miller with him to Las Vegas and they'll both get rich."

"I'm with that. Miller's psychic. Maybe that's part of what being a poet is; you know things you have no right to know."

"Could be. You guys cold down there? I can bring shelter halfs if you want. The guys on top are luxuriating with two each."

"No, we're OK. Would you put on some coffee before we come in? How's the wood?"

"Almost finished. You know, Shutzer was going to start burning down the château. He's some kind of Philistine-

Neanderthal. I had to threaten him with a grenade to stop the beast from ripping off these hand-carved, oak, two-century-old walls."

"Don't worry. I'll bring in some wood."

"Wont, try not to rip out anything that looks valuable, will you? Remember who the enemy really is."

"OK, Mother. I got it."

I hang up in the quiet. There's some wind now and the snow's blowing. Only twenty-five minutes more. I can almost smell and taste the coffee but it doesn't start my stomach rolling. Maybe I'm getting past it.

"Mundy, one last question. Why does an in-line character like you, practically sitting at the right hand of God already, want to worry about a mere set of First Fridays? What big sin do you have on your soul, anyway?"

Almost soon as it's out, I feel my foot in my throat. I'm doing it again, mucking around in somebody else's private world. There's a long quiet and I hope he's half asleep and didn't hear.

"Why do you think I dropped out of the seminary?"

I stay quiet. Even I know when you're not supposed to answer a question.

"In the second from the last year before ordination, we took our first vow. It was the vow of chastity. The vows of obedience and poverty are taken at ordination. I took the vow but didn't keep it."

"What do you mean, Mundy? Are you trying to tell me that there were *two* non-virgins in the squad back there at Shelby? I don't believe it."

"It wasn't that, Wont. It was . . . well, you know, self-abuse. I took the vow and then did it. I couldn't face up to telling my confessor either. Honest, I think I'm oversexed."

"You mean, that's all it was; you jerked off? That's what chastity *is*, Mundy. How else do you think priests manage it, anyhow?"

"That's not true, Wont. Self-abuse is a sin against purity. I could *never* say mass, touch the sacred host with the same hands that did such a thing."

Mundy actually holds out his hands and looks at them. Snowflakes settle on the brown leather fronts. They're huge hands, breaking out the sides of his gloves.

"You wipe your ass; what's the difference?"

"OK, OK, Wont. You'd never understand. But the worst of it was I couldn't tell it in confession. I could never serve as subdeacon at mass with that sin on my soul. And don't try to tell me it isn't a sin. I spent seven years learning all about sin; this is *my* specialty."

"So you're a great sinner, Father. I'm not going to fight you on that one. To be honest, I've never been able to figure out if I'm the biggest sinner since Cleopatra or I've never committed a sin in my life. It depends on which side of things you look. All I've got to say, Mundy, is if that's why you dropped out of the seminary and got drafted, it makes the ASTPR saga seem like poetic justice."

It looks as if it might snow all night. I get to thinking about our uninvited visitors. What made them come sneaking around, taking chances like that. They must be bored out of their minds; it's one of the worst things about a war: you're either scared shitless, bored to death, hurt or dead.

At two, Shutzer comes down; I'm pooped so I start right up the hill. I wonder what Shutzer and Mundy will talk about, maybe comparative religions. No, Shutzer will try to improve Mundy's bridge game. At least, it'll maybe get Father's mind off how big a lech he is.

I go and kick slats from the stalls in the stable. Miller comes in and scares me so bad I hit dirt in the dark. When I recover, we kick away until we each have an armful. At least we'll be warm. There aren't that many slats left; it's amazing how fast things burn up.

Inside, there's hot water ready for coffee. I open a can of sardines. We agree we'll each take an hour at the phone. I pull the second hour, crawl into my sack feeling not sleepy but go out like a light. When I'm awake for the phone, I'll make the call into regiment. That's my last thought.

The phone ringing wakes me. Miller's climbing into his sack; he points to his watch and turns over. His poem's on the floor beside his mattress. It's all crossed out and re-worked. He wouldn't mind if I read it, but I'm too tired. On the phone, Mundy says it's all fine down there; then Gordon calls, same thing; all quiet.

I warm up the radio. It's set for the regimental frequency. I get Leary. He's half asleep; there're no instructions he knows of. I tell him to tell Ware we've made contact with a German patrol but no exchange of fire. We go through the whole Wilco-Roger-out crap and I close down. Leary's reasonable but his partner Flynn's a bastard. One time Flynn reported me to Ware for sloppy procedure when I was on an OP. I'm crouched in a wet hole on the edge of a churned-up field, trying to see through steamy field glasses while he's sitting in a warm tent with hot coffee, worrying about *my* procedures.

I sleep again, but catch the calls when they come in. We're all half drunk with sleep. I dread going out in the cold; I wonder if it's stopped snowing.

This time I'm up on top with Wilkins. It's black cold, even though it's snowing white. I remember I haven't put on coffee water for the guys coming in; Miller forgot, too. I hate being dumb like that.

It's slippery going. The ground's hard with frozen leaves and about two or three inches powdered over top. I fall twice working my way up. Wilkins waves without challenging and goofy Gordon throws a snowball at me.

"Good snowball snow, Wont."

Nothing seems to get Mel down. Some people have it, some kind of inside rubber resilience that keeps them bouncing. He makes another snowball; I duck, holding my rifle close against my side, turning my back. The snowball hits lightly on the rifle butt and crumbles. Gordon does a perfect imitation of Hunt.

"What kinda sojur is you, there, Knott. That there coulda been a' enemy grenade. I oughta stomp the pissin' outa ya, mollycoddled lousy quizkid."

"Cut it out, Mel. I'm freezing already."

He folds up his shelter half, leaving mine.

"Out of my way then, if you don't want to play; I'm ready for a fire."

He slips and slides down the hill, grabbing trees to stay up, his rifle still slung on his shoulder. Wilkins and I decide we'll take turns sitting deep in the hole and change on the ten minutes. That's what he and Gordon have been doing. This manning two holes at night can't go on. I've got to work out something else.

I ask Wilkins about chess. It's something to keep us going and I've been wanting to know for a long time.

"Vance, why is it you won't play chess with the squad? Is it because there's no competition?"

Long silence. Am I doing it again? Is it any of my business, even? Vance is standing; I'm squatting in the hole; he looks down at me.

"Promise you won't tell?"

"Promise on Father Mundy's honor." He stares out into the dark.

"Because it's no fun. It's not because I usually win, but they don't *play* chess; they *work* at it."

He pauses; I wait.

"You know, the German word for chess is '*Schach*'; almost like their word for battle. That's the way Miller and the rest of them think of chess, as battle. But it isn't battle; it's seduction. The queen is trying to seduce the king, make him come out, be vulnerable. It's a lovely game played that way, and nobody really wins or loses. The secret is in the term 'checkmate.' It's mate, not kill or capture; it's all there. If you think of the game like that, chess is fun and easy."

I squat deeper. I find it hard to believe. Probably Mother's just a chess genius; no matter what he thinks he's doing, or why, chess for him is natural. It's like me and drawing. It always astounds me when a bright person such as Shutzer or even Wilkins draws like a four-year-old. Is that the way they see? I can't believe it.

Wilkins and I aren't scared enough anymore. We're tired and depressed. Phoning in gets to be the high point, something, anything, to do. I'm on till six and it seems impossible. Then my first day guard will be alone down at the bridge. Day guard, hell, it's still dark at eight o'clock. I wonder how the Germans are making it. If they're patrolling around, too, they can't be getting much sleep.

From six to eight, I sleep through, except for phone calls. We keep the fire burning low to save wood.

At eight, I'm down by the bridge. I watch the light try to

show itself through all the snow. At first, it seems only the snowflakes glow lighter and everything else stays dark; then the space between the flakes gets warmer, pinker, but it's still cold; maybe colder.

By the time Gordon comes to relieve me, it's full light but gray again. The wind has died and the snow's drifting down straight; softly, slowly, flakes big around as quarters, or wafers, ghosts of hosts; Ardennes manna. I kick the snow on the ground as I work my way back up to the château.

3
Foo Kit Lur

Gordon shakes me awake.

"Wont, it's Ware on the radio."

I swing my feet to the side of the mattress, still in my fart sack.

"What time is it?"

"Eleven-thirty. Ware insisted on talking with you, chain of command and all."

I slip my legs out of the sack; even my shoes are off. I thought I was in for a straight three-hour sleep and needed it. I still don't have it together in my head who's on guard and who's not. I look over; Miller, Shutzer and Mundy are around a bed with the bridge deal.

"What's up? Wilkins out alone?"

"Well, we figured we were all about to crack manning two holes, so we slacked off while you were asleep. OK?"

"Sure; fine."

What the hell else can I do; run around threatening to "stomp the pissin' outa 'em"? Besides, he's right; we can't keep it up; I was just too nervous, scared.

I squat by the radio. Gordon left it on and it's humming away, a little light glowing red. I switch to transmit and look around the room; there are more smashed chairs beside the fireplace. I hope we get them burned before Mother Wilkins comes back in.

"Able one calling Able four, over."

I get Ware. He must've been sitting in the radio tent waiting.

"What's this about your making contact? Over."

He sounds flustered, excited.

"They came to the posts last night and made noises, sir. They were yelling at us, sir. Over."

"Christ, Knott! What in hell'd they say? Over."

"It was in German, sir. Shutzer says they told us to sleep well. Over."

"Shutzer understands German? Over."

"Yiddish, sir. It's about the same, he says. Over."

"What the hell! Love wants you to locate their CP so he can put it on the operations map. It's total confusion here; there's talk about attacks and everybody being surrounded."

He pauses. He didn't say "over," so I wait. Procedure and all that, what ho!

"Sergeant Knott, I want you to take a small patrol and see if you can find their CP. Over."

"Wilco, sir. Over."

"Look first at that hunting lodge on the other side of the hill. That's the most likely place. Over."

"Wilco. Over."

"If they're not there, check the shack along the streambed downstream from the château. Over."

"Wilco. Over."

"This is pure recon; a three-man patrol should do. Don't take any unnecessary chances. Leave the rest of the squad at the château. Over."

Where the hell else did he think I was going to leave them?

"Wilco, sir. Over."

"Make it soon as possible; daylight if it looks OK. Over."

"Wilco. With this snow it doesn't make much difference, sir. We can't actually see much of anything. Over."

"OK, call back when you come in, or at twenty-hundred the latest. Over."

"Wilco, sir. Over."

"That's it, Knott; good luck. Over and out."

"Over and out."

The mob of them are crowded around me. One of the few events which could break up a squad bridge game would be talk of a patrol. Miller switches off the radio.

"You mean Ware wants us to walk out in the snow and muck around till we stir up a few of the friendly enemy? I don't believe it."

Shutzer wanders back and stares at his bridge hand some more. Miller and Mundy drift over and settle down with him. Gordon cracks the legs off a chair and tosses them into the fire.

"Who's it going to be?"

"You, Stan and me, I think. The rest will have to step up the guard, and, Bud, would you put chains on the jeeps? You never know, we might want to skedaddle away from here in a hurry."

Shutzer's still staring at his hand. Mundy's doing the same thing, scratching his head through his woolknit cap. He *sleeps* with that damned thing on. Whenever he takes it off, he carefully pulls out all the hairs stuck on the inside and saves them. He has a little pack of this hair in the bottom of his canteen holder; says he's going to turn it in after the war and claim a disability pension as an amputee. He's getting bald on top. Shutzer says it's a natural tonsure or maybe a flesh-colored yarmulke. Maybe Mundy will be a religious switch-hitter.

"Won't, what's the chance we finish our hand here first? Mother definitely outdid himself this time. I'm ready to propose he be drummed out of the squad."

Gordon's staring at his hand now.

"Maybe we ought to declare ourselves a firing squad and practice on Mother; I strongly suspect he's a German secret agent sent to destroy our minds, undermine our morale."

"OK, but soon as it's over, we'll go out, and Bud puts the chains on. Then when Mother's guard is up, you take it, Mundy. OK?"

I guess he hears. They've all settled back into the game, miles from patrols, chains, guard duty; they're wearing their brains thin on the possible combinations of cards. I wonder which one it is. No matter what they do, only Mother's going to have any satisfaction.

I'm already nervous. I go upstairs and crap; it isn't bad at all. I come down and scoop some water from the bucket with my canteen cup and put it on the primus stove. I open up my soap and well-used razor, last blade, both sides of both sides worn dull; but if I'm going to be killed, I might's well be a neat-looking corpse; my mom would appreciate it.

Afterward, to the background moans and complaints of bridge players, I heat up powdered eggs, spread orange marmalade on a biscuit and wash it down with coffee. By the time I'm finished, the game's over. I don't even ask what happened. Gordon and Miller look stunned. Shutzer won't talk to Mundy. I'm afraid to ask. Mother'd better stay on guard an extra two hours. Without a word, Miller goes outside to work on the jeeps. Maybe he'll hang himself with tire chains.

I pull out camouflage jumpers from the duffel bags. Shutzer, Gordon and I take off our webbing equipment while we slip the jumpers over our regular outfits. Then we strap the ammo belt, bayonet, canteen, aid kit back on again. We look like Arctic surgical soldiers. We should whiten our rifles and helmets but we don't; it's such a tough job getting that crap off afterward. So many of these things are extra, superfluous; we're carrying through with training routine, rituals to make us feel safer, help us not think what we're actually doing. We're going on an Ardennes safari, with guns, hunting humans, humans who are hunting *us*!

It's after one o'clock when we finally take off. We go down past the bridge, then automatically spread to a ten-yard interval. Shutzer's first as scout, then Gordon; I bring up the rear.

We drop into the streambed and push our way along the right bank. We've already decided to check out the shed or shack first; it's closer. Then we'll swing around and come up on the lodge from south. We're convinced that's where they'll be, so this shed part is mostly a bit of dry run in the wet snow.

I have our contour map tucked in my field jacket pocket under the camouflage cover. We all took a good look at it first. By staying with the stream we'll come close to the shed; it isn't more than four or five hundred yards, at most. The worst we can expect is the Germans will have an outpost there, but that's enough.

According to our map, it looks as if there's a saddle between two hills leading from the shed up to the hunting lodge. I'm not really scared, no shaking, but my tongue is dry. I grab a handful of snow from the low-hanging branch of a tree and stuff it in my mouth. The branch springs up and showers thin flakes of icy snow.

I keep one eye on Gordon's back and try enjoying the scenery. It really is beautiful. I wonder how I could ever manage the effect of snow masses with drawing. It would be mostly a matter of leaving white spaces. It'd sure be great if I could only finagle some typing paper. I can never manage an illusion of snow on gray insides of K boxes. Maybe I could draw first, then dab on rifle whitening for the snow. I'll have to try that; I'd be practically painting then. I could make a brush from some of Mundy's amputated hairs; he doesn't need them all. I'd attach them to the end of a stick with one of the rubber bands, like Benjamin West and his cat hairs.

There isn't as much snow falling and the visibility is better. There's a feeling sun might be up there above the clouds. The stream isn't frozen and is dark brown, almost black, against the snow. It's fast-moving and sometimes not more than a couple feet across. The protruding rocks are capped with snow, water rippling clear against the upstream surface. I'm having my usual trouble, noticing how beautiful the world is just when there's a chance I might be leaving it.

We stay on the right bank, generally, but cross over on rocks when it gets crowded with trees or bushes. Everything's quiet except our own noises. Inside a helmet you can hear yourself breathe or even swallow but it's hard to pick up outside sounds; another bit of brilliant army engineering. At least the Germans had enough sense to bevel out the sides of their helmets. I don't see how we're ever going to win this war doing everything so stupidly. The military mind seems to train soldiers for fighting the war just fought. We were trained to fight trench warfare. In World War I, they were all ready for cavalry charges. It never ends.

We're watching for tracks. There're rabbit skip-jump marks and we spot the trail of a deer but nothing of men. As we go downhill, the forest becomes more dense and the trees are bigger. In some places it's so compacted with trees, the snow doesn't penetrate and we walk on soft, brown pine needles only slightly powdered by blown snow.

Suddenly, Gordon stops and falls to his knees. In front, Shutzer's hit the ground. He motions back. I hurry in a crouch and drop beside him.

"I think that's it, Won't!"

He points straight ahead to a gray, weathered wooden shack with straw sticking out from cracks in the boards and from eaves under a slate roof. I roll on one side, reach inside my camouflage suit and pull out the map. I spread it on the snow. The shack seems to be just where it should be. I look up at the reality.

"Yep; looks deserted enough."

"Uh-huh. What'll we do now, coach?"

"You and Gordon stay here. I'll sneak around and look for tracks. If somebody's there, they'd have to make some marks going in. And, unless they're happy freezing to death for the *Vaterland*, there should be smoke, too."

I ease myself forward slowly toward a small rise on the left. I stay crouched over, keeping the rise between me and the shack. When I peer down the hill, I can see the shack and everything around it. There's nothing: no tracks, no sign of any kind. I pull out the scope and focus on it to make sure. I check especially the ground between shack and hunting lodge. Nobody's been near this place since it started snowing. I stand up, wave Shutzer and Gordon in.

We meet down at the shack. We peer through cracks in boards; nothing's in there except hay. It'd be nice having this place closer to the château; we could use it for firewood. Mother couldn't object too much to that.

There's a nasty little wind blowing and we shelter against the lee side of the shack. I take out my map again; this next part's harder.

We move out in the same order but with a twenty-yard interval. Visibility's still improving; we're heading almost due north now. I check Shutzer's watch. It's not two o'clock yet. According to the map, it should be about a mile from here to the lodge. With any kind of luck, we can get there, take a look, then be back in the château before dark.

We slink along in the trough of hills and come to a narrow road which isn't on the map. This shakes us. It's the kind of thing you don't want to have happening on a patrol. You're scared enough, without getting lost. We go over the map carefully but this road shouldn't be here. Still, far's we can tell, we're going the right direction. Unless we found the wrong shack, we should come on the hunting lodge within two hundred yards or so.

It isn't five minutes later when Stan hits the ground. He signals and I hurry on up. I drop beside him and peer out but can't see anything. He points. I lift my head higher and still don't see anything. Then I see it, a dark smudge in the vague smear of whiteness. We're close. Shutzer cups his hand over his mouth. I lean close so our helmets clink.

"Looks like Nazi smoke to me, probably burning Jewish wood."

We slither back to Gordon and have a powwow. The point is we've already done what we're supposed to do. There they are, there are Germans; and we know where they are. Gordon and I are for calling it quits. Shutzer wants to make sure. In the end, Shutzer talks me into sneaking up with him for a closer look. Mel will stay back to cover us. I tuck in our map, pull out the scope and give it to Shutzer. He's leading; after all, this part *is* his idea.

We creep back to where we were, then on up over the curve of the ridge. Now we can see down the other side.

Below, there's a long, low log-cabin-type building. It has a peaked roof and smoke is curling from a chimney on the east end. Bare-eyed, we can see a pair of German soldiers cutting wood with a two-man saw on a crude sawhorse. They're probably having the same trouble keeping a fire burning we have. They're not wearing overcoats and don't have any visible weapons. Shutzer's scanning the scene with our scope. Then he stops and concentrates on something up close.

I'm looking for outposts. They've got to have some kind of cover. I see a path of tracks down to the road between us and them. Also, there's another path up to a square of green canvas on a hill beyond the lodge. It looks as if there might be a latrine up there.

Shutzer hands me the scope and cups his mouth to my ear.

"Just this side of the road."

I adjust the scope to my eye. The tracks coming toward us, across the road, are fresh; there's hardly any snow in them. But we can't see where they go because they're blocked by the curve of the hill. Stan leans near to me again.

"Let's wiggle a little closer."

He's already moving before I say anything. I'm not exactly enthusiastic about being this intimate with Germans. In my opinion, four or five thousand miles is about the right distance. But I creep along behind Shutzer; me, the great leader, trying to keep up.

We move another twenty yards until we can see all the way downhill. Below us, less than seventy or eighty yards away, is a German soldier sitting on the edge of a hole. Shutzer brings up his rifle, sights, turns toward me, smiles. I shake my head. Shutzer leans.

"Don't worry; I'm only enjoying the pleasure of a fucking Nazi in my sights; I could get a hard-on."

My shakes are starting again. I brace my elbows down tight and scan with the scope. This one outpost seems to be all; at least the Germans are getting some sleep.

I concentrate on the ones cutting wood. With the scope, I can see they're much older than we are; they look thirty or forty years old. Their uniforms are wrinkled and even dirtier than ours. One's facing me and has his field hat pushed back. He looks like an older Max Lewis.

We can hear the sound of their saw and snatches of voices. We catch the smell of wood burning and something else. Then I know what it is; the one just below us is smoking. Gordon would've picked it up ten minutes ago; maybe he has. He might run down the hill past us, trying to stop this guy from smoking, save him from killing himself so he can kill us.

A soldier comes out of the lodge carrying something in his arms. I focus again. It's wet clothes and he's spreading them across a log fallen along the hill up from the flat space where the wood's being cut. We watch five minutes but these four are all we see. The rest must be inside by the fire; most likely sleeping.

We slip down to Gordon again and backtrack a hundred yards or so. Mel can hardly believe us; it isn't that often you get so close to the other guys without something happening.

We pull out the map and decide we'll cut straight to the château, over the hills, instead of doglegging the way we came. It's after three.

On the way back, my stomach gradually stops doing flip-flops. I know we could've killed those four guys and gotten away; that's what war is all about, after all. I'm also sure they could've done the same thing to us last night. I know I'd have an awful time pulling a trigger on the one cutting wood who looked like Max. Lord, please let me get through this stupid business without disgracing myself too much!

We mope along at a ten-yard interval, rifles slung barrel down on our shoulders, not much like real soldiers on patrol. I'm in the lead this time, and Gordon's bringing up the rear. After ten minutes, we stop again to check contours. We're coming out of thick wood into a cleared area sloping to our right, with a ridge and wood up on our left; it fits the map. Far as I can tell, we're still about a half mile from our château.

We start off again. We've just left the wood behind and are going across the clearing. I'm slipping the map inside my snow jumper along with the scope when I look up toward the ridge to our left.

There, at the edge of the forest, is a German soldier with his rifle to his shoulder, pointed straight at me!

I hit the ground so fast my face gets jammed in snow with my rifle caught under me! I slide downhill and roll. Everything's happening fast but in thick, slow motion and fumbling. Now it'll come: the impact, the pain, the blood.

I twist my rifle out, wiping snow from my eyes. Snow's jammed in the rifle sight. My helmet pops off and skids, rolls, downhill. I push the lock off my rifle and try to aim. The German, now joined by two others, is flailing wildly with both arms in the air, waving; signaling!

It's hopeless. We've had it. They've got us dead to rights; the war's over!

I drop the rifle and put my hands on my head. I look around; Gordon and Shutzer are doing the same thing. Shutzer's cursing out loud, slipping, crying.

"Fuck! Here we go! Dirty bastards!"

I'm watching the German. He brings down his arms, waves again, then turns his back, walks away from us into the forest and out of sight!

The others fade back with him, rifles at the ready. We're still, all three, standing there in the middle of an open snow-field with our arms up or our hands on our heads. The army doesn't give lessons on the proper form for surrendering. Gordon's rifle's dangling in the crook of his elbow. My face is wet from melting snow and sweat; maybe from tears, too. We're a sorry sight, not exactly Congressional Medal winners.

I pick up my rifle and start tear-assing, slipping and slid-ing down that hill. I scoop up my helmet, but don't put it on; then halfway I take a real header, belly-flopping at least ten yards, sliding into home plate. My helmet bounces away again. Gordon and Shutzer run past, then stop to wait. I pick up the rifle and helmet, run after them.

We don't stop till we can duck down in the cut of the streambed, about two hundred yards from the bridge. I flop and try getting my breath back. Shutzer and Gordon are pressed against the bank. Mel looks at me.

"You all right, Wont?"

I nod. They're both white, so white Shutzer's whiskers stand out black. It's then I notice I'm gummy between the legs. In all the excitement my plug gave out. Gordon points and squeezes his nose.

"Smells like those German gents up there stomped the livin' somethin' outen ya, Wont."

Shutzer takes off his helmet, knocks snow from the net-ting.

"I sure thought you'd had it when you went down. You could get a job in cowboy movies with a pratfall like that. Tom Mix couldn't do it better."

Then, uncontrollably, we're giggling, giggling on the

edge of hysteria, giggling, laughing, snorting so it's hard to breathe.

Finally we pull ourselves together; I begin feeling the cold. I realize I dropped the scope and map up there. Shutzer had a full clip spring from his rifle, too. Somehow, Gordon kept his stuff intact.

In a crouch, rifles at ready, we dash downstream, splashing, running back and forth on rocks, not running for any reason now except we're deep scared and glad to be alive.

Nobody's at the bridge but we pick out Miller on the upper post. We go on inside and Mundy's stretched in his sack by the fire. He sits up when we come in.

"How'd it go? Find any Germans?"

Shutzer sits down and starts digging snow from the action of his M1. I'm trying to figure some way I can wash out my pants, then get them dry fast enough to go back on guard. I slip them off, underpants, too. It's mostly fluid but stinks to hell. What the hell can I wipe with?

I rub and scrape with one of my K ration boxes. Then I tear off an ear from the D ration box and scrape some more. Shutzer and Gordon take off their wet boots. Gordon goes upstairs. Shutzer pushes his boots close to the fire.

"Found 'em all right, Mundy; then *they* found *us*. Krauts almost blew our heads off."

"Didn't hear anything here, nothing at all; and I was listening."

"Nothing to hear, Mundy, very quiet war."

Shutzer turns to me. I'm standing inspecting the inside crotch of my underpants. Below my field jacket, I'm wearing only wet boots.

"Damn it, Won't, that pickle head took one hell of a

chance just to prove his Goddamned, hot shit Aryan superiority."

"I'll say he did that. I think he was surprised as we were, Stan. There were three of them at least, you know."

"I know, I know. And they had the jump all right, sneaking out of a wood, uphill, like that."

Mundy's looking back and forth as we talk.

"Come on, what happened?"

Shutzer bangs his rifle butt on the floor a few times to shake snow off the webbing.

"Krauts jumped us, had us cold cock, Mundy, then didn't shoot. That's what happened."

"How come?"

"This Nazi bastard waves at us like we're a private parade for his amusement, then fades into the forest primeval. That's how come!"

"But you guys should be dead. What're you complaining about? I don't get it."

"Yeah. We're happy. We're happy. Hooray! Yippee! OK, Mundy. Make you feel better now?"

I know then none of us is going to admit we were ready to surrender. We talk about giving up a lot but mostly it's only talk.

Gordon comes down from the john.

"Boy, I only just made it. I don't think my heart and intestines will ever settle back to their proper places. Shutzer, you still taking it out on the nasty Germans?"

"Dirty Nazi Aryan super fuckers."

I go outside to rub snow on my spots. I rub till the snow doesn't come away brown. There's nothing more I can think to do. I slip the underpants back on and fast slide into my ODs. It also can't be too terrific for the shits having snow-cold underwear against my crotch. I back against the fire-place to warm myself, and maybe dry things out some. In five minutes I have to relieve Miller on top.

It's only then I realize I haven't seen Wilkins. I've been so busy, wiping up, I wasn't looking for him.

"Hey, Mundy, where's Mother?"

"Oh, he's tromping around upstairs in the attic playing dolls with the furniture. He's fine."

I should've known.

The back of my pants are warm now, but as they get warm, I begin to stink. I peek outside; it's snowing harder again. I grab my shelter half, helmet and rifle, then trudge up the hill.

Miller sees me coming and cuts across. He's kicking clouds of snow and trying to ski-slide in his boots as he comes down. Pretty damned impressive changing of the guard, yes, sir.

"King Kong cold wind up there, Won't, and you can't see a damned thing. I couldn't even make out the bridge. You'll be better off down there at the other post. At least when they shoot you we'd have some warning."

"You get such terrific ideas, Miller. You mean I'm sup-posed to be a sort of snowfield security early-warning alarm device."

"Well, you know what I mean, and you'd be a hell of a lot warmer. Maybe we'd even hear you shoot them first. When you think about it, that's what guard duty's all about, isn't it? You're out there so the rest of us have a chance to hightail into the bushes. It's your turn; lots of luck. How'd the patrol go?"

"OK. Only we almost got ourselves killed. Shutzer'll tell you about it."

I turn and face downhill.

"You're right, Bud, I *can't* see the bridge, not even from here. What's the use?"

"How'd you like a few extra cigarettes? I snitched them from Gordon's share before he could do his 'sacrifice to the gods' health ritual into that fire."

"Thanks! But when he catches on, don't tell him you gave any to me; I can't face the wrath of the righteous just now."

Miller and I start back on down together. He goes around behind the château to get more wood. There can't be much left of that stable. Wilkins'd better get things categorized for order of burning. I can see an intrasquad war coming up: hots versus colds, or something like that.

I walk on down the road and slide in against the wall. Bud's right; this is better than up on that hill. The wall blocks any wind and whenever I want, I can slump in a squat, lean my back against it, give my legs a rest. While I'm squatting like that, for sure, the only way they'll know the Germans have arrived is the sound of a bullet tearing through my skull.

But two hours standing up in the snow on a cold day can break you down. I light one of Bud's, or rather Mel's, cigarettes. I only have six matches left; I'll run out of matches before cigarettes. Bud has a lighter, a Zippo he traded something for. He might be the only soldier in the Ardennes Forest, either side, who can keep one of those lighters working.

If I were Miller and could handle all the poopshit little mechanical things in life the way he can, I'd be able to live a lot more comfortably with myself.

For me, just learning to dismantle and put back together my M1, the carbine, the thirty-caliber machine gun and the BAR was pushing the limits of my mechanical ability. I never did qualify on the fifty caliber. I did OK on the range, but couldn't reassemble the damned thing so it'd work without jamming.

I've watched Miller win bets tearing down those weapons blindfolded, getting them together faster than most people do with eyes open. It's something special, like his being psychic and a poet.

Nothing, but nothing, seems hard for Miller; he'd probably be a general in the German Army by now. No, they'd most likely shoot him. With Bud, you never know. Any minute, he might just refuse to obey a direct order. He's not contrary, only bullheaded; he won't do anything when he's convinced it's the wrong way. I don't think he's much on ethics, moral correctness or anything; but he has some kind of personal aesthetic which involves being logical, doing things the *right way*. In fact, Bud could probably do almost any wrong thing so long as it was being done right. Maybe it comes from being a watchmaker's son, but Shutzer's not like that at all. I don't know.

After ten minutes or so spinning like this, my cramps begin. I'm convinced it's from being scared all the time. When we were running down that hill, my mouth was filled with a sour, bitter taste. I had to keep swallowing just to stop myself from puking.

Somebody's coming down from the château. It's Shutzer. He has his snow jumper on again. I lean against the wall and watch him work his way along the road. He's lifting his feet high as he comes down, looking back at his own footsteps in the snow, like goose-stepping.

"Himmler's tits, Shutzer, haven't you had enough strolling around in this winter wonderland?"

"If it's OK with you, Won't, I'm going back to look for that scope and map, also my clip. We've definitely got to make out a Statement of Charges on the scope, so one of us should go check it out. Chances are they're still there."

"Hell, the scope's my problem, Stan. I can always sneak out later and look around."

"You'd never find it in the dark and this snow's going to bury everything, anyway."

"The hell with it."

"But it's OK if I go look?"

"I don't get it, Stan. What's the sense? Those guys *could* still be hanging around in the woods. They might even have a post up there."

"No, I'm sure they were only patrolling."

"Then they probably got anything we dropped. If it were a patrol, they'd come down to scrounge around after we ran."

"Maybe; but I'd like to take a look anyway."

"Rat's claws, Shutzer! It's just not that important."

"Somebody should do it sooner or later. I'm willing to do it right now, so relax."

I *know* I don't want to do it. Stan's not on for four more hours at least; now's good a time as any. But there's sure to be a bridge game going on, with me out here. Maybe that last deal cured Shutzer; maybe he's looking for some excuse to duck playing.

"OK, Stan; but take it easy. No fooling around. No one-man avenging Jewish army against the forces of darkness and evil. Mundy's our religious fanatic; remember that."

"I'll be back through here before you're off, and don't *you* shoot *me*."

"If you're not back by six-thirty, I'll send Mundy to sprinkle some holy water over your remains, like urine. A little Extreme Unction couldn't hurt either. We'll do it all kosher."

"Spoke, like in wheel, you, Won't."

Shutzer works his way down along the stream, same way we went out, under the bridge, then up over the road where our wall ends. Then he moves on to the other side of the road, and into the trees until I can't see him anymore. I light up my second cigarette, trying to breathe slowly and deeply at the same time. I'm painting the inside of my lungs black

with soot, according to one of Gordon's lectures. But sometimes I can stop the cramps that way. I don't want to crap in
the snow. It'd be much better if I can just hold out/in till I'm
back inside.

I'm just beginning to get worried when Shutzer crosses
the road farther down, at the turn in the road. I watch him as
he comes toward me. He slides down off the road and joins
me against the wall.

I've just phoned in and it's all OK except they're about to
form a lynching party for Wilkins because of the last bridge
deal. Mother's upstairs and Miller suggests we lock him in
and slip a little food under the door once in a while. But
Father Mundy says we'll all starve if Mother doesn't cook.

"Find the stuff?"

"Just my clip."

Stan takes out a cigarette and I give him one of those last
matches. It isn't often Shutzer smokes. It's then I notice his
forehead is dripping sweat, his hands shaking and his mittens
soaked.

"They came down after we left, I guess, because there's all
kinds of tromping around. They took the scope and map; war
souvenirs for the *Fräuleins* back home."

"I'm definitely in for a Statement of Charges then. I hate
making out those things. Normandin, the company clerk,
acts as if I'm stealing the stuff to start a war surplus store
when I get home."

Shutzer pulls off his wet mittens. He's the only one in the
squad who has these new mittens with the index finger separate for firing a rifle; the rest of us still have old-style, wool-
backed, leather-fronted, five-fingered gloves, designed to

encourage frostbite. I've never seen anybody except officers and Shutzer with these new mittens. Shutzer wrings them out before shoving them in his pocket.

"Looks as if you really did a good hunt for that scope, Stan. OK if I use you as a witness to prove I didn't hide it in my duffel bag or bury it somewhere?

"What've you been doing anyway, walking around on your hands and knees? Or just praying in the snow for Mundy's soul?"

"Nawh. I could see right off the stuff wasn't there."

He looks down at himself. He's wet from boot tops to crotch.

"I got wet working out a little surprise for our Teutonic friends."

"Grenade trap?"

I say it and hope not. Shutzer might just do a thing like that. He's the only one of us fighting the war on purpose.

He smiles and blows two smoke rings. He can blow the most solid, holding-together smoke rings I've ever seen. These two he churns out now are blue and thin against the snow. A draft skittering along the gulley bends, then tears them apart.

"Built a snowman."

"Come on, Stan! Don't *you* start bucking for Section Eight, too. Save some space for me."

"Built a life-size snowman right where we dropped our stuff. This is perfect snowman snow; rolled two big balls in no time at all, piled one on top of the other, the way people do in kids' books. Then I made a face with pinecones for the eyes, nose, mouth. Finished the whole thing off using pine needles for a mustache, then a long pine branch, with a flat snowball on the end, stuck out like an arm giving the Nazi salute. I even plastered a few pine needles falling over one eye. Damned good resemblance if I say so myself.

"You know, Won't, maybe I won't start an advertising agency after the war. Maybe I'll buy myself some rocks and try it as a sculptor. I'll tell you, I built me a genuine masterpiece out there."

"Come on, Shutzer. You mean you built a snowman in the open field on that side-slanting hill. Those German crazies could've snuck up behind the mad artist at work and made a few well-placed critical comments with a burp gun. One more ventilated ASTPR whiz brain."

"If those Nazis were going to kill me, they already had their chance. I figure they're dogging it the way we are. They don't want any trouble; they're getting all their thrills sticking yellow stars on Jews, herding them into cattle cars, locking them up in concentration camps, using them as slave labor. They're not going to do anything against anybody with a real gun in his hands."

"You really believe that shit, Stan? You really think the Nazis are killing Jews?"

"I *know* it. It's hard for a goy like you to believe, but I *know*. I have relatives who were there. These Nazis are bloodthirsty monsters. It's a whole nation of shits like Hunt and Love."

"OK. So maybe you're right. But what sense does it make building a snowman in the middle of a forest? Tell me that, and no more Zionist sermons, please. I don't want to hear it; I don't want to believe anything like that."

"All right, buddy; but you'll see.

"By the way, I stamped out a message in the snow just in front of my snowman. It faces the forest where they came out at us. If they go by there again, they can't miss it."

"OK. So what's the message?"

"FUCK HITLER!!!

"I made the exclamation points with pine branches."

Shutzer stands and slings his rifle on his shoulder. We've

been sitting against the wall out of the wind, waiting for warning bullets through our skulls.

"Stan, you're nuts. Tell Gordon and the rest about the snowman, and don't forget your love note. They've been threatening to lock Wilkins in the attic; maybe they'll lock you up there with him. He can catalogue furniture while you make paper airplanes inscribed with messages in Yiddish to throw out the dormer windows for the Germans. This whole squad is going quietly berserk."

Shutzer starts up the hill. I think of lighting another cigarette but don't. I'm feeling rotten. Cigarettes, breathing, nothing seems to help. My stomach's rolling, rumbling, and my back hurts.

I can't stop thinking about things. Everybody's saying the war's almost over, the Germans are supposed to give up, maybe even by Christmas. But it's never going to end.

When you think how long it's taken to come this far; how the farther we go, the closer the Germans are to home, fighting for their lives, with short supply lines, it looks impossible. With all the murder and looting they're supposed to've pulled on the Jews and Russians, I don't see how they can ever give up either. They'll fight to the last crossroads, the last railroad station, the last city.

And after that, the Japs. The only chance to stay alive is get hit, be captured or go ape. I admit I'm afraid of being captured by Germans. Maybe it's all only propaganda but something inside me is afraid of what they'd do. Seeing those bodies, the one leaned against the tree and the others pushed together in the woods on the way in, didn't help. Maybe Shutzer's right; maybe they are different. It had to be the Germans did it. What could they be thinking?

But we were all ready to give up today, even Shutzer. It

was so easy, nothing to do. And God, you can get killed fast; I was expecting it, tight inside, feeling my last time slipping past me, waiting, helpless.

I've got to stop. If you think about what's happening or what might happen, you'll never make it. If you start looking at those ideas, then soon you're waiting and if you start waiting, you're finished.

When I go off at eight, I'm dead tired. I'm feeling dry-skinned, my lips feel tight, as if the skin will split and fester. I've been fighting off cramps the last hour.

Gordon comes down for the first night guard. We talk. We reach the conclusion to try two on a guard but only one post, phoning in on the half hour. That way, we can get some sleep. We should really have two posts but what the hell, if that's how the squad feels, OK.

I tell Mel the new password is "snow—man." We laugh about Shutzer's crazy snow sculpture. Mel says he hopes the Germans don't find it; all we need is a hot and bothered enemy slavering after our blood.

Up at the château, Mundy, Miller and Shutzer are settling in for a game of Shutzer's PANTRANT.

I say I'll probably join in soon as I make my call to regiment. I warm the radio. When I get through, Leary says to sign off and call back in five minutes; Ware wants to talk with me.

I turn off and spread myself on one of the mattresses. There isn't enough time to go for a crap but the cramps are already beginning. There's a big pile of shiny, splintered wood leaning against the fireplace. I wonder if Mother knows about this. I should go up in the attic to find out just what the hell he's doing. What would I do if he's decided to give it all up and hanged himself? Here I'd have Miller hanging by tire chains and Wilkins dangling in the attic. Maybe I ought to skip the game and check out Mother; that's what a sergeant is supposed to do, I think.

The fire's burning fine; chunks of cast metal are attached to some of the wood and are glowing red in the heat. What could it have been? They wouldn't burn a piano or anything like that, would they? I don't think so; I hope not.

At quarter past, I call again and get Ware.

"Everything go off OK, Sergeant? Over."

"OK, Lieutenant. Shutzer, Gordon and I took it. We checked the shed, nothing there. We found them at the lodge. There were three Germans plus an outpost on the road just under us. Over."

"Good work. You only saw four of the fuckers? Over."

"No, sir. After that, on the way back, we made contact with an enemy patrol. There were three or more of them; they were about a half mile from the château. Over."

"You made contact? What the hell's that mean? Did they see you? Over."

"Yes, sir. They pinned us down, could've picked us off, but didn't. I don't understand it; none of us does. Over."

"Well, I'll be Goddamned!"

There's a long pause. My cramps are coming on so hard I'm bent double over the radio. I hear the word for the first part of the game. It's Miller and the word's "brinkolar." He gives the spelling. I think about ice skates, candy bars, stars. Anything but think about what's happening just north of my asshole. If Ware doesn't sign off soon, I'm going to crap my pants again.

"Sergeant Knott, things are still confused here. Nobody seems to know what's happening. I'll report this to Major Love now. He's climbing the walls of the S2 tent; at least this is something. Over."

"Yes, sir. Over"

Please! Let me off before I explode.

"OK, Knott, stay in there. Over and out."

I turn off the radio and wait for a strong cramp to let up. Shutzer's gathering in the slips of paper with the different definitions. Mine would have been "the nearest edge of a frozen star." I loosen my field jacket, my belt, the top buttons of my pants. I work out some toilet paper from my helmet liner on a mattress beside me. Then slowly I get up and start toward the stairs, leaning over, holding my pants with my left hand. I make it to the top of the stairs, then stand there while a bad one bears down on me. I hold till I get my pants down and my ass jammed into the toilet.

I sit there and let the cramps roll. I'm bent in half, head between my knees. I keep feeling if I can only get it all out, whatever it is, then I'll be OK, but it never works. I hate going on sick call, but I'll do it when we get back.

I work my way downstairs for the first call-in from Gordon. Nothing. Mundy's on next. The PANTRANT game is over and everybody's catching up on sleep. I ask Father to listen for the next call and I go up to find Wilkins.

The door to the attic is open and I can see the light from one of the flambeaux. Mother is sitting on the floor surrounded by at least fifteen paintings in big gilt frames. He doesn't turn around when I come in. I lower myself onto the floor beside him.

"Look, Wont. Look at these paintings. They're actually not much good, but they're such a comfort. I can feel the calm and concern of some person who took the time to see and then make something to help me see with him. That's love, Wont; sometimes I almost can't believe there's any love left anymore. These paintings make me glad I'm a human being."

I look around at the pictures. They're mostly forest scenes with pine trees and snow, or meadows with flowers in spring. There are two with deer browsing or looking up at us just the way the deer I saw did. There are also pictures of pots and pans, one of some vegetables falling out of a basket. I start out only worried about Mother sitting up here in the dark but then feel myself falling into it with him.

Up to that moment, all my experience with art had been limited to drawing. I never had an art course in high school; everybody was pushing me into math or science; trig and spherical trig, solid and analytic geometry; special classes at Drexel Institute. It wasn't particularly hard but it wasn't fun either; only more work, learning new games, tricks for non-thinkers, preparing myself to make a living.

But drawing has been a lifelong private joy. I'd draw on anything, hide drawings everywhere; my schoolbag, note-books, even textbooks were filled with them. My poor mother would frantically clean out the drawers and closets of my room every few months and throw them out, piles of scratch-ings. I didn't mind much; for me it was the process of draw-ing, not the drawings, that I loved.

I used to run around the art museum at the Parkway in Philadelphia but I never looked at the paintings on the walls. We were only interested in finding secret hidden doors or passages in the wood-lined rooms, getting scared by Egyp-tian mummies in the basement when we played hide-and-seek.

It's hard to believe a person could get to be nineteen years old and never even *look* at a painting, let alone *see* one. But with me it happened. The shock of discovery was over-whelming.

It might only have been because I was so miserable, scared, the reality around me so unacceptable. I'll never

know all the reasons, but these intimate presentations of another world, another time, through a mind not my own, had
an unbelievably profound effect on my deepest psyche. It
changed my life. There, murmuring with Wilkins in the
voice of lovers, after love, I knew an aesthetic experience. I
dimly perceived what it was all about. I'd never be the same
again.

Much later, I bring Mother downstairs with me. He's
agreed to try arranging everything up there into three cate-
gories. First, what can be burned without committing too
great a sacrilege. Next, what could be burned in dire emergency but shouldn't be. Last, the things we can never burn
for any reason, things that must be defended to the death if
we want to maintain any status within the species.

It's almost ten o'clock. We've been up in that cold, dark
attic, in another place, more than an hour.

I call the squad together, except for Gordon, who's out on
post. I tell them I think tonight we should have two on but
only one post, the bridge. Nobody argues. I think none of us
was looking forward to being out there alone in the dark.

I'm glad we don't argue; I'd've been forced to pull rank,
and that I dread.

I'll be on down by the bridge with Mundy next. It'll only
be two hours; then we'll have four off sharing the phone. It
won't be bad. After all, there's a war on and we're right in the
middle of it, more or less.

I'm still feeling very slow. Looking at the paintings
helped but I'm drained, weak. Mundy and I slip on the
snowsuits; it'll make us less visible and also keep that vicious
biting evening gulley wind from blowing through us. The
snowsuits have hoods we can tie tight over our helmets and
around our necks. The trouble is they're made from some

kind of crinkly, noisy material. It makes a sound like Dacron sails when they're being pulled up. I'm probably the only person in the world who thinks of snow, cold and fear when he hoists his sails on the sunny marina in Venice, California.

When we go out, the snow has stopped and the sky is clearing. There's an almost full moon, and clouds are racing across in clumps. Shadows of clouds roll over the trees and snow as we walk downhill to the bridge. Gordon challenges and we all move together against the wall.

"Any noises out here tonight, Mel; owls, Indians, wood elves?"

"Quiet; nothing except that spooky banshee wind blowing through the trees like background sound effects for a Frankenstein movie. And wait till that moon starts ducking in and out clouds; it's as if you're on some kind of shadow-crashing roller coaster."

Gordon picks his grenades off the wall. Seeing that makes me glad we've decided on a two-man post. He starts up the hill. Mundy leans against the wall with his back hunched and his shoulders pushed forward. I stand my rifle against the wall and tighten the string on my snow-jumper hood. Mel's moved the telephone up onto the ledge. I pull it down again to the base of the wall. We don't want the post looking like a doctor's office. Mel's also rolled himself a big snowball to sit on. He was almost ready to receive patients. Mundy slides over and sits on the snowball chair; I begin rolling one for myself. Shutzer's right; this is perfect snowman snow. I roll it in a few minutes. We both sit on our snowballs, like two guys side by side on johns in a barracks. I don't know about Mundy, but I'm not up to much talking. It's going to be a long two hours. If Mundy starts up again on his save the sinner's soul crusade, I'll just tell him to can it. I want to think some more about those paintings.

We've just finished our first call-in at ten-thirty when I think I hear something moving on the other side of the road! I push my snow hood back and rip off my helmet. I unhook grenades from my pockets and put them on the wall; Mundy does the same.

I don't know if he heard anything, but he can tell for sure I did.

The moon's bright just at that moment and we stare hard but can't see anything. But we can hear it, there's no doubt now. There's something moving around in the brush just inside the trees on the other side of the road, less than forty yards from us!

I'm trying to decide if I should call the château. I'm afraid whatever's out there will hear me; it's so close! There's the sound of something big moving, so big I almost convince myself it's some kind of animal, not a man; then there's quiet again. Next we hear the sound of what can only be digging. There's also the sound of shuffling and puffing. It's human all right. We're tense waiting. Cranking up the damned phone makes too much racket; I take it off the hook so they can't ring us here. This might be one of those "Miller" cases where the signal will be the sounds of shooting and screaming. We wait.

Then we hear voices, loud whispering, tails of "s" sounds. The moon goes behind a dark, dense cloud; shadows of trees bend as darkness sweeps over them. It's deeply dark, just snow glow on the ground and everything else invisible, dark. We're both holding our breath so we can hear. I'm *sure* I see something on the road, something standing up etched in the dark. We hear voices again and we wait.

Then, just before the moon finally comes out, there's a voice, a louder voice, almost a shout, and more scurrying, snow-muffled cracking of pinecones and branches under foot. When the moon comes out strong, we see him on the road.

It's a German soldier with a rifle to his shoulder pointing straight at us! Mundy and I duck fast. Nothing happens! I reach up, snatch one of our grenades from the ledge and pull the pin. I lob it up over our wall and count. There's concussion, a bright flash, the singing thrump of fragments, the smell of nitrate.

Somebody laughs!

Mundy and I look at each other. We slowly, carefully, push our heads over the edge of the wall. The soldier is still standing in that same place with his rifle pointing at us! We duck down again. What the hell do we do? Maybe they *are* supermen. That guy should be riddled with fragments and he hasn't moved!

I peek again. I hear somebody, not the soldier standing there, somebody in the trees on the other side of the road, trying not to laugh. Then there's a yell. First one voice, then at least three.

"FOO KIT LUR!" "FOO KIT LUR!" "FOO KIT LUR!"

There's more laughing. I pick up the phone and dial the château. With all the yelling and thumping going on, one little phone cranking will hardly be noticed. I get Shutzer.

"Hey, Won't! What's going on?"

"I don't exactly know, Stan; maybe we have a zombie or there could be a looney bin near here for totally bonkered-out German ex-soldiers and some of them escaped. The noise you just heard was me throwing a grenade."

Across the road they're still yelling, now in unison like cheerleaders at a pep rally.

"FOO KEET LUUR!" "FOO KEET LUUR!"

I hold the phone receiver up over the edge of our wall, then bring it down again.

"Can you hear that, Stan?"

"Hell, yes, we can hear it *without* the phone. What're they yelling about this time?"

"You won't believe it, Stan. I think they're yelling 'Fuck Hitler, FUCK HITLER' the way your grandmother would say it; that is, if she'd ever say such a thing."

"Bull toads!"

"Serious, Stan. I don't know what to do."

"Want us to come tearing down, San Juan Hill, Charge of the Light Brigade, anything like that?"

"I don't think it would do any good. So far, except for the yelling, nothing's happened. There's just this crazy guy standing out there on the road pretending grenades don't hurt. Maybe somebody should bring down a few strait-jackets. If we can't put them on the Germans, we can use them ourselves. This is all insane!"

Then it happens; a grenade comes sailing over the wall and lands near Mundy. I drop the phone and hit the ground. Then I see it isn't a grenade at all; this is a snowball with a stick pushed into it. I work myself into a sitting position against the wall, unscramble phone wires.

"Stan, this is too much. Honest to Christ, now they're throwing snowballs."

I look over at Mundy; he isn't listening; he's picked up the fake grenade. He pulls out the stick, packs the snowball more tightly, tosses it back over the wall and across the road.

"Wait a couple minutes, Stan. I'll call back. If there's a lot of combat-type noise, have Miller rev up our jeeps and get the hell out of here!"

Of course, you'd know it, a few seconds later more snow-balls come flying over the wall, this time without sticks. Mundy's taught the Germans how to make honest-to-God

American snowballs without handles. Every time they throw one, we get the FOO KIT LUR yell.

Mundy's busy picking up snowballs, packing and throwing them back. I even throw a few myself. We can't see the Germans and I'm not about to stick up my head higher than our wall. I stay crouched and sling most of the snowballs underhand. But Mundy's standing straight up, zinging them across the road and into the woods. Theirs are lobbed to drop in on us. I've got to say there's nothing much of hurting anybody with these snowballs. I scrunch down by the phone again and crank.

"Shutzer?"

"Yeah, Won't! We're all set. Just give the word. Miller will roll on down in the jeep with Gordon behind the fifty. The rest will close in behind."

"Well, we're having a Goddamned snowball fight."

"*What?*"

"Stan, you don't think maybe the war's over and nobody's telling us? I just finished talking to Ware and he sounded peculiar. They wouldn't do that to us, would they; end the war and keep it to themselves?"

"You're sure you're OK down there? Mel snuck halfway downhill and along the ridge. He says it looks as if somebody's put up a scarecrow in a Kraut uniform near the bridge. He couldn't be sure but that's what it looks like."

"A scarecrow! Damn it, Shutzer, you started all this FOO KIT LUR shit; now it's snowballs and scarecrows. Why don't you take over this whole sump hole of a war, just send the rest of us home?"

I hang up, then stand straight to take a good look. To be honest, at this point the only thing I'm afraid of is being hit in the face by a snowball.

Sure enough, it's a scarecrow. What we thought was a rifle is a stick with a piece of paper flapping on the end. From the corner of my eye I catch a movement and somebody steps onto the road from the forest. He waves both arms. He's far enough away so in the dark I can't make out his face, but it isn't the one who looks like Max; that much I can tell. He's smiling and has a Schmeisser slung upside down over his left arm.

"*Schlaf gut, ami!*"

He waves again and slowly steps back into the forest.

"Slaff good, Kraut."

It's Mundy standing beside me waving both arms, an Irish windmill. We hear them crashing through the brush uphill on the other side.

My insides begin unwinding. I stoop, pick up the phone and crank it. I stand leaning against that wall and jam the phone box between my elbows. I'm perspiration-soaked from the top of my head down into my boots. It could be from the snowball throwing but I think it's pure fear. All my clothes are saturated with fear sweat, so it'll just dry and that's that. We all smell the same; there's no use washing. I get Shutzer again.

"What's up now, Won't? You two started building snow castles yet? German misplaced castles on the Rhine?"

"Don't rile me, Stan; this is your war. I'm only reporting it, right? We said good night, politely as sugar pie. You can go beddy-bye now; it's been settled. You know, we might just end this war ourselves, privately, out here in our forest. We'll all move into the château together and defend it against the crazies who *like* wars. Maybe declare ourselves neutrals."

"You're *sure* you're OK there? Gordon's been applying his instinctive, humanist mind. It, combined with Miller's analytic approach, can be deadly on unsolved problems; but nobody's come up with any answers that make sense. The bad news is neither of them thinks the war's over. Maybe we need some of your creative, gooey thinking on this project."

"I'll work on it, Stan."

"Yeah, and Foo Kit Lur."

After maybe ten minutes more, with the two of us staring into the dark, hoping not to see anything, I decide to slip along the streambed, creep up on the scarecrow.

All the way I'm watching for mines. I work my way along until I'm beside it. They've made their *own* version of Adolf Hitler. That's what all the hollering was about. This scarecrow is decked out in a beat-up uniform. The head is made from a good-sized snowball with pinecones and pine needles arranged the way Shutzer said he did it on his. It could even be the same head. On the end of a stick tied to the arms is our map. At the foot of the scarecrow is our scope.

I scramble up onto the road and signal back to Mundy. He sees me and waves. The fool doesn't even have his rifle covering me. I pull our map off the stick and pick up the scope. Then I dash back along the road and jump over the wall. I grab Mundy's wrist and look at his watch; it's time for the eleven-thirty call-in. This time I get Gordon.

"Mel, tell Shutzer we got the scope and map back; we can forget the Statement of Charges."

"He's taking a crap. What'd they do; trot up and offer them as Christmas presents, gift wrapped?"

"They were out there with the scarecrow. By the way, the scarecrow is another Shutzer special, a German version of the great leader. What do you think's going on, Mel? I can't figure it."

"I admit I've given up on any idea the war's over, or is even about to be, but that's what I keep wishing."

"Wouldn't it make a great Christmas present? OK this is it, folks. Noël, No Hell, go home! I've got to say this is one creepy place to spend Christmas."

"Looks real goyish to me, Wont. Here you've got the whole thing: Christmas trees by the thousands, snow, pinecones, fireplace, the works. What else could you want?"

"How about a small-size, dried-up Douglas fir nailed to the living-room floor, with artificial icicles and tinsel, a sheet underneath for snow, trains running around the tree and some colored lights with a few shiny, colored Christmas balls?"

"All very commercial, no real Christmas spirit there. What's the opinion of our spiritual adviser, Father Mundy himself? This will probably be the first time he's missed midnight mass on Christmas Eve. Do you think we could fly him out, sir?"

"Don't worry, I'll work out something for Mundy myself. I remember all the Latin, both give *and* take. I'll do a midnight mass with a canteen cup of that wine and a few K ration dog biscuits. It's the spirit counts; isn't that right, Mundy?"

Mundy smiles and shakes his head; the letdown's set in.

I hang up and wait for the next half hour to crawl by. Father and I work around a semi-conversation about the best Christmases we can remember. He tells how he believed in Santa Claus till he was twelve years old; used to fight kids in school proving it. I feel sorry about what I said when we were discussing faith; I didn't know how close I was. This kind of insensitive accidental cruelty is something I wish I could outgrow.

At midnight we see Wilkins and Shutzer coming. Mundy stands up, stretches and yells, "Merrrry Christmas!"

Mother is scrunched up inside his pieces of blanket. He looks at Mundy.

"Come on, it can't be Christmas yet, Paul. Don't tell me that."

Mundy bangs his split gloves together and stamps his feet.

"Can't be long, Vance."

He pulls back his field jacket sleeve, glances at his watch.

"Give or take a week or so."

Shutzer leans his M1 against the wall. He looks wiped out; he should be, after all the cockeyed stomping around and playing in the snow.

"Let's not rush the season, huh, Mundy?"

Wilkins has moisture dripping from the end of his nose. His eyes are watering and he's blowing on his gloved hands. I wonder if he's going to make it through two hours. Shutzer will keep an eye out and if Mother can't do it, one of us can come down. Mother seems so frail, almost invisible out here in the dark and cold. Stan stamps his feet.

"Buttered udders but it's cold. You guys get on up there where it's warm. If we throw any grenades, we'll probably only be keeping ourselves warm."

There's no snow falling now and the moon's lowered close to the tips of pine trees. The damned wind is gusting again, making whirls of loose snow. Mundy and I tromp uphill. I'm not having cramps and I'm hoping I'll get in some sleep.

Miller and Gordon have hot coffee ready, along with soup Mother cooked up. I sip the soup, feel it glow inside and gradually bring me back to life. Soup will most likely go straight on through, but it's worth it. Wilkins's used our leftovers from the hash and beans; also, I taste something of sardines. It sounds like a weird combination but tastes good after two hours in the snow.

Miller wants to know all about the snowball fight. I let Mundy tell it; I'm slowly collapsing.

"You mean they were lobbing snowballs in on you for no reason at all?"

"That's right."

"You're sure, Mundy? You guys aren't making this up?"

"Honest to God, Bud, cross my heart."

Mundy actually crosses his heart. Not only that, but Miller doesn't laugh.

I slip off my boots and slide carefully into my fart sack, head away from the fire. My feet are numb and starting to tingle. All I want is blank sleep for three or four hours. This craziness is wearing me down more than some kind of actual firefight. My mind's a jumble, my nerves shot. I always have trouble dealing with something I don't understand.

I listen to Miller, Gordon and Mundy talking. The last thing I remember is Father putting more wood on the fire. I can't even get excited about what we're burning. I know it doesn't look like something from a stable. I've gotten to the point where there's no resistance left.

The next thing I know, Shutzer's shaking me awake. It's six o'clock in the morning. I've slept six solid hours. Somebody covered for me on the four o'clock guard. My first thought is it has to be Mundy bucking for martyrdom, but it turns out to be Mother. I'm worried about *him* making it and he's doubling up to cover for *me*. I wonder if my shaky condition is visible to the whole squad.

Shutzer and I are on the next two hours. I've lost all track. I don't know when Shutzer was last out but he looks fresh enough. We gather grenades, bandoliers and M1s, start down the hill. It's still pitch dark and the temperature seems to have dropped. It's so cold now there's not much chance of snow.

There's a feeling in the air of mornings when we'd trudge off to early Christmas mass. We'd sneak down past the Christmas tree without looking, smelling the pine and peeking squint-eyed, just enough to see the tree lit, but saving everything until we came back. This morning has that same feeling of morning about to happen. There's nothing you can put your finger on, only a sensation of anticipation and imminence. Mel's probably right; this is as close to Christmas we could ever find in the middle of a war.

One year I got a two-wheeled bicycle, a new one from Sears Roebuck, with balloon tires and the most glowing red paint and shining chrome that's ever been put on any machine. That year it was snowing, too, and after mass I rolled the bike down the snow-packed steps of the porch. I rode that bike along the still, dark street between row houses in the falling snow. I'd never ridden a two-wheeler before but managed to get it rolling through sheer exuberance. Then I couldn't stop; the bike had coaster brakes and I had no idea how to use them. Dad came out in the snow and stood in front of me so I rode between his legs while he grabbed the handlebars and held me.

"Won't, would you let me look at that map? Do you have it with you?"

I reach inside my field jacket and pull it out.

It was wet from the snow but is almost dry now after six hours against my chest inside the fart sack, beside the fire. I'm too tired to even wonder what Stan wants with a map on a guard post.

Stan ducks down against the wall and lights some matches. What can he be looking for? We know where we are, more or less. He stands up, his eyes wild.

"See, Won't! It's just as I thought! I've been thinking about all the crazy things that've been going on ever since the walking dead, and only one answer makes sense!"

He ducks down and lights another match. I get down with him. Shutzer points at some markings on the map. They're in dark pencil; it looks like a 4B or even softer. It's thick writing, which I guess is German. There are about four lines, and they're on the back. Shutzer lights another match. He runs his fingers along the words.

"OK, this first part is easy. It asks if any of us speak German. That's no trouble. But then there's something more; it looks like a number and a word. It's either S A N D K A R T E or L A N D K A R T E. The fucking Krauts write such pointed letters."

The match goes out again. I look around to see if there might be some German standing around who can help us decipher. Shutzer has another match lit. Maybe I'll ask him if he'll lend me a few; he seems to have boxes in every pocket. Shutzer's turning the map over. He lights another match and runs it across the surface. He stops and puts his face close to the map just as this match goes out. He stands and looks at me.

"Well, I'll be damned. There's an X marked beside the shack down on the stream and the number twelve hundred. I'll be damned."

"You think maybe they've buried some treasure there and we're going to play treasure hunt? What's it all about this time, Stan? Why don't we just pull out of here and let these crazy characters have the forest to themselves?"

"Shit no, Won't. I think at least one of those Krauts wants to surrender, maybe the whole pack."

"Aw, come off it, Stan! Things are bad enough."

"Listen! Let's start at the beginning. First there's the frozen soldier Wilkins shot down. Just suppose that soldier was like this scarecrow here with a piece of paper stuck on the end of his rifle like a surrender flag. Remember, there was a piece of paper on the ground beside that corpse."

"Look, Shutzer. *I'm* the creative-imaginative type around here. You're our businessman. I'll write the stories and draw the pictures."

"Remember, Won't; I'm a sculptor now. I've even started a sort of fashion here in this forest with the Krauts imitating my masterpiece. But if I'm right, then those two soldier stiffs hooked together, dancing—an American and a Kraut— were a message, too, telling us they want us to get together. Crude, I admit, but then remember the kind of minds we're dealing with. Pushing corpses around for these fuckers is as ordinary as playing dolls for little kids."

"OK, I'm listening."

"So then they come around with the '*Schlaf gut*' bit the first night to let *us* know *they* know we're here and they're not too mad about it, right?"

"Very good, Stan. And when does the woodsman come through and save Snow White from having her heart eaten out by the big bad wolf?"

"No, I'm serious. Listen! Think of some other reason why they didn't mow us down or at least take us prisoner on the side of that hill? Hell, they're still telling us they want to make a deal. Don't you get it?"

I'm beginning to. Shutzer's right; it's the one answer that makes everything else fit.

"Then, Stan, all this FOO KIT LUR crap is part of the same bullshit; they built that thing up on the road to show us they're agreeing with your lovely message out there on the side of the hill."

"Right. It all fits. Now, if I'm right, they want us to come meet them by that shack or shed we checked out today. Look!"

He scrunches again and I get down with him. He lights another match. There must be over fifty matches still left in that one box alone. I don't remember if there are matches in D rations. Maybe that's where he got them.

"See. It's right here. There's the X and the number twelve hundred. What else could it mean?"

The match goes out and we stand up again. There's the beginning of some light starting in the sky.

"Crushed mush, Stan. It could be a trap. I must admit I'm not a big truster of Germans."

"Now you're cutting in on *my* territory, Won't. I'll leave the creative business to you but I'm the Kraut hater around here. Don't forget that. Still, if we can pick off this bunch it wouldn't be such a bad idea either."

"I'm scared, Stan; we can't risk the squad on a wild-haired guess like this."

"Look! If they wanted to kill us, they could've done it easily yesterday. They could've done it last night when you threw the grenade. If they could lob snowballs in on you, what was to stop them from dropping in a few mashers?"

"Maybe they're just nice guys, Stan. There could be some good Germans."

"Christ, you sound like Mundy!"

"OK, I'll mention it when I call in. Ware will tell us what to do."

"Let's think about it a minute here first, OK? We don't want any officers screwing things up. We can probably make something good out of all this for everybody if we use our heads."

"What'll we do, surrender to each other simultaneously, take turns walking in with prisoners? It sounds like the fox, the chicken and the grain problem."

Shutzer lights up and lights one for me, too, saves a match. By Gordon's standards, the whole squad's going downhill. I guess everybody's feeling the strain. It's quiet and I swear I hear a violin playing. It sounds like the music of the celestial spheres. I take off my helmet and tilt my head different ways trying to locate the sound. Sometimes it seems to be coming from the tops of the trees. I don't know whether to mention it or not; Stan'll be convinced I really have totally flipped.

"That's only Gordon, Won't. Mother found a violin up there with all the junk. This violin's in a hand-carved wooden case. When Gordon opened it, he did everything but get down on his knees and pray toward Mecca. He says it's the most beautiful violin he's ever seen and he's probably not good enough to play it. I had a big argument with him while you were asleep about how no object can have a memory and what's the difference even if he plays it or not; for that matter if even *I* play it. Gordon's convinced it does something to the wood or the strings and a good violin should only be played by a true violinist. I don't know whether he's decided the violin isn't as good as he thought or he's better than he says he is."

I leave my helmet off. We stand there quietly, listening. Paintings, violin concerts; we're leading the cultured life. Maybe this *is* a bunch of high-class Germans trying to make peace. I'm ready to believe anything.

"Look, Won't, suppose you and I go out there just to see what's going on. We'll play it careful and it's only the two of us. I'll take all the risk; you hang up there on the ridge, where we came in, and cover me. How can it hurt to check things out? What if there is a bunch of shit sniffers wanting to give up. Why not?"

"I should call Ware first. I could just tell him we have a chance to take some prisoners."

"And what do you think Ware will do then?"

"I guess he'll tell Love."

"Then you know Goddamned well Love will come charging out here and arrange the whole affair so he looks like General Patton winning the war single-handed. He'll probably organize and lead some kind of phony tiger patrol, too. Right?"

I know he's right. Max Lewis was on a one-man job, checking a bridge for mines, and got captured by two Germans. In the bombardment, the Germans gave up to him. He trudged in with them and passed through Captain Enders at battalion, who phoned back to regimental headquarters. Love jumped in a jeep, drove out, then went stomping into division with his side arm out covering the prisoners. Lewis pulled three days' loafing around the kitchen truck, but Love got himself a Bronze Star.

"Sure, Stan. That's the way things are in the army. We can't do anything about it. Wait a minute; what time is it? I have to make the phone-in."

We're five minutes over. I crank and get Mother.

"Everything OK out there, Wont?"

"Sure, things're fine here, Vance. Shutzer's working out details for the armistice. He's giving the Germans Texas, Mississippi, Louisiana, Georgia, Alabama, North and South Carolina for all of Germany, including France."

"Honest, come on, Wont; what do you think's happening?"

"Maybe the Germans know they have us trapped and are playing cat-and-mouse. Once there, when it was quiet, I thought I heard big artillery from the south and even behind us. Do you think the Germans could be building up some kind of attack?"

"Relax, Vance. The only thing I've been hearing is Gordon playing his violin. I'm beginning to think the war might be winding down."

"Lord, I hope so. I've about had it."

"Just get some sleep. And no more taking two guard schedules, but thanks a lot. You get some sleep yourself now."

"I couldn't sleep anyway; my mind keeps spinning on all this craziness. I can't stop it."

"OK, Mother, but just stretch out and try. Listen to Gordon and pretend you're at a concert with Linda. You'll be home before you know it. Try to just let go."

"OK. Thanks. I'll try."

Mother's tying up again, all right. He's not joking, not seeing the funny things. I'm bad enough but there's a difference. We've got to do something. I hang up. Shutzer's still leaning on the wall; he's so short he can just get his elbows over the edge.

"Now listen, Won't. Suppose we try a scenario like this. We pretend one of us, all alone, like Sergeant York, captures this bag of Germans. Then we build that person into a second Audie Murphy. It'd be at least a Silver Star; maybe even a trip back home as a returning war hero for the home front morale. He could make speeches at high schools, and decorate some recruitment center all dressed up in a clean, pressed uniform dripping medals. How's that sound?"

"Sounds like a court-martial."

"How would they ever catch on?"

"We'd need a citation from an officer."

"Ware'd go along. We could even call him out after it's done and give him a piece of the action. Maybe Ware could drive one of the jeeps back full of Krauts. I can work that part out; leave it to me. For Wilkins's sake, we should at least try."

"Wilkins?"

"Sure, who else?"

"Jesus, Shutzer, what a brain. Let me think. Boy, would that ever be perfect. We'd all testify how we were pinned down or something and Wilkins came in the nick and saved the show. Ware's having trouble with Love about our not being aggressive enough. This'd look good to him. And what's Ware going to do anyway, call the entire squad liars? And we'd have this mob of genuine German enemy soldiers to back up our story. What could he do? It'd sure solve things. Christ!"

Shutzer lights cigarettes for both of us, two on a match again. I smoke my way through most of the cigarette, running things over in my mind. Shutzer keeps quiet. He's going to make a great advertising executive or management man. He knows when to press and when to let up.

"OK, Stan. How's this sound? I tell Ware we're taking a patrol out to check the shack again because we heard some noises from over there. I'll even tell him they were around again last night."

"Don't say anything about the snowman or the scarecrow or the snowball fight."

"Right. And we won't say anything about all this to Wilkins yet, either."

"We don't tell anybody till we find out some more. Maybe I'm all wrong and they don't want to give up. Maybe you're right and it's just some kind of addled, baroque way they've thought up to take *us* prisoner without too much fuss."

"Jesus, Shutzer! I'm just beginning to feel good about this and you bring that up."

"Sorry; only want to keep things in focus. It'll be the two of us; if it doesn't work, so we tried. How the hell else do you end wars? Somebody's got to take a few chances."

"OK, then, just the two of us, for now."

We talk about it some more. The best fun is building up the citation part. Mother's going to come out looking like the tiger of the Ardennes; he'll become a legend. Maybe we can work this up into a Congressional Medal of Honor. Wilkins's name will be inscribed on the dollar bill. The trick, as I see it, is getting Ware to go along; but that's Shutzer's job. With

Miller and Gordon chipping in, the fantasy sections will be easy. We can probably even get Father Mundy to contribute some bits. He's up to a couple reasonable lies for a good cause.

At ten I radio back to regiment. This time I get Flynn. In his nasty arty-farty voice, he tells me to call back in five minutes; Ware wants to talk with me. I switch off and stretch out on a mattress. I make the effort to wait out this five minutes without a cigarette, without a watch, too. Maybe I'll make it ten minutes, build up some suspense.

When we came in, I gave Shutzer one of the replay hands, and they've ripped Gordon away from the violin long enough to get a game going.

The violin is in its open case propped against one of the grenade boxes. It's a beautiful thing all right. I'd love to try a drawing. Getting those strong, gentle curves wouldn't allow for any fudging at all. I'd want to draw it just as it is, in the case, with the lid up, the bow lying across the strings.

There's a round ball of something orange with a worn groove. I walk over, lean down and sniff; it smells like pine trees. The case is lined with dark green velvet and there's a small green velvet cushion hooked to the back of the violin and off to one side. Under the violin strings there's light powdered dust on the red-brown wood. Cut in the wood on top are two twisting curves like musical notes.

It's the first time I've really looked at a violin. No wonder Gordon got excited. It must be wonderful to hold a beautiful thing like this against your neck and stroke music from it. I'll do my drawing on the side of an empty D ration box; the K boxes are too small.

At least ten minutes go by before I get back to the radio. Ware comes right on.

"What's been happening out there? Over."

What could he know?

"We had some harassment of the post at about twenty-two-hundred, but that's all, Lieutenant. Over."

There's no answer. I open after ten seconds and repeat.

"There's something big going on, Knott. We've had some unbelievable reports. The fucking Krauts are attacking everywhere. It could be the biggest thing in the war. They're all excited here; talking of pulling the whole regiment back. Over."

"Wilkins said he heard what sounded to him like heavy artillery to the south and behind us but none of the rest of us did, sir. We also thought we picked up some noises down by that shack last night. Shutzer and I'll check it out. Over."

"Major Love's sent the first squad on a tiger patrol north to capture a prisoner. Over."

Hell! Edwards and the whole squad out in this weather trying to pull down a prisoner. Fucking Love!

"Things are quiet here, sir. Over."

"OK, hold your squad in there, Knott. We're having a staff meeting in two hours. I'll give you the situation on the next call. Over."

"Roger, sir. Over."

"Over and out."

"Over and out, sir."

Nobody seems to have paid much attention to the call-in. They're all wrapped into the game. Only Shutzer looks up and gives me a wink. I stretch on a mattress and try to think. Those jerks at regiment panic over anything; there's probably nothing happening. I've seen those signal corps guys totally screw up things more than once.

Still I'm scared. I'm scared thinking about going out and maybe actually talking with Germans. Finally, I'm dropping off to sleep. We're one in a hole on the daytime guard now, so I can sleep long as I want; but if we're going to try making contact with those Germans I'll only get in about an hour. I drift off as Mundy's wanting Miller to talk about *A Farewell to Arms*. Miller refuses to discuss it. None of us except Mundy thinks it was much of a book. And there's no book around to read now except one called *Forever Amber* and that's with Edwards's squad. They're never going to finish it. From what I hear, this is one Mundy *isn't* going to like. Or maybe he will, but he'll say he doesn't. With that I'm gone.

It only seems minutes later Shutzer's shaking me. Mundy, Miller are asleep. Wilkins is upstairs again. Gordon's on guard.

"What do you say, Won't? If we leave now, we can get there by noon."

I'm groggy; at first I don't know what he's talking about; then I remember. I sag in my sack on the side of my mattress and the thick taste in my mouth feels as if I've thrown up. I struggle my feet to the floor; I can't really think of anything to say that'll keep us from going on this crazy voluntary patrol. We'll stop by Gordon and tell him where we're going. We've *got* to tell Gordon; hell, he's second in command; he's even got some stripes in one of his pockets to prove it. Supply *had* corporal stripes.

We don't put on snowsuits; I think we've both lost confidence in these Germans' trying to kill us. We're both pretty much believing the story Shutzer's made up. But we take our rifles, bandoliers, grenades, the works; we're not into pacifism that much, yet.

On the way out we stop by Gordon.

"Where in hell you guys going; maybe going to build a fat Göring snowman so tonight it'll be FOO GURR INK? He's a perfect subject for Shutzer's snowball sculpture."

I stand there while Stan explains what's been happening and shows our map with the marks.

"You mean you two are going to tromp on out there and set up an armistice conference with a bunch of Germans? Who do you think you are, Churchill and Roosevelt? You must be out of your minds. And you, Shutzer, my favorite Jewish German-hater; what are you doing sticking your neck out to help a bunch of Knockwurst Knickerbockers get back to some nice warm POW camp while we're out here freezing our tootsies off? I don't get it!"

I look over at Shutzer. Far as I'm concerned, it's his show. I'm still not sure what the hell we're doing.

"Listen, Mel. Just suppose they really do want to surrender. Suppose we can arrange it so Ware and Love think Wilkins alone, six-gun ablazing, did it himself. Suppose all of us write up Wilkins for every medal they've got reserved for hero types. He's the closest thing to a hero we've got around here anyway. What do you think of that?"

Mel stares at Shutzer. Mel has the most incredible way of absorbing anything while not showing much on his face. There's something unflappable in him.

I'll bet Mel's one hell of a good doctor today. Maybe when I'm a little older and start having serious health problems, I'll look him up, move to New Jersey; let Dr. Melvin Gordon ease me carefully, comfortably, into the grave with a minimum of screaming and hollering, something more or less dignified. He'd do that for me.

Now he only shakes his head. But I can tell it's gotten to him.

"What makes you think Ware or Love is going to take

part in this great farce? And the Germans, I can't see them giving up like that. Besides, no matter what you diplomats plan, Wilkins will never go along with it."

It's something we haven't thought of too much, how to talk Wilkins into this whole scheme. We're quiet, leaning against the wall, not smoking, mulling this one over. It's Mel himself who comes up with it.

"We could always have a playoff, like Saturday night bingo, to see who's this week's lucky hero. He might go along on that basis. No matter what we play, bridge, poker, chess, tiddlywinks, Wilkins will win. To make sure, the rest of us could play less than our best."

Shutzer looks at me, winks quickly.

"Hell, Wilkins will win no matter how hard anybody plays. Especially chess. I don't think he's ever lost a match, even against Evans in the first squad, and that freak's a human calculator. I think he sees colors as numbers."

I look back and forth. Mel and Stan are so different in the way they perceive life and still there's a strong bond between them. It isn't Jewishness either; it has something to do with love, not sticky man-to-man love or even brotherly love, but they love themselves, and can let that feeling flow over into other people. I don't really think Shutzer actually even *hates* Germans. He only hates what some Germans have been doing, the way Bud hates doing things the wrong way.

They're waiting for me to say something.

"Well, do we tell Wilkins or not? He's so nervous he'd never even agree to our going out now to talk with them. He's convinced we're surrounded and in some kind of trap."

It's then I tell Stan and Mel what happened back in the dent at headquarters: the run through the forest and all. I try to tell it straight, without leaving anything out, and still not elaborating. They listen carefully, looking at each other, not believing what I'm saying and at the same time knowing I have no reason to lie. When I'm finished, Stan's the first to speak.

"I don't think we should tell him. When we've got the Krauts all here, prisoners, then we can have the chess competition playoffs. When we go out to get the Krauts, we leave Wilkins here to guard the château and mind the radio. It'd all be perfectly natural."

Gordon takes this in his usual way, as if he didn't hear; no expression on his face.

"I still think we should tell Mother; we'll have such an advantage and it wouldn't be fair. But I see what you mean; let's think about it. For now, if you guys want to take the chance, you'd better dash on out there to see if there really are Germans 'underneath the lamplight by the village square.' I'll keep my ears open and if I hear anything, we'll come charging out to help. Give two quick shots, count three slowly and fire once more if you need us. OK?"

Shutzer looks at his watch and we both nod. We're really going to do it.

"If you guys aren't back by one-thirty, I'll phone regiment and tell them you went on a recon patrol."

"Ware's in a staff meeting. If he calls before we get back, tell him we're just doing a little reconnaissance-mission-type thing."

"Right."

Shutzer and I go out the same way we went the first time with Gordon. About two hundred yards from the shack, Shutzer motions me to a fifty-yard interval so I can just see him through the trees. The whole thing is even more spooky than I thought it would be. I've been completely conditioned not to trust Germans. I imagine they don't trust us much either; I don't think they even respect us; at least, not as soldiers, probably not as anything. I've got to say I respect them, at least as soldiers. If there were as many of them as there are of us in this goofy war, I'd hate to think of how it would come out.

Shutzer drops to one knee and stops on the ridgeline where he can see down to the shack. I drop and wait. Then he gives me an OK sign with his thumb and finger, a soft motion forward. He starts slowly over the ridge with his rifle at ready. I move carefully up after him, my rifle ready too, the lock off. At least we learned something from that mad scrabble in the snow.

When I get to the top, sure enough there are two German soldiers standing in the lee of the shed. They look unarmed. One, probably a noncom, probably the one with the Schmeisser the other night, is talking to Shutzer.

Shutzer's slung his M1 on his shoulder. I let myself down just at the turn of the ridge to stay out of sight. After three or four minutes, Shutzer comes trudging back uphill to me. He's sweating the way he sweated in that bathroom back in town at Shelby when he was waiting his turn with the girl.

"Well, there they are. The main guy, the noncom, wants to talk with our officer in charge. Between my Yiddish and his German we can get most things across OK."

"I don't understand that lingo, Stan. Besides, I don't have any stripes or anything. He's never going to believe I'm an officer."

"Maybe he's just not happy talking with a Jew, especially about surrendering. Let me go back. I'll tell him our officer in charge isn't with us. There's another guy, a younger one, and I don't know why, but I think he understands some English. Unless they have side arms or rifles hidden on the other side of the shack, they look unarmed."

"God, Shutzer! What should we do? Have they said anything about surrendering?"

"Nope. Only the business about wanting to talk to our commanding officer."

We stand there a minute, thinking it out.

"Look, Won't, you come down with me. We'll tell them our officer is back in the château. I'll translate whatever he says and you try to watch the other Kraut and see if he's picking up on what we're saying. You look goy enough; maybe he'll come out with more if you're there."

So we go back down the hill, trying to saunter casually as if this were an everyday thing, talking to Germans. As we get closer, I see they aren't the ones we saw at the lodge. These must be the ones who jumped us on the hill. The soldier leaning against the shed is smoking a hand-rolled cigarette in yellow paper.

We walk straight up to the one Shutzer's been talking with. My God, he looks like a German soldier from a Hollywood hate-the-Nazis movie; only worn down, ragged-looking. He's almost a foot taller than Shutzer with deep-sunken, pale gray eyes. His blond eyebrows are so thick they almost block his vision, he must see the world through a screen of hair. Maybe he combs them down over his eyes so we can't fathom the devilish torture schemes he has in mind for us.

The skin on his face is tight against bone and there are deep wrinkles, long lines coming down the side of his face from the outside edges of his eyes almost like scars, deep runnels from the sides of his nose to the bottom of his chin. He could be any age from twenty-five to forty. When he opens his mouth, he has a wedge-shaped broken upper front tooth and one eyetooth missing. There's something of an often beaten club fighter about him. He's wearing the gray-green field uniform and even in this cold he isn't wearing an overcoat or a helmet, only an overseas-type field cap, frayed, greasy and fitting tight to his head. I have the feeling he might be mostly bald.

He and Shutzer start talking. They have a hard time getting things across but work it out with hand movements and trying different words. The German has a tendency to repeat a word only louder when Shutzer doesn't understand, but Shutzer plays it almost like a game of charades, searching for new ways to say what he wants. The Kraut's pointing to his stripes and the insignia on his shoulder boards. I figure he's still trying to get in touch with our officer.

Shutzer takes out two packs of four cigarettes, along with some of his inexhaustible matches, and passes them around. The soldier leaning against the shed leaves what must be their hidden cache of weaponry and comes over to take one. Shutzer lights all four cigarettes on one match, even with the wind blowing. We move close against the shack, out of the wind. The other German smiles at me and I smile back.

This one's younger and his face is white, thin. His eyes are long, dark and wet along the bottom rims, almost as if he's been crying, or is about to. Wilkins's eyes are like that sometimes. Both Germans are wearing the usual black leather boots with thick soles and hobnails but these are soaking wet, cracked and worn.

We're standing there and the first German begins a long speech. It goes on and on. He doesn't raise his voice or even particularly look at us but goes through his speech as if he has it memorized. We're almost finished the cigarettes before he shuts up. Shutzer's been interrupting him at different times when he didn't understand, so that slows things down, too. Shutzer turns to me.

"OK, I think I've got it. First, he wants to talk to our officer. He's only told us the stuff he's told me now so our officer will know he's serious.

"These guys are tired of the war. They've been shipped across Germany from the Russian front, where they had the shit kicked out of them. He says the Krauts have started a big, new offensive here on the west, just south of this sector. They're part of something like a battalion I and R outfit, and they're all sure the war's about over. They don't want to be killed in the last days after getting through five years. He thinks their outfit is going to push off in a day or two and the whole bunch of them don't want anything to do with it. They're convinced even if they live through this attack, they'll probably be sent back to the eastern front. They don't want to be captured by Russians."

"Did he actually say they want to surrender?"

"Not in so many words, but that seems to be the gist of it. He keeps wanting to talk with our commanding officer. I explained we only have a noncom like him with us. He says that's good enough. There are seven of them all together."

"What do you think, Stan?"

"Well, we can always go back to the squad and talk it over. I'll tell him we're checking with our commanding officer."

"OK, you do that."

The Germans are standing there during this. They're on second cigarettes Shutzer gave them. The noncom takes a last deep drag, then grinds out his cigarette in the snow with the heel of his boot. Shutzer begins yakking away. I watch the other one; I still can't tell anything. It doesn't even sound like Shutzer talking when he spouts the Yiddish; it's more singing, rolling sounds. In English, Shutzer talks in quick spurts, almost as if he can't get his tongue to go fast as his mind. He comes back to me.

"OK, we're on. I told him we'll bring our commanding officer here the day after tomorrow at ten a.m. Wait a minute till I check that time again."

Stan goes back and gabs a few more minutes.

"That's right, ten o'clock, with our officer, right here, day after tomorrow. He wants it to be tomorrow but we've got to work this out."

The Germans have already started back up the hill. I didn't see from where, but they've picked up a Mauser and the Schmeisser. The younger one turns, waves, smiles as they go. Stan and I turn and go back the way we came.

"What're we going to do for an officer, Stan; bring Ware out here?"

"Don't be crazy. We've got the most perfect officer type in our own squad, better than the whole German Army can produce. They'll come crawling in on their bellies when they meet our officer."

"Miller?"

"Of course. Who else?"

When we get back, it's just lucky Wilkins is on guard. I guess they had to wrestle him out of his attic. I call everybody together and Shutzer explains what's been going on. Miller butts in.

"You mean you guys've been out there in the bushes talking with Germans?"

"Drinking beer, eating pretzels and dill pickles, out there under the old *Tannenbaums*. Yes, sir, Buddy boy."

Mundy keeps shaking his head and smiling all through Shutzer's spiel.

"You guys are crazy, but what a terrific chance. Imagine Wilkins with medals all over his chest. He can have a Silver Star for the top of his Christmas tree. Far as I'm concerned, he's been overdue for a medal since he climbed over Hunt in the barracks that day. God rest his soul."

"You mean Hunt's soul, Mundy? Hunt didn't have any soul. He was heel solid through."

"OK, Shutzer, sorry I mentioned it. There's no sense talking against the dead."

Mundy blesses himself.

We push the idea around for ten or fifteen minutes. Everybody has wild fantasies about Wilkins capturing the prisoners. If we're not careful, we'll be writing a novel to include everything. We can call it *All Cuckoo on the Western Front*.

"And, Miller, you'll be our commanding officer. There never was and there never is going to be an officer like you."

"Fuzz that. You're the one, Won't. You get the extra pay, you be the officer."

"Come on, Miller," Shutzer butts in and saves me. "No Kraut's ever going to believe a hundred-thirty-pound weakling like Won't is an officer. Besides, he has brown eyes. You can't have brown eyes and be an officer. You're the only logical candidate."

"How about Mundy; he's big and tall, sort of soft like an officer. Besides, he's older. I'm too young."

"Damn it, Miller. You're not young; you were born old, came into this world checking the doctor's instruments, telling him how to hold the forceps."

"Then what's wrong with you, Gordon? You're tall enough and you have that Buddha shit-eating smile all the time. You look like the natural leader type; besides, you have corporal stripes in your pocket. I saw them fall out once while you were unhooking grenades. Stop hiding your light under a bushel basket man; be proud, strut a little, maybe even get a swagger stick."

"Listen, Miller. Those Germans have Jews like me worked out to the 'J.' They have pictures, maps, diagrams spread all over Germany: Jewish noses, Jewish lips, Jewish eyes, Jewish ways of talking, walking, spitting, combing hair, tying shoes.

Any Kraut worth two cents would see through me in twenty seconds. No, you're our only pure Aryan type. You're elected commander-in-chief by acclamation."

Miller finally succumbs. And do we ever do him up right. We put together the best, cleanest uniform from everything that will fit him, mostly Gordon's stuff. We take Gordon's sets of two stripes; then we tear off all our PFC stripes. We use Wilkins's sewing kit to sew together a conglomerate of stripes, three up and three down, both arms; only all stripes, no rockers. There never was a rank such as we give Miller; he's our "bastard sergeant minor." Shutzer screws out a lens from the scope for Miller to wear as a monocle, but he can't keep it in.

We empty all the crap from the field jacket pockets and tuck folds in back so he looks somewhat tailored. It'd be great having a pair of Love's form-fitted shirts and pants. Even so, Miller looks more like an officer than Love ever could; when we're finished, he's damned impressive.

We have him strut around the room practicing jaw thrusting and general arrogance. Stan assures Miller he doesn't need to say anything, just nod his head or shake it and act like an S.O.B.

Before Mother comes off post, we shuffle our clothes back and hide the field jacket with all the stripes. We're excited about Wilkins being a hero. Mel keeps harping on the idea we should tell him, but by now we're all so wound up with secret planning and wanting to surprise Mother, Mel can't get anywhere.

That night passes fast. It's a feeling of Christmas, hiding presents. When I'm not on guard, I sleep like a dead man and when I wake up, even manage a regular solid-type crap.

. . .

I'm beginning to feel better about things. Around ten, I make the call to regiment. This time, Ware's waiting for me.

"How're things out there, Knott? Over."

"Quiet, sir. We took a two-man patrol down to that shack and did a brief recon tour but didn't see anything. All quiet here, sir. Over."

Gordon, Shutzer and Miller're hanging over my shoulder. Only Father's on guard and Mother's upstairs. Gordon's even put down his violin for the call. It probably wouldn't sound so great to Ware, hearing violin music in the background.

"Well, things're tough here. We're packing to pull out. We're not sure we aren't completely cut off. There's no intelligence coming in we can count on. We're going to drive west with the third battalion as point. Nobody knows anything. We can't locate the first battalion, and our first squad still isn't back; must've run into something. Over."

"The whole first squad not back, sir? Over."

"That's right. I'm telling you, Knott, things are rough. Fucking Krauts are pumped up. People here talk about divisions of tanks and infantry pouring through a twelve-mile break, moving up units from the south to close the gap. But we don't know anything for sure; communications are all snafu. Germans dressed up in American uniforms with American jeeps are cutting phone lines, changing road signs, confusing troop movements. The best we have here is reports from isolated units. Over."

"Did the first squad take the other 506? Over."

"It's out of commission. We've got the communications section working on it, but so far, no luck. Over."

"Maybe they made contact with another outfit and just can't get back, sir. Over."

"It doesn't matter. Love wants your squad to stay out there so we'll have some idea if anything breaks. Keep your jeeps ready to run. But most of all, Love wants a prisoner. You go out to that hunting lodge and pick one off. If there's an officer or a noncom, try to grab him. Since the first squad didn't get back, we need some kind of intelligence and fast. Over."

Right here, I don't know whether to mention this big, new Christmas attack the Germans talked about. How would I explain knowing a thing like that? Also, the Germans could be lying.

"All right, sir. With so few of us, we'll make it a night patrol; have to jump a guard or something. Over."

"In any case, call in soon as you have one. We'll either come out to get the fucker or you can bring him in with one of the jeeps. Over."

"Wilco, sir. Over."

"Over and out."

"Over and out."

For more than ten seconds nobody says anything. Then Miller puts his hands over his eyes.

"Holy mud! The whole first squad!"

Shutzer starts pacing, pounding his fist in his hand or against the side of his head.

"This lousy war's never going to end!"

Gordon sits, then lies out on one of the mattresses. He stares up at the high ceiling.

"Think of it. Bergman and Kelly, Moser, Evans, Edwards; the whole squad. Maybe they're only *dogging* it. With Love running amuck and Ware charging around in circles, maybe they figured it'd be best to find some calm corner of the world and hide. I'll bet they're tucked into holes tight up in a wood somewhere."

Shutzer's still stomping back and forth. Once he walks the entire length of the room away from the fireplace.

"What the hell's going on? I thought this festering war was about finished; now it's boiling up again!"

Gordon's voice is calm.

"What'll we do about the prisoner deal and Wilkins? Maybe we ought to call it off. You know, that idiot Love's almost wiped out the entire I and R platoon."

I flop on a mattress. I'm scared. I didn't like the sound in Ware's voice; there was something desperate, the edge of panic. I try getting myself calmed down, stop the butterflies. I remind myself how Love was convinced we were surrounded and wanted to abandon Metz when all we had to do was gather in thousands of prisoners. You almost *have* to be a fuckup to get in S2 or G2; it's where the tough-ass soldiers tuck the sissies. This could all be nothing.

But we might just be walking into some kind of convoluted trap. Maybe we should do the whole thing simple as possible: forget the Wilkins part and only take our prisoners. Love'd be happy as hell having seven prisoners to play with and we'd look like conquering heroes. He might even get off our backs for a while. Wilkins and Gordon could march the prisoners back while the rest of us stay out here to see what's happening.

At two I'll be on post again. I feel gritty, dirty. The flambeau smoke and smoke escaping from the chimney make my eyes sore, my throat rasping dry. The shits are holding off, but I have a pain on my left side like a stitch and all my innards feel twisted tight. I need some more of that deep, calm sleep. I wonder if it's still snowing.

4
Throw Me a Why Not

I slip and slide down the hill. There's a new wind, a wind from the east. Thin bits of snow are flying in the cold air but it could be only from the trees or blown up off the ground.

Mel's on, waiting for me. It's just getting dark. Next one will be two-man. I try to think up a new password. God, the whole business seems so ridiculous, like merit badge tests in the Boy Scouts. Sometimes I can't force any sense into things; this gets to be a lifelong problem.

Gordon's waiting; his rifle slung on his shoulder. Even he looks pooped.

"God, Wont, the outside of my foot where I had trench foot is killing me. It's like somebody's twisting a pipe reamer in there; then when I go in to the warmth, it hurts like hell."

He's walking in a circle stamping. I hadn't thought how this cold weather must be for his bad feet. He starts uphill.

"Wait a minute, Mel."

He comes back.

"Tell the rest of them the pass for tonight is 'jingle—bells.' "

"OK, 'jingle—bells.' Did you call me back just for that?"

"No. Mel, what do you think's happening? I'm so confused I'm not thinking; I don't want to think."

"Wont, this war's such a mess it doesn't pay thinking too much. Try relaxing. There's nothing you can do except get killed, wounded, or drop out of it somehow. That's all there is, worrying doesn't help."

"But about Shutzer's 'solve the war' plan. How's that fit in with Ware wanting a prisoner and everybody going ape at headquarters?"

"That can wait. But, no matter what, Wont, I still think we should tell Mother. He's got to know.

"Look, I'm freezing and my foot's killing me; I'm going up. Don't worry; relax."

I lean against the wall. It's good to be alone for a while. So much is happening and I want to do the right things. I roll over all the possibilities. Somehow, my brain isn't working. The cold has done something to me; the cold, the fear and the worrying. When I close down against the cold, my mind shrinks from thinking. It only wants to remember what it was to worry about geometry tests or track meets. It seems like ten thousand years ago; a huge rip has been made in my time band.

On the half hour I phone in and mostly get Miller. We talk about what might've happened to the first squad. It's impossible to think around; none of us can let ourselves believe anything bad's happened. We're *all* turning our minds off.

I watch and listen to the dark come on. Melting things start freezing; you can hear it, a clicking, clinking sound. I try to figure out the date; maybe we're on the up side now; every day will be a little longer. And how many days before we stop counting? We haven't even been in combat half a year; think of those poor sad-assed Germans.

Miller and Shutzer have the next guard; at least I think they do; the squad's running itself as usual. They know more about what's happening than I do and I don't care much. The time passes; it's totally dark. I'm cold.

When Miller and Shutzer come down, I challenge with "jingle," trying for some military semblance. Shutzer counters with "hell's bells." They come to the wall with me. Shutzer gets right into it.

"What do you think, Won't? Miller and I've been talking. We think the three of us should carry through, go out at ten tomorrow and set things up. At the very least we can get prisoners for Love. We could even just ask for one volunteer prisoner now, gather up the rest later; like jacks or pick-up-sticks."

"How about Wilkins?"

"There's no sense worrying him more than we have to. He's happy up there in his attic, pushing furniture around, fighting Miller or me when we go for wood. God, he makes *me*, Stanford Shutzer, feel like the ravaging Hun just because I want to burn an old bed or some broken-down chairs to keep warm. Why don't we leave him alone? We don't need anybody flipping out on us right now, anyway."

I look over at Miller. He's already lit a cigarette. He's staring down at his boots in the snow. He glances up; I have the feeling he's with Shutzer. It's OK by me; we aren't breaking any particular laws I know of.

"OK, Stan, we're on. If you and Miller are for it, I am, too."

. . .

It's raunchy going inside; our smells are filling the place. It's hard to remember how I felt when we first walked into this room. The whole place is a mess. With Wilkins upstairs most of the time, nobody's keeping things straight.

There are open number ten cans and German sardine cans thrown around. Pieces of equipment and clothes are piled up on the mattresses or on the floor. I try not to look. I pick up some of my own stuff; stack my rifle and equipment by the door.

I take two flambeau bottles out to the jeep and fill them. The outside might be cold but at least it's clean and smells good. I'll ask Miller to turn over our jeeps and check if they start; maybe we can stuff pillows around the batteries to keep them warm. No, that's dumb. I inspect the jerry cans; we've actually only used less than half of one can, so we have plenty of gas. I can't stop worrying. I breathe in the clean air but mostly only smell gasoline.

Back in the room, I settle onto one of the mattresses. I close my eyes and try to make myself be somewhere else. I'm not cut out to be a noncom; that's for sure. I don't care about things enough to make other people do them. I have hardly enough energy to do things for myself. Both Max and Louis were always running around following up, seeing things were done and letting you know if they weren't; Edwards the same way. Those guys were natural noncoms. God, I hope the first squad's OK.

Now it comes back again; sometimes I can't shut it out, turn it off.

Gordon and I were the first ones to reach Max. It was after we'd worked Morrie away and back to the medics. At first, we didn't know anything was wrong; not serious, anyway. He was doubled up on his knees. We couldn't see, except he had his hands locked in at the bottom of his gut with his rifle beside him. His helmet was on the ground in front of his face. He wasn't screaming or even groaning. His eyes were squeezed tight.

Mortar was still coming in, plus eighty-eight. Gordon and I are glued close against the ground, afraid to move.

Max looks more like a football player who's had the wind knocked out, or been kneed, than anything else. Gordon inches close to him. Lewis only shakes his head and doesn't move. Suddenly, he jerks up, almost standing, then falls over on his side. The blood gives two or three stiff spurts all over Mel; then each pumping is slower till it runs in a thick stream.

We fast pull his pants down and there it is, a piece of shrapnel, half the size of a Ping-Pong paddle, only curved, cut deep into his groin and halfway through his leg. He's had it pinched in his fingers but couldn't hold any longer.

We try everything to stop the bleeding. We even tie his canteen against it with his belt, but nothing works.

Max never says a word, only moans or cries. We can see the cut artery, like a piece of plastic tubing, but we can't squeeze or hold it. Gordon tries giving wound tablets, only Max can't swallow; he's already a long way to being dead. I'm sure he's gone before we get him back.

Carrying him in, we see the other Louie, Corrollo. He's not more than thirty yards away, but in a small depression, out of sight if you're keeping low to the ground. Gordon sprints crouched over there and comes back green. After we get Max in, we go back out and get the other Louie. He has a jagged piece of cast metal wedged into the space between his open eyes.

That was some recon patrol; it turned into a full-scale

war. Love must've read the map upside down or inside out. I can't even remember what we were supposed to be doing that morning, above a crossroad, on a slippery wet meadow with an old white cow munching muddy grass.

I said I wouldn't tell about that stupid day but there it is. I can't trust myself.

The phone rings and I'm still not asleep. Mundy picks it up.

"No, this is Mundy. Yeah, OK, wait a minute."

Father pulls the battery box close and pushes the phone over to me.

"It's Shutzer; he wants you."

I work out of my fart sack and take the phone. Already my stomach's tight; what in hell can it be now?

"What's up, Stan?"

"Our German friends are here again. They're down the road there by the scarecrow. Maybe they're going to build us a snowman, a snowman with a cigarette in a long cigarette holder, a sitting-down snowman. Folks, we're having the snowman war! FOO KROO SIF FELT!"

"It's too much; I give up, Stan."

"Hell no, you got it all wrong, Won't. *They're* the ones who are supposed to give up. Damn it, they don't seem to care whether we see them or not; far as I can see, they're not armed."

"Remember, Stan, how they hid the rifle and the Schmeisser. After all, these are 'the enemy,' your Nazi murderers."

"Yeah, I know. Wait a minute."

I hold the phone away from my mouth. Gordon's up on one elbow and Mundy's leaning his elbows on his knees, looking at me. I explain what's happening. Wilkins is already pulling on his boots and webbing equipment. He's looking scared again.

"Relax, Mother, it's only our local crazy Germans playing some new kind of game."

I hope I'm right. I wait.

"Won't?"

"Yeah, what is it?"

"It's too dark to see exactly what they're doing but there are at least five or six of them down here working like fury. They've got something big with them and it's *not* a snowman. Could be a mortar! I think maybe you'd better have somebody man that upper post to cover us here."

Gordon's out of his sack and dressing quickly. Mundy's pulling on his boots.

"Mel, you and Mother go up top. Stan claims there are five or six of them, and he can see they're working on something, maybe setting up a mortar!"

Mother and Gordon grab their rifles and are out the door before Stan comes on again.

"Won't, Miller says they've definitely got something tall they're putting up along the road."

"Stan, Gordon and Wilkins are on their way to the other post. Do you want me to come down there?"

"No, I still don't think it's anything serious; it's just so weird. We'll hold on and let you know what we find out. Miller's creeping along the wall to get closer."

He hangs up. I ring the upper post. It's lucky we left that phone in place. I get Gordon.

"What can you see, Mel?"

"Can't see much yet till our eyes get used to the dark, but it looks as if there's a whole road crew down there working on the bridge. Mother here's about ready to crap his pants."

"Can you see what they're doing?"

"Hell no! All we can see is there's a bunch of them; it looks like almost a whole squad.

"Wilkins wants to know if we should open fire if they make a move toward Shutzer and Miller."

"Put Mother on, will you?"

The phone rattles, bangs against Wilkins's helmet. His voice is a whisper.

"Sarge! Our guys are in a bad spot! If those Germans want, they can rush over and wipe them right out!"

"Don't worry, Vance. They've both got grenades and I'm still in contact. Shutzer's not worried, says the Germans aren't even armed; in fact, he thinks they might be building a snowman to match his, claims we're in the snowman war."

"I don't get it, Wont. What the devil's happening around here anyway?"

Mother usually keeps the vow even under stress. Except for Father himself, I guess he's the only one who really does.

"Take it easy, Mother. Let me talk to Gordon again."

"Wont, I just saw a light. Somebody struck a match right out in the open and didn't even hide it.

"Wait a minute! There's another light, and another. What the hell? There're at least six lights burning now. Jesus, there's another. Wait, hold on, here's Wilkins again."

I'm anxious now to talk with the lower post. This is beginning to sound serious. But I listen to Wilkins.

"It's a Christmas tree! Those Germans are standing out there in the snow in the middle of the road lighting candles on a Christmas tree. I can't believe it; what's this all about?"

"Christmas, I think, Mother. Hang up; let me talk to Miller and Shutzer."

I ring the other post. It's Shutzer.

"Can you see it up there, Won't? It's a fucking Christmas tree. These crazy Krauts have stuck a Christmas tree in the snow, smack in the middle of the road, and they've tied a bunch of candles to it. The candles are all lit and there are apples and potatoes hung on the branches. There are even stars cut out of cardboard.

"Come on down! Wait a minute! Now one of them's putting stuff on the snow next to the tree. It's that noncom we were talking to yesterday. The rest of the Krauts are standing by the other side of the road with shit-eating smiles on their faces. My God, they're a sad-sack-looking bunch; they make *us* look neat.

"You've got to see this, Won't, or you'll never believe it."

"We'll be right down. Don't take any chances. Don't shoot us."

I hang up. Mundy's standing with his boots on, finally. He slings his rifle.

"What's going on? What's happening down there?"

I realize Mundy's the only one who doesn't know what's happening. You can't hear the phone unless you have the receiver against your ear; it isn't like the 506.

"Our German buddies have brought us a Christmas tree, Father, and we're all going out to sing carols and maybe celebrate midnight mass for you. Come on, let's get going."

I swing a bandolier around my head and pick up my rifle. I consider stationing myself behind the fifty caliber in the jeep to keep everything in control, but it doesn't seem right. I guess I'll never make it as the big bad killer.

I'm down with Stan and Bud before I realize Mundy isn't with me. Maybe it's just as well; we need somebody on the phone. Those guys up top will be cut off otherwise. I should've thought of it.

They don't challenge me when I come up, just turn their heads and motion me on. The light from the candles is strong enough so I can see them easily. I can also see the Germans lined beside the tree. We could probably all get court-martialed for something like this, consorting with the enemy.

Later, after the war, they used the term "fraternizing" to condemn any uncalled-for familiarity with the Germans. Most of it was with women and they threw the book at some soldiers for it. Fraternizing always seemed the wrong word; it didn't have much to do with "brothering." I've always felt consorting was more what was going on. We were sure consorting with the enemy that night.

Miller, Shutzer and I walk to the edge of the bridge. We're down in a gulley, so the base of the tree is at eye level. We have our rifles over our shoulders and I even forgot to bring a grenade.

Then they do it. They begin; slowly, first, only one or two voices, then all together, they sing a Christmas carol. It's in German but I know the song. They're singing "O Tannenbaum"; it's the same as "O Christmas Tree." The Germans stop singing and it's quiet; the candles keep burning. Then they start again. This time it's "Adeste Fideles." Miller leans close to me.

"Those are Christmas presents under the tree. See? There's a loaf of bread, a bottle of wine and what looks like one of Corrollo's sausages."

When they finish singing this time, the noncom steps into the center of the road beside the tree. He picks up the wine and bread, holding them out toward us. I don't know what to do. I can't get myself to vault up and stand there on the road with everybody watching me take presents from a German. He's there alone, arms spread, looking into the darkness, searching for us.

Just then, Father Mundy comes loping down the road, singing "Adeste Fideles" at the top of his lungs. He has things in his hands and other stuff tucked under his arm. He forgot his rifle. He goes straight to the German and hands him our last bottle of wine; at the same time, he takes the loaf of bread. Then he gives him another bunch of little packages and takes their bottle. The German leans down and picks up his sausage from under the tree. He gives this to Mundy, too. All the time they're chattering away at each other, smiling.

Then, suddenly, the German reaches inside his uniform jacket and pulls out a Luger! I start trying to unsling my rifle but it's too late. The German passes the Luger to Father, handle first, or, I mean, he tries to pass it. Mundy's pushing it away! I pick up a loud "No, sir!"

Is the Kraut speaking English or has Mundy been holding out on us all this time and is fluent in German; maybe he speaks Yiddish, too, an Irish Jew infiltrating the Catholic church. No, that's too much.

Now Mundy unhooks one of the grenades from his field jacket pocket. Sometimes he even forgets to take them off when he sleeps; as I said, Mundy doesn't care enough. He passes that Goddamned grenade to the German. The German turns around and hangs it on the Christmas tree. The branch bends to the ground. He and Mundy are laughing.

The other Germans don't move while all this is going on. Then they break out with "Silent Night" in German. Miller, Mundy and I sing in English.

After that, Mundy shakes hands with the German and jumps over the wall back down with us. The German joins his mob on the other side; we're all still singing. We need Judy Garland in a pink frilly dress, or Sonja Henie to come skating along the creek. I hear singing behind us and it's Gordon. I figure Mother Wilkins is still up there on the hill keeping us covered. There wasn't anybody on the phone, after all, so he has no idea what's happening, but he must hear us singing.

The candles on the tree have started sputtering. There's a fair wind and they burn fast; a few have even blown out. I'm watching the candles and I'm lost somewhere deep inside my mind. I don't see any signal, but the Germans slowly back into the forest, trudge up the hill and away.

There are only a few candles left lit. We turn, then walk back uphill to the château. Miller and Shutzer still have another half hour to go. We don't say much; speechless is the word, I guess.

When we get inside, Mundy spreads the German presents on one of the mattresses. Gordon parks his rifle and sits on another mattress. I didn't realize how nervous I was but now I'm shaking. I can't seem to absorb these things the way the others do. Probably the imaginative-creative type isn't cut out for playing war, or maybe I'm only a garden variety coward.

I'm glad to be inside and I still have over two hours before I go out again. I take a deep breath. I wish Gordon were out on post; I'd take a smoke right now. Gordon's pulling his boots off.

"Come on, Mundy. What is this, did they teach you German in the seminary so you could go to Berlin with the Papal Nuncio and train the savages, some missionary kind of thing? Or maybe you're a German spy, sent into our midst to destroy our morale with all this Christian crap. What in hell were you two guys talking out there, anyway? He didn't speak English, did he?"

Mundy starts working on his boots. He stretches, yawns,

lifts his woolknit cap about two inches and scratches his head.

"Well, I just kept saying, 'Merry Christmas and Happy New Year.' I maybe said it fifty times. 'Merry Christmas, Happy New Year.' "

"And what was he saying to you? What was he actually saying anyhow?"

"It sounded something like 'Throw me a why not.' He said that a lot. Then when he gave me the bread, he said, 'Why not go shrink.' That's what I think it was anyhow. I don't savvy that German lingo. I can say a few words in Irish and I've memorized a lot of Latin, but nothing in German."

It's years later, when I spend Christmas on the Starnberger See, near Munich, with my family, I realize what Mundy was hearing. *Fröhliche Weihnacht* is Merry Christmas, *Weihnachtsgeschenk* is Christmas present. We were so close. I wonder what the German thought Mundy was saying.

There's a noise at the door. It's too early for Shutzer and Miller, so I jump. It's Mother Wilkins. He's stayed up there on the hill all this time and we forgot about him. His face is drawn and white. He has his usual dripping pearl on the end of his red nose.

"Is everything OK? What was happening? Mel and I couldn't get anybody to answer the phone. It sounded like somebody singing."

Gordon jumps up, goes over and helps Mother swing off his two bandoliers, lifts the rifle and grenades off him.

"God, I'm sorry, Mother. I forgot all about you up there. It was fine. The Germans only wanted to spread a little Christmas cheer, that's all. Father Mundy here even went out and did some present exchanging."

It's pitiful to watch Mother stare at Gordon when he says this. He looks over at me.

"Is he making this up, Wont? Is that what happened?"

"That's it, Vance. This particular branch of the German Army seems to believe in calling the war off every once in a while, like 'no fighting on Sundays' for knights in medieval days."

Mother sits on the edge of the mattress beside Mundy. Mundy's trying to open the bottle he got from the German. Mother still isn't finished; I'm about ready to confess the whole affair. He might go along with the idea anyway; maybe Mel's right.

"Gosh, Wont. I don't know if I can keep up with this 'now you see it, now you don't' kind of war. I'd rather we kept out of each other's way except when we have to fight. I can't take it."

Gordon's wrestling with the tough skin on the sausage. He pulls out his bayonet.

"Come on, Mundy. Just what the hell did you give those Germans besides our last bottle of wine?"

I glance over at Mel's watch. It's time to change guard. I decide we'll cut it to one on a post if everybody agrees. I don't remember who's supposed to be on next. I think it's Mundy and Wilkins.

"I didn't give them much. There's not much around here worth anything; at least, not anything we actually own and can give away. I gave him some of those scrambled eggs nobody eats, then six cans of that fish we found and *all* the lemonade packages. Oh yeah, I also gave him ten of those four-pack cigarettes. What the devil, it's Christmas, isn't it; or almost, anyway. I gave him a grenade, too.

"I wanted him to know we weren't going to throw any

more grenades, that's all. It was a sort of peace offering."

Mel comes over and shakes Mundy's hand, laughing.

"I've got to admit it, Mundy, you're sly; imagine, giving away all those cigarettes. But then, killing people for Christmas isn't quite in the best Christian spirit, you know."

Mel hands Mundy the sausage.

"Come on, Gordon; a few cigarettes aren't going to hurt that much."

Gordon takes the German bottle from Mundy. He pulls the cork out. Mundy takes out his penknife and starts cutting slices of sausage. Gordon sniffs the bottle carefully.

"Wow, this is the real stuff. This is like gin or vodka, really strong, white lightning."

He takes another sniff, then a small slug. We watch as he shakes his head and his eyes water. It's a few seconds before he can talk.

"Holy cowpiss! That'll keep anybody warm. Where the hell do they get something like this?"

He hands the bottle to Mundy. Mundy's passing out the salami. He gives a slice to each of us, another communion, salami wafers. Schnapps for the blood.

"Watch out, Father! That's not the stuff for saying mass. I'll bet it's at least a hundred proof. But it'll keep *your* blood moving in the dark out there."

Mundy looks at his watch.

"Holy mackerel, why didn't you guys tell us? We're already five minutes late. I think I was waiting for the phone-in."

He's up and throwing his stuff together. Wilkins starts up, too.

"You stay here, Vance. You've been out in the cold enough. We'll go one on a hole for tonight. Nobody's going to come crashing in on us. Is that OK with you, Father? I'll come down if you'd rather not be alone."

"No, I'm fine. I want to do some thinking anyhow. We priest types call it meditating but it's really thinking, our own private kind of thinking. You stay here. By the way, what's the password again?"

" 'Jingle—bells.' But a few bars of 'Silent Night' in *English* will do."

When Shutzer and Miller come in, we pass around the bottle and cut some more off the sausage. This sausage is delicious, better than Corrollo's mom sent and better than he took off bodies. This must be a sausage sent to a German straight from home, no ordinary GI stuff. Shutzer can't believe it.

"No shit. This is genuine kosher salami. It's good's Katz's. I think I'll take up Christmas."

Gordon pulls another long guzzle from the bottle. We're all going to be zonked if we keep at it. Maybe that's the great German plan: get us all looped, then wrap us up. Gordon passes the bottle to Wilkins.

"Sure, Shutzer. Then that explains this whole thing. Why didn't I think of it before? These aren't real Germans out there; these are Jewish spies dressed up in German uniforms and trying to escape with important information. These are their last rations they brought from back home on the ghetto.

"Be careful of that salami, Wont; there might be a roll of microfilm built into it; revealing the location of Germany's secret weapon. Check the bottom of that bottle, too."

Shutzer takes a slug, looks down into the neck of the bottle.

"Yeah, like a Chinese cookie. But, Gordon, your whole theory's out. How could a bunch of sheenies put on an entire Christmas scene like that, down to the last candle? It isn't fitting. No, these are plain down-home Krauts, but they've got good taste in salami, I'll say that."

We save half our bottle and most of the salami. Things like these can make ordinary rations almost edible. Shutzer puts on some water for coffee. Miller crawls into his sack about the same time I do. It feels like Christmas Eve whatever day it is. This will be my first Christmas away from home if I live that long, or maybe I already have.

5
Don't Tell Mother

Miller shakes me and I swing up into a sitting position on the edge of my mattress. I'm groggy. I look around; the fire's roaring. We're burning picture frames now. While I watch, Shutzer pushes down on one, cracks it at the corners, levers it into four parts and throws one chunk on the flame. We must be getting low for Wilkins to have sacrificed these frames; they're oak and hand carved. He made a point of that when we were looking at the paintings. I glance over and the violin's still there, so we haven't gone totally barbaric.

"How about it, Won't? We still on? Do I go in the green room to dress up? Mother's upstairs. He's on the edge all right; we had to practically wrestle these frames from him. He called Stan a traitor to everything 'his people' stand for. We've got to do something before he cracks up completely."

"How about you, Stan?"

"Ready and raring to go."

"OK, be right with you."

I go outside to take a piss. I could go upstairs but I want

to see what the weather's like. I figure it's about nine a.m. It'll only take half an hour getting out to the shack, at the most; so there's plenty of time.

It's clouded over. It's not snowing but the clouds are heavy and could start dumping any minute. I'm amazingly calm; maybe I'm like the rabbit cornered by the dogs and I've stopped fighting. I watched Jenkins go that way. He quit caring about things. He'd walk around on an exposed hill eating a chocolate bar. Thank God, Edwards caught on early and sent him back. I don't think he was bucking for anything; he'd given up; he didn't know what the hell he was even doing.

I come inside. I grab Miller's arm and look at his watch. It's later than I thought, twenty-five to ten. Shutzer and Miller are waiting. Miller's being pinned in and spruced up by Gordon. If we had makeup, Gordon'd probably paint a dueling scar across Miller's cheek. Miller looks so much like a movie version of the cruel German soldier he scares me. I have a hard time believing he's on *our* side. He's slipped completely into the role; maybe *he's* the Nazi spy in our midst.

In a few minutes I have all my crap on. Getting decked up as a soldier going on a patrol is a scene in itself.

As a street painter now, in Paris, I often get a *déjà vu* feeling when I pack to go paint. Going out with an easel on my back, with bottles of turpentine and varnish stuffed in my pockets and a canvas strapped to the easel, is one hell of a lot like being weighed down by military hardware. In fact, I use the same term; even if I'm only going painting up some alley or in a courtyard, I say I'm "in the field."

But there's a big difference. Even though painting's a challenge and physically exhausting, it's one hell of a lot more comfortable. People might hang on my back or ask stupid questions, but I never feel somebody's behind me with my life in his hands. The clicking I hear is cameras, not somebody pushing off a safety.

When we go out, we don't even go in interval. We have our rifles slung and we're walking along as if we're going to school or maybe going ice-skating after school. For smart guys, we're slow learners. I consider exercising those three stripes but don't. After all, in this deal, I'm distinctly the supernumerary.

We get to the shack just before ten, but they're already there. It's the same two, the noncom and the one with pale face and drooping eyes.

Miller and I stay up near the ridge while Shutzer strolls on down. Miller does everything but put one hand between the buttons of his field jacket. He's Napoleon watching the battle of Borodino. He even has one foot slightly stuck out. We decided he shouldn't carry a rifle, so he's unarmed except for a grenade we hung on his belt under the field jacket to look like a pistol bulge.

Shutzer turns and motions us on down. I hang back, more or less covering, rifle still slung on my shoulder but ready to swing up and fire. They have no weapons we can see, the same as last time.

Shutzer does a great job introducing Miller. He does everything but curtsy. The German noncom does a short nod and Miller pulls off a perfect imitation. They're liable to draft him into the German Army if we're not careful. Shutzer draws us all back a few steps.

"I can feel we're about ready to get into the crux of the matter. Miller, you just look severe and nod or shake your head when I talk to you. Won't, I guess Miller will have to make the decisions here on the spot. I can't see how we can do it any other way. I'm still not sure about that other guy. I think he's the one who's engineering all this, but I doubt he actually speaks any English."

All this is sotto voce, not far from the Germans, as if we're making casual conversation. Miller has his hands on his hips.

"OK, Shutzer, let's get on with it."

Jeee—sus, he *sounds* like a general. He doesn't even crack a smile. Shutzer goes back to the Germans, and Miller swaggers behind him. I bring up the rear, still somewhat wary.

Shutzer and the noncom start talking. The noncom keeps his eyes on Miller. Miller stares into the noncom's eyes as if he knows what's going on, but then he turns to Shutzer. Shutzer looks serious as a ghost.

"OK. They want to surrender all right. In fact, they want it tonight. But here's the kicker. They're convinced if they surrender without a fight, their folks back home will suffer or they'll be discriminated against after the war.

"They want us to take them in a fake firefight. At least that's what I think he's saying. Do a few questionable nods, Miller; maybe stroke your chin like Plato dialoguing with Aristotle."

Miller carries through. Perhaps it's all the bridge and games; they don't seem to know the difference between life and death or some game. They're *playing* at all this. Shutzer turns to the noncom and opens conversation again. I still can't fit this Shutzer, using his hands, shaking his head, singing his words, with *our* Shutzer. Which one is real? Which is the real Miller? Which one am I? I *know* I'm not a sergeant in the I and R squad of an honest-to-God infantry regiment.

I watch and listen as Shutzer and Miller go through their act. I listen when Shutzer translates for Miller and I listen to what Miller answers. The gist of it is they're not enthusiastic about letting us have a single prisoner now. I guess they don't trust us *that* much. Shutzer explains how our officers are pressing for a prisoner to question about what's happening to the south.

On this note, the other German moves closer and the pair of them powwow. Shutzer breaks out cigarettes and spreads them around.

In the end, they insist we come tonight, make a lot of noise with small arms fire, maybe a few grenades, then take them in. They say they'll have to leave most of their equipment in the lodge or it won't look as if they were surprised. They're convinced the big attack will charge through here soon.

So, after a lot more dickering, Shutzer and Miller join me. The capture scene is set for midnight tonight. They'll line up on the space in front of their lodge and we'll be on the hill where we peeped down on them with our scope the first time. We'll have an enormous advantage. It doesn't sound like a trap at all, just a complicated surrender. I'm still scared, but there doesn't seem any reason for it; everything's working out perfectly. I don't know why, but I'm deep scared. I'd like to read Miller's poem about fear. I think I could make some personal contributions.

On the way back, Shutzer and Miller are in stitches. They keep going over the discussion, the negotiation, as if they're dissecting a bridge hand. It's a hand I wish I'd made up myself so I'd know better what's going to happen, what's in the cards.

When we get back to the château, everything's fine. Wilkins has ducked upstairs again, so it's easy to get the squad together. I even pull Mundy in off post. Miller's gone back to his ordinary clothes and Shutzer's explaining what happened. Mundy looks dazed.

"You mean you really did it. You went out and talked with

them again and they're all set to come in with us, without any trouble?"

"Right. Only we have to pull off the whole business of having a firefight. It actually makes things better for the Mother Wilkins Win the War Plan. It'll add an element of realism. We'll get them back here, then have the chess play-offs to determine our local hero."

Mundy stands up and strides his forty-inch stride up and down outside the mattresses a few times.

"You know, Vance'll never go for this on the basis of winning at chess. For him that'd be taking unfair advantage. We've got to make this look like random, dumb chance, and I know how to do it."

We all stop and wait for Father to go on. He's right. Wilkins can win at chess, playing us all at once, different games or the same game, without even trying.

"Here's what we do. We'll draw straws. Only all of us will know which straw is the winning one and we don't draw it, maybe the second one from the end. I'll hold the straws; Vance will trust me. I'll work it out so he draws last and is sure to win. That way we won't be sitting around here running a chess tournament with a house full of Germans while Ware or Love could butt in any minute. What do you think?"

We look at each other. Shutzer goes tiptoe over to Mundy.

"Let me kiss your armpit, Mundy. That rarefied atmosphere has not addled your brain as I've been convinced it had all these months. That's just how we'll do it. We know Mother'll go along with this. He must know how much trouble he's in. I think he'll grab at the chance."

Mel is still shaking his head, but he's with us. I start warming the 506; I want to find out what's happened to the first squad, if there's any word yet. They crowd around me. God, we're a mixture of smells, mostly bad. I think stinking feet is the worst of it; practically everybody has his boots off.

We have it in our minds we've practically retired from this war.

There was a move-a-minute chess game going on when we came back from the patrol but it's abandoned for my call.

I get Ware right away.

"How is it with the first squad, sir? Over."

"No word yet. Over."

I hope he doesn't pick up the general moan behind me.

"They didn't get back at all, sir? None of them? Over."

"Nothing. Things are so bad here the motor pool and kitchen are packed up ready to take off; nobody knows which direction. Even the third battalion is engaged south. We can't pull them out or the whole flank will collapse. We don't know a Goddamned thing. Have you got that prisoner yet? Over."

"We reconnoitered last night, sir, and I think we can pull one down tonight. We'll hit the outpost about ten o'clock, just before they change the guard. Over."

I turn my head, wink at the squad.

"Well, make it for sure. I'll come out tonight, maybe Love, too, and we'll pick up the prisoner to bring him back. Over."

"Love's coming out *here*, sir? Over."

"Right. At least I think so. Over."

"Things must be serious, sir. Over."

"You have no idea. Love figures a Jerry squad on an outpost like that might be close to intelligence and know what's going on. Love's desperate; the Colonel's climbing all over him. It's like a madhouse around here. We keep having staff meetings and nobody has any idea what to do. Hennessee, the S1, has disappeared; nobody's seen him in almost twenty-four hours. We have double perimeter guard all around headquarters and the perimeter's pulled in tight. Over."

"OK, sir. I don't really think you have to come out. Tell

Major Love we'll have his prisoner for him sometime after twenty-four-hundred and we'll jeep him straight to head-quarters. No sense his taking a chance coming all the way out here; these woods are full of wandering patrols. Over."

"I'll tell Major Love that. I'm not exactly enthusiastic about driving on those roads at night in the snow without lights. Over."

"We have o ir jeeps ready, sir, with chains. Miller turns the motor over ev .y couple hours to keep the battery and water from freezing. We're OK. We'll get that prisoner in for you, sir. Over."

Tinker's balls, the last thing we want is Ware and Love roaming around out here. We'll never get it worked out for Wilkins.

"OK. You do what you can. If your squad can pull this one off, you'll square the whole I and R platoon with Love, that's shit sure. Over and out."

"Over and out, sir."

I switch off the radio and watch the light fade. I look up. Mel's standing behind me, his fists jammed into his sides.

"The entire first squad gone? God, there are only six of us left in the platoon. It's like World War I; it keeps going on. My mind doesn't believe I'm letting this happen to me."

"Mel, we'll just go on the patrol, do the shooting match, pick up our gremlin friends, then dash back to our castle before the dragons get here. We'll leave Wilkins on the radio. That all makes sense to me."

Gordon turns away.

"None of it makes sense. How can you make sense inside something like war which is basically nonsensical?"

Miller, Mundy and Shutzer have heard everything; there's nothing more to say. My first impulse is to dash right out with Shutzer and get it over with. It'd be the simplest way. But the Germans want shooting noises; it'll sound better if the whole squad's there.

So we'll leave Wilkins on the 506. We'll pull it off fast, get back, run through Father Mundy's straw pull, and we're home free.

I figure we'll go out at eleven; then we should have time enough to work over the whole business before Ware shows up. I still can't believe Love will come scrambling around in the dark with a jeep where there's any danger of an actual, real-life German patrol.

Before ten-thirty, we start getting ready. I tell Mother we're going out to try for a prisoner. I tell him if we're not back in two hours to call regiment. He's obviously glad not to be on the patrol. Half-assed tiger patrols like this are the worst.

None of us is talking about the first squad. There's nothing to say. I've pulled in the guard, so Wilkins will be alone at the château. I think of telling him to man the bridge post just to make it look good in case Ware does come. But I don't. If things go right, it shouldn't take us very long.

This time, we all put on snow jumpers. The room looks like hell. Maybe while we're gone, Mother will straighten things up. He won't have much else to do, and since he'll be on radio, he can't hide upstairs. I've got to admit I'm worried about him; as Mel said, he's at a terrible disadvantage. It's like one of those party games where everybody knows some secret or password and one person is being made a fool because he doesn't know. It's not fair but I'm hoping it'll come out right.

We check rifles and grenades, sling on bandoliers as if we're going on a serious patrol. Mostly it's theater for Mother, to make it look good, but also you never know. Then again, Gordon and Mundy haven't had much contact with these Germans except for the Christmas tableau and caroling; they could still be scared. All of us *should* be scared, but it's so unreal we aren't functioning properly. I'm still wishing they'd've let us have one prisoner for now, and push off the big capture scene till later. But maybe they know things we don't. Maybe there *will* be an attack coming through here. Ware sure sounded scared enough.

I'm more nervous than I thought I'd be. Still, when we get outside, and moving, it isn't so bad. It isn't snowing and there's strong moonlight. It's the same as the night when the Germans built the scarecrow; fast-moving low clouds, opening and closing the moon, bending shadows, white, blue and black. When there's a moon, with the snow, it's almost light as day, moon sparkling on frozen crystals. I spread us at a ten-yard interval. Shutzer's out as scout and I'm behind him. Mundy's in back of me, then Miller, with Gordon bringing up the rear. It's a regular patrol formation, only abbreviated. Around the bend, we stop to dress Miller in his costume.

The snow's deep and powdery; it flips up with each step into the tops of my boots. There're stars and a cold wind. I've had some fun ice-skating on nights like this, brooming off the surface of a creek and building a bonfire, but tonight seems quiet, unrelenting and expectant.

We head downstream toward the shack. I've decided to do the same dogleg we made the first time we came up on the lodge. This route we know, and we come in on the uphill side with the outpost below us. Even though they must be waiting for us, I'm worried about our first contact with that German outpost. We want to come down slowly, without scaring anybody. I'm still spinning wheels, expecting the worst.

. . .

When we get to the bottom of that last ridge, I signal the rest of the squad to stop; that is, Gordon and Mundy. Miller comes up in his costume. Shutzer agrees to approach the outpost first while we wait on the ridge. He and Miller will do all the arranging. It's too dark to see much now, because the moon's ducked behind a huge bank of clouds. We can just make out the white shining line of the road down at the bottom, between us and the lodge. We still can't see the outpost we found the first time. Maybe they're not manning it anymore. Maybe they're like us, not so scared, more interested in preparing for the big surrender. Shutzer leans close to me.

"Well, here goes. I don't know what to say so they won't shoot at me. I'm just going down shouting 'comrade.' "

Miller's standing behind me.

"Sounds as if *you're* the one surrendering. You sure you know what you're doing here, Stan?"

"Don't bug me, Miller."

Miller stands back of me while Shutzer goes downhill. Stan's saying "comrade" out loud as he goes, but not actually yelling. I hear a voice from the dark say *"Kamerad"* back. I motion the rest of us farther up the ridge till we all have a good field of fire over the lodge. I tell everybody to cover Shutzer and be ready to fire if anything goes wrong. We definitely have the advantage in case of a firefight. I'm becoming more and more convinced the Germans are being honest about this.

I keep my eye on Shutzer. I watch as he walks to where the outpost was last time. Then I see the outline of a German as he crawls out of his hole; the two of them start downhill toward the lodge. I'm looking for some sign from Shutzer but there's nothing. I see them cross the road and work their way up the other hill. The moon's come out again and it's perfectly clear as Shutzer walks across the flat area in front of the lodge and goes inside.

We wait. There's nothing else to do. Shutzer had his rifle slung on his shoulder the whole way, so he must feel confident.

After maybe five minutes, Shutzer comes to the door of the lodge and waves us on down. I check to see if Gordon and Mundy are in position.

It's not much for fire cover if something goes wrong; but there's nothing else we can do. I could just send Miller but I want to know what's happening, what the arrangements are going to be.

Miller's watching me. He saw Shutzer and he's waiting to see what we do. I signal and we both start walking downhill. The German on outpost, the one who took Shutzer into the lodge, is coming back toward us. We pass at the edge of the road. It's a weird feeling in the flitting moonlight, so close, both of us armed, passing like that, smiling at each other in a secret way; it really is almost as if the war's over.

We work our way uphill to the open space. Shutzer's waiting; the Germans are all inside.

"What's the deal, Stan? Everything still all right?"

"They want to talk to our officer, Herr Müller, here. I'll bet it's because I'm a Jew."

Miller does a near-perfect jaw thrust.

"Fuck you, Shutzer."

We're on the edge of giggles. It's the first straight-out intrasquad "fuck you" in months.

"OK, you inferior-type, nick-pricked Jew, take me to our real leaders. How many of them are there anyway?"

"Six, plus the one who went to the outpost; seven altogether. If they're actually going to give up, why keep one on guard? Who the hell are they guarding themselves from anyway?"

"Maybe other Germans. Who knows. Maybe they have a Major Love of their own; Übergruppenführer Liebe, or something."

I look around and take a deep breath. I'm trying to keep control. I'm between rushing into things and abandoning the whole project.

"Seven, that fits. OK. We're on. Let's go see how we do it. By the way, where's Snow White?"

"We'll negotiate that one. Miller, you get seconds. Won't here doesn't know what women are for, anyway."

We go inside. It's smoky and smelly but better than our place. There are bunks along the walls. In fact, except for practically no windows, it's like a barracks. At the foot of each bed is a neat pile of equipment. Hunt would've been happy to see this; it's almost as if they're ready for some kind of Saturday inspection. I wonder if they always keep it this neat or they've neatened things up for us. These Germans are even good at surrendering. That's what I call *real* soldiering.

At the far end of the room there's a fire burning. Most of the Germans are standing around it, murmuring to each other. They look over their shoulders when we come in. The moonlight coming through the door behind us is blue and hard cold; bright compared to the dark yellow-orange blackness of the inside. The noncom comes away from the others, toward us. After he and Miller exchange those peculiar short head-jerk nods, he starts talking with Shutzer.

Miller and I try looking as if we know what's going on. The other Germans have drifted closer. They nod and murmur to each other as the noncom goes on with his spiel. I wonder what else can be coming up; I thought it was all settled, was going to be simple. Shutzer turns to Miller, gives me the eye.

"Somehow we got our signals mixed. They're still worrying the idea of turning over one prisoner. I think that scared them. They insist on pulling off the whole affair now, tonight. I'm playing hard to get; it's all coming off perfectly; don't worry. Miller, act as if you're not enthusiastic, stroke your chin some more or put on a mean stare. I think they expect it."

Miller takes his "military" stance. What would happen if I broke out laughing? Those Germans might insist I be court-martialed, hanged by the thumbs. But Shutzer's playing things straight. He's concentrating as if he's pulling off some kind of exotic pseudo squeeze in a bridge tournament.

"They say if we take one prisoner now, they'll have to report it and somebody might come out. They don't have any radio contact I can see, so that doesn't make sense either."

The noncom looks back at us and Shutzer goes to talk with him again. Miller takes about two steps forward. I crack open some crappy Chesterfield cigarettes and pass them around. One of the Germans whips a bottle off a shelf, along with tin cups. He pours drinks for everybody. It's that same white lightning they gave us last night. This guy pours me a full cup. I'm liable to get so drunk I'll hit someone when we start our little firefight. Shutzer comes back with Miller in tow.

"They're all worried about the big attack; want to get on with the show right away. Sounds great to me. Miller's given the OK. They'll gather their things together and we'll go to it.

"One of them was back for supplies this morning and saw lines of weapons carriers and tanks. I can't tell if they're bullshitting or not; I just can't see any kind of attack coming through here, can you?"

"I don't know, Stan. I'll believe anything. The Germans have generals and colonels, the whole shitload of leader types, too. Anything can happen."

I give Stan a slug of my schnapps. The Germans are wandering around the room packing; they aren't taking much. I watch as the noncom slips off his watch and jumps up to hide it on a rafter. I don't think anybody else sees him do it. Maybe when I come back for my drawings, he'll be looking for his watch. Everybody trying to save something personal.

The Germans are lined up by the door. They're stamping out cigarettes and checking rifles. Each of them opens one of the little leather cartridge holders they wear the way we wear ammo belts. All the German equipment is worn, brown showing through fake black leather, square edges rubbed down round and smooth.

By the quick way they get ready, you know these would be tough customers in a *real* firefight. It scares me watching how they go about it: no nonsense; quietly slipping cartridges in their rifles. The noncom slings his Schmeisser under his arm and takes out his Luger. He pulls back the bolt to check his load. He looks over at Shutzer and Miller, nods his head.

Shutzer gives me the details.

"Here's how it'll go, Won't. They're going to line up on the open space in front of the lodge. Miller and I will stay here with them. You go back up to the squad on the hill. When he gives the signal, we all start firing. Maybe have everybody fire off about two clips; that should be enough. Then the squad'll come down, we meet on the road and take them in. That's when we disarm them. The noncom wanted to hide his Schmeisser but we said no deal. What the hell can he want with a gun like that after the war? It's not exactly a gun to hunt rabbits.

"He and I will put up our arms to stop the shooting and that's all there is to it. Seems OK to me."

"Sounds fine, Stan. I'll scoot back uphill to brief Mundy and Gordon. You and Bud play it close, now."

"Nothing to worry about; it's in the bag. This might be the high point of my war."

I go out past all the Germans. They have their weapons at the ready and it's almost like being the groom at a military wedding. The outside is silvery, the moon bright; clouds racing past in a fast moving sky. I think the moon's about one phase before full and it's lighter outside than in the lodge. I struggle uphill and pass the guard in the outpost coming down. I wonder how they signaled him? Maybe there's a phone in his hole. I peer in as I go by but don't see anything. It's a good hole, with a fire step. Huge roots on the sides look as if they've been hacked through with a bayonet.

I work my way up to Gordon and Mundy. I grab hold of Mundy's wrist and check the time. The moon just then is clear of clouds and Father's watch hands are straight up, midnight. The snow on the hill across from us glistens with refracted moonlight, tiny flashes of blue, violet, crimson in glaring moonlight whiteness against the dark. I send Mundy off right, above the road to our château. I stay in the middle; Gordon goes lower and off left twenty or thirty yards. I can see everything, including both of them. We wait; it's absolutely silent.

I'm feeling unreasonably calm when they walk out from the lodge. Shutzer and the noncom come first. The noncom lines his men in an evenly spaced line. Miller stands behind the noncom and Shutzer. The three of them are on the edge of the clearing with their backs to us up on the hill.

Shutzer looks up to see if we're all ready. I wave my arm.

Shutzer and the German put their arms over their heads. The German soldiers lift rifles to shoulders and point at the sky. I swing my rifle into position aiming out over the lodge. Gordon and Mundy've done the same thing. They don't look at me; they've got their eyes on Shutzer.

Then Shutzer and the German bring their arms down. The Germans fire simultaneously, almost like a salute at a military funeral. First the military marriage, now the funeral. I fire off a clip, one at a time, trying to space them unevenly. Mundy and Gordon are doing the same. The Germans are reloading. At least we've found one thing we do better than they do: running a fake firefight.

The next round, the Germans fire more irregularly, as they individually shove new cartridges into the chamber and fire. It begins to sound like a real battle.

I'm pushing in my second clip when one of the Germans goes down! Honest to Christ, the way things've been going, my first thought is he's faking it, pretending, the way kids do playing cowboys and Indians or cops and robbers. But then I see this is for real: he's not playing; he's kicking his feet, rolling, and blood's spurting from his neck! I scream at Gordon and Mundy to hold their fire. Shutzer has both his hands up. All firing stops and it's quiet for two seconds. Then there's another single shot; another German goes down, buckles and pitches face forward.

I see Mundy breaking fast off our hill and down to the road. He's farthest forward and is yelling as he runs. He's holding his rifle over his head; running along the road, waving his arms, yelling.

"Wilkins! Mother! Stop it, for Chrissake, hold your fire!"

There's another shot. Mundy drops on the road. This time it's a Luger. The noncom turns and shoots Shutzer, who still has his rifle slung. Miller drops to his knees and fires; the noncom bucks, spins and falls. There's a few seconds' silence after that. Then the other Germans begin firing into the hill at us. There's nothing else to do. I pull off all seven shots in the clip, with Gordon firing away beside me. Miller's flat on the ground. Shutzer sits up once, then stretches out and rolls over. With our position and semi-automatic rifles, the Germans don't have a chance. In ten seconds they're all down; only one's moving. He'd tried to run uphill toward the latrine. He's dropped his rifle, but now he's been hit and is screaming on the side of the hill.

"Mel, you check Shutzer and Miller! I'll go after Mundy! Watch out none of the Krauts is faking it!"

I'm yelling, crying and running. It all came on so fast. I fall twice sliding downhill till I get to Mundy. I flop on the road beside him. At first I can't see where he's hit. He's turned on his back with his knees pulled up, his arms locked around them, rocking back and forth. He's breathing but he rattles with each breath. Blood is starting to roll out the corners of his mouth. He's not crying and he's not screaming. He's only saying over and over in a low voice, "Jesus, Mary and Joseph. Jesus, Mary and Joseph."

I manage to straighten and roll him onto his stomach. He's been shot in the back and I want to get at it. There's a deep melted patch, black from his blood, in the moonlit snow. Mundy pushes himself up onto his knees. There's a great flowing hole in the middle of his back.

I unhook my bayonet, slit up the field jacket. Mundy's on his knees and elbows, his head on his forearms. He's still rocking.

"Hold in there, Father. I'll get you fixed up."

I pull off his aid kit, cut away the edges of his shirt. His back is white and black in the night. There's a hole about a half inch round just to the left of his spinal cord. When he breathes, air sucks in and out the hole, making blood bubbles. I can hardly hear his voice against the snow.

"Anybody else get hit?"

"Everything's OK, Paul. Don't worry."

I sneak a look toward Shutzer and Miller. Miller's up and seems OK. Gordon and he are working over Shutzer. Shutzer's sitting. Mundy tries again, not much louder than the sound of breathing and slow, slower than usual even.

"All the Germans dead?"

"I think so. Don't worry about that. We'll get you wrapped up and out of here. Just relax; don't think too much. You warm enough?"

"Yeah, I'm warm. May the Lord have mercy on those poor Germans and on all of us. Boy, we really fucked up."

Fucked up? Mundy? Holy shit! I've plugged, patched the hole with my bandage, and now I'm wrapping Mundy's over top to hold it down and tying the strings on the other side across his chest. I feel around to see if the bullet came out but there's nothing. By now, my hands are so sticky and wet I can't tell much. I've dumped both packs of sulfa into the wound. I'm sure, at the very least, there are broken ribs and the lung's punctured. Who knows what else? Father twists his head, looks at me.

"Don't tell Mother."

"OK, Paul. We won't tell anybody."

So now I'm telling everybody. But for a long time I did keep it to myself.

I glance up to see just where Wilkins is. Maybe he got it, too. Maybe one of those Germans figured out where the firing was coming from and put one into Mother. But then I see him coming along the road. He's moving cautiously, from tree to tree; I think if anybody moved he'd shoot, no matter who it was. Wilkins still has no idea.

"Don't worry, Paul, we won't tell Mother. He'll never know."

I take off my belt and Mundy's. I hook them together and strap that whole thing around to hold down the bandages. The blood seems to be slowing but it's thicker. Mundy begins coughing.

Huge gobs of blood are coming out of his mouth with each cough. He slides forward so the side of his face is against the snow but he's still on his knees, rump in the air. He's trying to say something through all the blood. I take off my helmet and get down so my ear is against his mouth.

"Looks as if those First Fridays didn't do much good."

"You don't need 'em, Father."

I can't be sure he hears me. His eyes are still open, almost transparent with the moon shining through them. I dip my right thumb into the mixture of snow, slobber and blood beside his mouth. I make a cross on Father's forehead, close his eyes, make crosses on them, a cross for his lips, then crosses in the palms of each hand. I can't think of anything to say I could live with.

Then Mundy, without opening his eyes, his mouth just moving against the snow, is trying to say something more. I get down closer; I can only just hear him.

"Remember, don't tell Mother."

He stops breathing; there's a bubbling and a last sigh of a breath. He lurches forward, thrashes, kicking his feet; then he's still. I look up and Wilkins is there, standing over us, crying.

"Is he dead? Is Paul dead?"

"I think so, Vance."

"He ran out to warn me. I heard him call my name just before he was shot. I don't understand. I heard the firing and had a perfect position. I could've put down all those Germans with no trouble at all; they didn't even know where I was. I don't get it."

Mother's crying hard, racking sobs; he drops on his knees beside Mundy on the road.

"You know how Paul is, Vance. He does crazy things without thinking. He was always making mistakes."

"I feel terrible. It's like it's my fault somehow."

"There's nothing you could've done, Mother."

I try folding over the cut in Mundy's jacket. He isn't bleeding anymore. When he fell forward on his face, his arms went under him and are crossed on his chest. I turn him over onto his back and put my face next to his mouth to be sure, but he's stopped. He's gone.

Wilkins and I drag him by shoulders and feet from the center of the road. I know I have to go help with Shutzer. Gordon and Miller are still working over him. None of the Germans is moving, but that one up on the hill is moaning.

"Vance, go see if you can help the German. I'll check what the situation is with Shutzer. Make sure that guy doesn't have a knife or a pistol or anything. Be careful."

I run uphill to the clearing in front of the lodge. God, it looks like a massacre; it *is*. At least seven people killed in less than ten seconds. We didn't mean it, none of us, but there they are. I'm crying and having a hard time breathing but I'm not shaking. I'm still doing the things I have to do. I'm mostly trying not to think. I only know we've got to move out of here fast. If those Germans thought their own people would hear the firefight we put on, they can't be far away. They could come charging out here in a hurry.

When I get to Shutzer, his face is white-green; Gordon has his canteen out and is giving him wound tablets. He's split Shutzer's field jacket up the arm and there's blood over everything and seeping into the snow. It looks practically black, the way Mundy's did. In some strange way, it doesn't look like real blood; more like motor oil. It's partly because there's so much and it's thick. There're two bandages wrapped over Shutzer's shoulder and his arm is tied twisted across his lap. There's yellow sulfa powder over the front of his jacket.

"How's it going, Stan?"

"God, Won't, what a mess. Shit, it looked so easy. I never thought Wilkins would come charging out like that."

"How's it look to you, Mel?"

I lean closer. Stan's shoulder's smashed and somehow the arm is twisted around, dislocated. Gordon's got the blood stopped with a tourniquet.

"I'd say our friend Shutzer here got the million-dollar wound. Your days as avenging Jewish warrior are over and done with, Stan."

"Me, the one guy who wants to fight these Nazi bastards gets the million-dollar wound. Isn't it the way?"

Shutzer swallows hard, winces. He's about ready for heavy shock.

"How's Mundy?"

"Dead, Stan. He died fast. Nothing I could do."

I can't help myself, I'm crying again.

"Fucking Kraut!"

"Come on, Stan. What the hell else could he do? He thought he'd been double-crossed."

"Shit, what a fuckup."

"That's what Mundy said. He also said not to tell Wilkins."

"Fuckin' Mundy."

"The story is we were pinned down; Mother got us all out. OK?"

Shutzer and Gordon look at each other, nod. I help Mel

settle Stan onto the ground. We've got to get moving and I'm starting to drift. I head uphill to where Wilkins is with the German. I figure we'll go straight back to the château down the road. It's going to be some trick moving three bodies with only four of us. We can't leave the German out here and we're not leaving Mundy.

I pass the German noncom. He's on his back with his arms and legs spread like a dead actor. His helmet's been blown off; above his right eye there's a bluish dent around a small hole, and there's not much blood. He is bald. Miller really did it. The snow around isn't thrashed up and the noncom probably didn't know what hit him. I hate to think what his last thoughts were. Boy, if he lived, he'd be a one-man beginning for World War III.

I get to Wilkins. The German's propped on one elbow with his head uphill. His eyes are open and he's watching me, watching the trigger on my rifle. I realize I've been running with my finger inside the trigger guard. I check and the safety's on but I don't remember doing it. I'm going to make some mistakes for sure, but how big a mistake can you make after one like this?

The German's scared out of his mind. It's the same one I watched cutting wood on the first patrol, the one who looks like Max.

"He hurt bad, Mother?"

"The bone's broken just above his knee and the bullet tore a chunk of flesh from the back side when it came out. I've made a tourniquet, so there's no hard bleeding now. He won't take the wound tablets. He even knocked the sulfa out of my hand."

"Can't blame him."

"Wont, is there any chance Shutzer can talk with him so he won't be so scared?"

"There's not much we can do, Vance; Stan's in bad shape himself."

"We've got to get him out of here fast or he'll freeze."

"You stay here, Mother; I'll go look in the lodge for coats or something we can wrap around this guy and Shutzer."

I'm distinctly losing momentum. We're in a bad spot and I'm running out of steam. I sprint toward the lodge trying to start my blood moving. Inside, the fire's burned down. I prop the door open; enough moonlight comes in so I can see overcoats hung at the bottom of each bed. These are the heavy, high-collared, long Wehrmacht overcoats. They look even more bulky than ours. I guess when you've come from the Russian front, this kind of weather seems like spring.

It's right then I get the first good idea I have all night. I gather six overcoats and stumble out into the snow with them. I call Gordon and Miller over, explain what to do. It's the only way I can think for all of us to get out and away. I go back to Wilkins and give him two of the coats. We're going to look weird but it might work.

Going back is miserable. We've slipped Mundy, Shutzer and the German onto overcoats, then covered each with another coat. Using the arms, we drag the coats like sleds. If we keep moving, it goes OK, but when we stop, the coats stick to the snow. Also snow gathers on the bottoms and front edges. Since there are four of us, we take turns pulling, three at a time. The one not pulling watches that nobody falls off, and cleans away snow from packing in front of the coats. Even though we've never come straight along this road before, I figure we must be half a mile or more from the château.

Wilkins tells us why he came out after us. I should have known. Ware and Love are at the château looking for their prisoner. Well, we've got one, so long as he stays alive. Mother strapped a tourniquet on him, using the *Gott mit uns* belt. Not tonight. Mundy's favorite joke was "We got mittens, too"; somewhat sacrilegious for an almost priest.

Shutzer's still conscious and the pain is coming on strong. The German moans for a while, then goes quiet. Every time we stop to change on the pulling, Gordon lets up the two tourniquets. I look at Mundy. In one way he looks like a real corpse, his arms folded across his chest, but he's smiling. It must be some facial muscle spasm pulled up his lips.

We're almost reaching the ends of our endurance, the changing and stopping getting more and more frequent, when suddenly a voice calls out of the dark.

"Stop! Who goes there?"

I've already hit the ground before I realize who it is. It's in English; it's Love.

"It's we, sir. It's the second squad. This is Sergeant Knott here."

"Rhythm?"

"We don't know the counter, sir."

There's quiet. I hear Ware's voice, then Love's voice again. I'm at the breaking point. Maybe I should just sob, cry, scream, let it out. Maybe then they'd know I can't do it anymore.

"Advance forward slowly to be recognized. Keep your hands over your head."

I struggle up off the ground with my hands on my head. My hands are raw from pulling on the sleeves and are numb cold. I walk down the road. Lit by the moonlight I see where they're crouched in a gulley.

"All right, Knott, you can put your hands down. How come you don't know the password?"

Ware speaks up. I don't think I could say anything without bawling. I'm in a bad state.

"They've been out on post five days, sir. We didn't think it wise to give the pass over the radio."

"With German infiltrators all through here, in American uniforms, speaking perfect English, we can't be too careful, Lieutenant."

"Yes, sir."

"Where's the rest of your squad, Sergeant?"

"Back on the road, sir."

"Did you manage to take a prisoner?"

"Yes, sir; but he's badly wounded."

Ware steps forward. He has his carbine in his left hand.

"We heard firing maybe fifteen minutes after we sent Wilkins out to bring you in. Did you make contact?"

"Yes, sir. Mundy's dead and Shutzer's badly hurt. Could we please bring them into the château now, sir? Shutzer and the prisoner are in shock."

"Jesus Christ. Why the hell didn't you tell us that before, Sergeant?"

Love flips open his holster and pulls out his side arm.

"The enemy may be in direct pursuit. We'd better get out of here, Lieutenant. Let's get moving on the double."

"Except for our prisoner, sir, the Germans here are all dead. We were pinned down in a firefight when Private Wilkins broke us out. I'd like to mention him for a citation, sir. He saved the squad."

"Wilkins? Ware, is that the soldier we found here at the château?"

"Yes, sir."

"He didn't look like much of a soldier to me."

"Sir, he stood alone in plain view and shot down six of the enemy with eight shots."

Why go through all this now? We need to get Shutzer and our prisoner into the château. Somehow Love and Ware have to move out of our way.

"My God!"

"Yes, sir."

"We'll see about any citation later; after this is all cleared up and we know what happened."

"Yes, sir. Is it all right if we move the wounded into the château now, sir? Both of them are bleeding badly."

"Did you give them their wound tablets, Sergeant?"

"Not the prisoner, sir. He wouldn't take them."

"All right. Let's get those men in, and make it on the double."

Love breaks into a shuffling jog through the snow along the moonlit road toward the château. His leather pistol case has a dangling thong and bounces against his leg. He keeps his pistol out as he runs. He also has a carbine slung over his shoulder. Ware stays back.

"How did Mundy get it?"

"Fast, sir. Right through the chest."

"How about Shutzer?"

"Shoulder wound, Lieutenant; probably bones broken, a bad dislocation. Gordon fixed him up. We've got it tied down and a tourniquet on it, sir."

I'm afraid I'm going to cry again. It's all so stupid.

When I get back, the rest of the squad's busy. Miller's covering the German; he's unconscious, could even be dead. Gordon and Wilkins are working on Shutzer. His eyes are half open, but when I speak he doesn't answer. He's breathing hard; it's almost like snoring. I look at Mel; he shakes his head. I wonder if my face is white as his. Against the snow, with the moonlight, we look like pale greenish ghosts, almost transparent.

We start out, Ware bringing up the rear. He's walking beside Mundy and not saying anything. Mundy's smiling his idiot smile.

It takes a good struggle uphill to the château. Our fire's

almost out but two of the flambeaux are burning. How long have we been gone? It can't be much more than two or three hours. It's hard to believe how fast things change.

First we carefully carry Shutzer and the German in. Even Ware helps. Love is standing with his back to the fire rocking up and down on his toes with his hands behind him, staring around. Our place looks like hell. It's for sure Wilkins didn't have much time alone before Ware and Love showed up.

While Gordon, Miller and I carry Mundy in, Ware warms up the radio. Mundy's already beginning to stiffen. It could be only the cold. Miller cracks a few more frames for the fire. He eases behind Love and throws them in. Love turns around to watch. Then he turns to me. He starts pacing back and forth with his carbine in one hand. He's put his pistol back in the holster but hasn't fastened it.

"Sergeant Knott, get some men out on post. We can't be sure the enemy didn't hear the firefight and won't be sending out a patrol."

"Yes, sir."

Now I've got to tell it. I'm spinning wheels to tell it right; not actually right, the way it was, but so it sounds right.

"Sir, before the prisoner went into shock, he told Shutzer there's supposed to be a big attack through this sector soon, maybe tomorrow."

"Holy shit, soldier. Why the fuck didn't you tell us that right away? I thought this was an I and R platoon."

Well, at least he got something right. We *are* the I and R platoon now, Wilkins, Miller, Gordon and I.

"Yes, sir."

"Lieutenant Ware, get regiment."

Love flips his wrist and looks at his watch.

"We just have time. They're closing down all radio communication at o-two-hundred."

Ware's switched on the radio. While they're hanging over

it, I go to Mundy, kneel beside him and slip off his watch. It's an expansion bracelet on that Benrus. I ease it over his big hand and slide it onto my wrist. Mundy wouldn't mind. I don't think his parents would want it back, and I'm not sure it would ever get that far.

Ware reaches Leary; Love takes over.

"This is Major Love, Corporal. Write down this message and rush it to the regimental commander immediately. Over."

"Wilco, sir. Over."

"Have contacted enemy. Have taken prisoner. Prisoner badly wounded. Have suffered casualties, one dead, one wounded. Have destroyed enemy outpost.

"Prisoner informs us impending enemy attack through this sector, perhaps tomorrow. Repeat TOMORROW! Leaving immediately with prisoner and wounded. Will contact you directly at regiment. Signed Major Love. Repeat the message, Corporal. Over."

Leary reads it back.

"Correct. Get that to the Colonel on double-quick time right now. Wake him if necessary. This is urgent. Over and out."

"Wilco. Over and out."

Ware flicks off the switch. It's all so embarrassing. Shutzer moans and Mel wraps a quilt closer around him. We pull the fart sacks from the other beds to cover Stan and the German. They're both shivering violently. It doesn't make sense but I cover Mundy, too.

Love's pacing like a lion now. He won't look at Shutzer or the German; or, particularly, Mundy.

"We've got to get out of here fast, Lieutenant. We'll take the prisoner and the wounded soldier with us."

He turns to me.

"Sergeant, have the chains transferred from one of the squad jeeps to mine. We have a long way to go and the roads out there are rough. We had a hard time getting through to you."

"Yes, sir."

I look over at Miller, but he's already on his way out. I'm glad he's getting out, because I can feel he's about to say something that could grow into a general court-martial. I know myself that if he starts I'll join in. We could wind up killing Love and Ware, bang bang! We could cover up; who'd ever know? But I know I won't do it myself. The essence of the peasant mind is resentment without courage or initiative to strike back effectively. I've learned to live with it.

"Sergeant Knott."

"Yes, sir."

"I'm shocked with the condition of the quarters here. This is private property and the United States government is responsible."

Ware surprises me by speaking up, actually lying.

"It was in bad shape when they came in, Major."

"Nevertheless, Lieutenant, there's ample evidence to indicate dereliction of duty, conduct not becoming American combat troops. I wonder if these men realize there's a war going on. At this very minute, the entire American military presence in Europe is endangered. If it weren't for extreme extenuating circumstances, I'd see that this soldier, as noncom in charge, was brought before a military board and severely disciplined.

"And where are your stripes, Sergeant? You've had enough time to sew them on. You should be proud to be a sergeant in the U.S. Army."

"Yes, sir. I'll get to it right away."

God, I hope Miller rips all the garbage off Gordon's field

jacket. If Love ever sees that, we'll have a court-martial to end all court-martials.

"You get out there now, Sergeant, and hurry that soldier with those chains."

He flips his wrist. Looks at his watch again.

"We don't have much time. Lieutenant Ware, be prepared to move the wounded and prisoner into the back of my jeep."

Gordon and I make a four-handed carry. Mother props Stan so we can get him up and out to Love's jeep. Thank God he's unconscious, because we must be hurting him. He moans each time we shift or move too fast. When we get him sitting in the jeep, Gordon loosens the tourniquet once more and lets it flow. The blood's still flowing, so he's still alive.

"What do you think, Mel? Will he make it?"

"Let's hope. Shutzer's strong. With a careful drive back and quick medical help in a warm place, he'll be OK."

"Maybe we should keep him out here with us. What can they do for him right now we can't do?"

"He needs morphine more than anything. He's got to go back. It's mostly a question of how much beating he takes getting there."

We go inside to move the German. He's not fighting us anymore. He's conscious when we pick him up but there's so much pain he passes out again. When we get him propped beside Shutzer in the jeep, Mel lets up on his tourniquet. He isn't bleeding much.

I go back inside and pull off one of the satin covers. I'm out again before Love can think of some other asshole thing. Miller's stretched on his back, flat on the snow in the dark trying to hook the chains. He's pulled off the stripes. I wonder when he did it. Miller always does the right thing and way ahead of when I would.

We tear the satin into strips and tie Shutzer tight to the German so they support each other. Then we tie the two of them to the handholds and the jerry-can clamps. We tie securely so they won't fall out, but not so tight we block circulation. Gordon's a genius at this kind of thing. I'll bet he's a high-class blood-and-bandage man today.

I wrap all the extra satin tatters around Shutzer and the German's hands. They're both already ice cold. Gordon brings out Stan's sleeping bag and we tuck it around both of them the best we can.

Love and Ware stand beside the jeep talking. Love's smoking a cigarette in a short holder. Gordon moves off down to the bridge post. Wilkins is on post above the château. I guess Love thinks I sent them out; he'll never know how this squad runs; self-contained, automatic drive.

Love stamps his feet and uses a stick he picked up somewhere to scrape snow from his boots. Those boots, combat boots, are waxed ten coats thick.

Miller crawls out from hooking the chains. Love climbs into the front passenger seat. Ware walks around back and stops by me. He looks at Shutzer.

"Sir, I think they won't fall out if you're careful but it's going to be a rough trip. It'd help if you could stop once in a while and loosen the tourniquets on each of them."

"We'll do what we can, Knott."

"Sir, you won't forget about Wilkins?"

"We'll do everything we can."

"Thank you, sir."

"You're doing a good job, Knott. Don't worry about it."

"I don't think so, sir."

Ware looks at me. I wonder if that's in the category of insubordination. I don't care much.

"Major Love wants you to keep the squad here until the Krauts start their attack. Try contacting us by radio, same frequency, then pack up and get the hell out."

"What about Mundy, sir?"

"Take him with you if you can."

"Yes, sir."

"Headquarters will be moving out at o-eight-hundred. I'll leave a jeep with a radio to pick up your message, then guide you in."

"Yes, sir."

Major Love turns around in the front seat.

"What's going on back there, Lieutenant? We can't stay around here all night. Let's get going!"

"Yes, sir; be right there, sir."

Ware goes around to the front of the jeep, gets in and turns the motor over. They roll off the terrace in front of the château, downhill and over the bridge. Even here, where it isn't particularly bumpy, Shutzer and the German roll back and forth. They look weirdly like lovers, locked together rocking back and forth, synchronized puppets on a hayride in the snow.

The scarecrow's still there near the bridge, casting a long shadow in the moonlight. I wonder what Love thought of that. Probably pulled off a couple shots with his carbine. I should talk!

The moon's all the way across the sky now, and some clouds are beginning to drift in. My feet and hands are freezing but I hate to go inside. I'm feeling empty, drained. Miller's standing behind me. I'm not only feeling empty; I'm feeling dirty, hollow, cheap and shallow.

"Bud, you go down and get Mel. I'll go up for Mother. We're not going to keep any guard unless you want to or one of them does. None of this makes sense. If Germans are going to charge through here, we'll hear them. Maybe tomorrow morning when we can see something we'll take turns on the upper post; that's enough."

Wilkins and Miller bring more stuff down from the attic to burn. I can't decide whether to cover Mundy's face or not. I decide not to. I'm about ready to crack and don't know what to do. I only want to climb into my fart sack, zip it all the way up, cover my head and breathe my own breath. I also want to run. My legs are quivering, jumping to run.

I pick up one of the flambeaux and go upstairs to the toilet. Nothing comes and it hurts; it's the beginnings of latter-day piles. I almost start sobbing out loud on the toilet and it's not the pain. I know I can't go downstairs like this.

I go up into the attic, Wilkins's hideout. We've really cleared out most of the junk, burning. Wilkins has lined up along the walls everything he thinks is too good for us. The rest of the stuff is piled in the center. The paintings he took out of the frames are leaning against one wall. I spread them around me and sit in the middle of them, the way I did with Wilkins. I try to let the calmness come into me again. I sit in that dark, dust-smelling room in the attic cold for a long time. I cry up there alone. It would've been so much better for me, for all of us, if we could only have given each other the comfort and support we needed so badly, but it's hard for young males to share real emotion. It's probably part of what allows wars to happen in the first place.

Finally, I go downstairs. I look at Mundy's watch. It's three-thirty. Wilkins and Miller are sleeping; Gordon's playing with the fire.

"How's it going, Wont?"

"Better. But lousy."

"I've been sitting here thinking maybe Mundy's the lucky one. He won the big prize."

"Yeah, could be."

"Is the whole world run by shits like Love? If we get through this, is that the way it'll be?"

"I can't even think about it."

Mel pushes some burnt ends into the heat of the fire; they flare and throw light on his face. He looks bad as I feel.

"Mel, you think Wilkins has a chance?"

"You mean the citation?

"Most likely it's up to Ware, and he'll need to let Love write himself in. You heard him on the radio. He's Buffalo Bill and General Robert E. Lee rolled in one. He writes his own citations. But maybe Mother will get something after all."

I go over and kneel beside Mundy again. I remember doing it and trying to put him in my mind but it doesn't work. Like looking for a star on a moonless night, it has to happen from the side. The blind spot's in the center of the eye.

"Ever think about how many dead people there must be, Mel? Mundy's gone and joined the great majority. I'll bet there are thousands of dead people for every live one. I'd like to stay in the minority a while longer."

"You're not doing much about it; me neither."

"For some reason I can't figure, we don't pay enough attention to important things; like Mundy here."

"So what's important?"

"Really being alive, I think. If I ever get through all this, I'm going to do the things I want. I'm going to look at a lot of paintings, and listen to music, really listen, not just hear it. I love to draw, always have; I might even become an artist. That'd sure be worth living for. I know damned well I don't want to be an engineer; that's just what my dad thought he wanted, and I don't think he really knew either."

"My folks want me to be a dentist, take over the old man's practice, make *his* life seem to make sense. I think I'd puke every time I brushed my own teeth; I don't even like the sound of *other* people brushing their teeth. I'm taking my chances at getting to be a doctor; that'd be important to me. But what's the difference; what chance do we have, anyway?"

"Mundy told me he still wanted to be a priest. He only dropped out because he thought he wasn't good enough. Can you believe it?"

We're both talking to Mundy. I'm still kneeling on the floor beside him. I cover his face. I remember now thinking how somebody had to get something out of all this. I wanted it to be me. And it was.

That night, the darkness lasts forever. We're worried about Shutzer. Mel says if Stan makes it back to regiment, he'll maybe only get a stiff shoulder out of it. It's his left arm. We try to remember if he's right-handed; we're both almost sure he is.

Wilkins and Miller sleep away. I lie out on a mattress but my head spins. The Germans could come and blow us away. I'd have a hard time even getting excited about it.

At eight, just as light is breaking, I try getting through to regiment but nothing doing. Love said they were closing down, but I'm hoping to reach that jeep Ware promised. I try on and off for almost half an hour and finally give up.

We agree somebody should be out on the hole; Miller volunteers. I'm still not hungry but I'm dead tired at last. My eyelids are dropping over my eyes as I pull off my boots, jacket, helmet, and climb into the sack. It's the first time I've been this undressed since we left regiment. I go out cold.

6
A Statement
of Charges

I wake, it's dark and I don't know where I am. I see the fire burning but it doesn't mean anything. I look at my arm and I'm wearing Mundy's watch. It's hard to believe but I *still* don't catch on. The hands are straight up and down. I don't know if that's o-six-hundred or eighteen-hundred. I hold the watch to my ear but it isn't ticking. So I don't have *any* idea of what time it is. I don't know much of anything; something in my mind is keeping me from knowing.

This is the first time I experience a separation of the physical and mental.

The second time is later, when our first child was born. My wife went through forty-eight hours of hard labor; I was driving home along the Pacific Coast Highway in California and woke up grinding over sand into the Pacific Ocean. It wasn't that I fell asleep; my mind became detached from me.

A cop saw the whole thing, watched me drive across the

oncoming lane, over curbs, through a parking lot, over tire bumpers, down an incline, and chug along the sand. I'd probably've wound up in Hawaii if the motor hadn't stalled.

Now, that was a nice cop. After I got myself together enough so I could explain, he took me home in his squad car. Then, somehow, he got my car pulled off the beach and drove it to Topanga Canyon, to our house. It was there when I woke up and I never even got a towing bill. It was the kind of thing that gradually tuned me back into life and people.

I look around. Somebody's cleaned and straightened things up, arranged our rations along the high mantel over the fireplace. They've also somehow dragged that copper tub down from the bathroom upstairs and stood it beside the fireplace. There are bucketfuls of steaming water hanging on hooks over the fire. There's no one there but Mundy and me.

"Hey, Father, where is everybody?"

I remember while I'm saying it. I'm not even sure if I finish the sentence. I'm back. It's all on me again, with a feeling of green slime dripping from my brain into the back of my mouth. I cry again.

When I'm finally pulled together, I swing out of the sack, slide on my boots without lacing them and go outside to take a piss. Things like needing to piss are what bring you back. It's dark out. From the moon I can tell it's evening, not early morning. I've slept about ten hours.

Wilkins and Miller are struggling and slipping uphill from the bridge with that German Christmas tree on their shoulders. I button up and wait for them. Miller looks through the branches at me.

"Well, well. Sleeping Beauty's awake."

He isn't. I hold back one curtain so they can push the tree through the French door.

"What's up? Who's on post, or have we given up the whole idea?"

Miller and Wilkins stand the Christmas tree in a corner on the other side of our fireplace. Miller's knocking snow off branches.

"We've more or less kept somebody out there. It's OK. Don't worry, Won't. You're alive, right?"

"Thanks. When am I on?"

"If you're really gung ho to sit in a cold hole for a couple hours, you're on at eight. We've about convinced ourselves no patrols are coming through here anyway. If they come in force, it'll most likely be in the morning."

"What's the tree for; going to try burning it?"

Miller looks quickly at Mother, then at me.

"Vance and I here were getting depressed, figured we need some Christmas spirit; so we cleaned this place up. Now we'll decorate our tree, roast chestnuts, crackle a Yule log or two and stuff ourselves with turkey, cranberry sauce and all the trimmings.

"We also decided to have a real Christmas washup all around."

Miller and Vance are wearing gloves and lift those buckets off the hooks, pour steaming water into that tub. They head on out to get more water; I go over and peer into the bottom of the tub. They have it about a foot deep; I reach in and the water's not exactly hot but it's good and warm. They have the tub close enough to the fire so the near side is almost hot to the touch. I hear them staggering back with full buckets. I look around the room; they really did a job on it all right; it looks as good as when we first came in.

They put the buckets on the hooks and then each of them dunks a hand into the tub. Wilkins smiles at me.

"Almost there. We've decided you get 'firsts.' You aren't

the rankiest but you do have rank on us. Besides it's a Christmas present."

"Oh no, Vance. We pull straws the way we do for everything. No sucking ass around here."

God, it's all so artificial, we're trying to pretend nothing's happened, that Mundy's not there dead beside us, that Shutzer isn't hurt, that the first squad isn't missing, that the whole gruesome war isn't going on out there.

"Did you hear what Love said to me about a court-martial? What a shit."

"Fucking Love couldn't wipe his own ass without an orderly. Forget it, Sarge."

Mother's standing back admiring the tree he's jammed in the corner beside the fireplace. It's surprising how fast the smell goes through the room; there *is* something of Christmas, despite everything. I know I'm trying not to look over where Mundy is; I'm glad I covered his face. Mother turns the tree a quarter turn.

"We need some decorations, Bud. Just those apples and potatoes with the paper stars aren't enough."

"God, I hate to think of those poor shithead Krauts."

Miller turns toward me.

"Don't then, Won't. For Chrissake, it's over; we can't go back."

With Mundy gone, we're talking like rear-echelon barracks cowboys. Miller goes outside. Wilkins spreads one of our satin covers under the tree. Miller comes back, his helmet filled with ammo for the fifty caliber. They're brass and the tips are painted different colors, red for tracer, black for AP. We pull cartridges from the belt and tie them onto our tree with bits of wire Miller's hauled in from his magic jeep. The brass reflects flickering light from the fire. I'm still drifting.

We call Mel in from post. I talk them into pulling straws using thin strips of K ration box. The Mundy plan is being carried through, not for a bath of medals but for a bath in a metal bathtub. I win, Gordon's second, Wilkins third and poor Miller, engineer of the whole affair, last. That's the way things seem to work out in this world. I can't imagine how they ever maneuvered that damned tub downstairs but I'm sure it was another piece of Miller genius. He's even found soap for us.

In the tub, I actually do feel like Claudette Colbert. I'm rubbing warm, soapy water all over my body. Miller, Wilkins and Gordon are piling wood in the fire till it's blazing; Mother must have lowered his standards. The whole room is light for the first time. I wash myself, leaving my filthy clothes on a mattress. We'll wash clothes last. We've definitely turned off the war.

Each of us takes a turn. We keep adding more hot water till it's sloshing over the sides. It works out OK for Miller. His water's got the most dirt but it has the most suds and there's more of it. None of us wants to get back into stinking clothes so we wrap ourselves in quilts. It looks like a Roman party with all of us in golden togas. Boy, if Love could see this. All of us have washed our hair for the first time in months and we've rubbed ourselves down with the quilts. Wilkins is fitting his glasses back over his ears and staring at Mundy.

"I feel rotten being clean, with poor Mundy there."

We're all quiet. I'd been pushing the same idea out of my mind. Miller goes over to Mundy. Miller has one corner of his quilt looped over his shoulder and then tied somehow high under his armpits.

"If we can only get the clothes off him."

He lifts Mundy's arm. It's stiff as a board, the whole body moves.

"Come on, Won't, give me a hand here."

So the four of us, in the blaze of the fire, shift and push Mundy around, slipping off his field jacket, unbuttoning, sliding down his shirt over his shoulders. Gordon unbuckles his pants while I unlace and pull off his boots and socks. He has holes in both socks, heel and toe.

When we get him all undressed he looks white, like a statue, and stiff, so we can stand him up. We rock him on his stiff legs over to the tub, then struggle him up till he's standing in the tub. I want to put more hot water in but Miller says it doesn't make sense. We'll save it for washing clothes. Gordon rips some strips from the bottom of his toga. Wilkins and I start sudsing Father while Miller and Gordon hold him up straight. There's less blood than I expected; most of it's caked on the shirt and field jacket. We wash his hair and get him generally scrubbed off. Vance reaches down into the water to clean his feet and between his toes.

Mel goes back upstairs and brings down another quilt. We lift Mundy out and stretch him onto the quilt on his mattress. We dry him off and wrap the quilt tightly around him. Then we slide him into his fart sack. The army calls them mummy bags; this time it's appropriate.

Now somehow I feel better. I think we all do. It's been like playing dolls where you carefully dress the doll in pajamas, and tuck a tiny blanket carefully all around the doll in the doll carriage.

We pour four new buckets of water into the tub, then dump in our clothes, field jackets and all. We hand slosh them around for a while until Miller tells us to get out of the way. He pulls off his toga, jumps in the tub and starts jumping up and down, bare ass.

"See, this is the way a washing machine works. You push the water under pressure through the cloth fibers."

He's jumping up and down, stomping in the tub, flickering light and glintings from the burnish of the tub and the brass cartridges on the Christmas tree behind him; it looks like a primitive rite.

We take turns, stomping in the water. We keep bailing out dirty water and adding new hot. I think we stomp around like that for more than an hour; our feet have never been so clean. If any Germans come in while this is going on, they'll turn around and run fast as they can just to preserve their sanity.

After we've got the clothes all washed, wrung out and hanging around the room, we go to sleep. I never would have believed I could sleep as deeply as I sleep then. And I think it's the same for all of us. Bad as everything is, at least we're going to be clean and ready for what comes.

At seven-thirty, I wake and try calling regiment again. Nothing. If Ware hasn't left a jeep to convoy us, we're really up shit creek. Everybody's still sleeping soundly.

Quietly, I dig into the D ration box and cook some hash with chunks of cheese cut into it. I eat one of the fruit bars. It's the first fruit bar I've tried in months. My stomach seems to have given up on me; it's quiet and there's no pain. I finish with a full canteen cup of coffee; pushing it all the way. Maybe not eating for so long has helped. The clothes are all pretty much dry; I pull mine on. They're almost like new, only the bottoms of my sleeves and cuffs are damp.

At eight I go up on post. I need to be alone, get some fresh air in my lungs. The inside, with the windows and doors closed, the smoke, the fire, the steaming clothes and Father in the middle, wears me thin.

At about nine o'clock, it begins snowing again. I phone in, get Mother. Everything's fine. The rest of them are awake. Mother's cooking breakfast.

"Wont, how're we going to get Paul out of here when we take off?"

"I don't know, Vance. Put him in a jeep, I guess."

"He's stiff as a board."

"Right."

"How about if we take one of the bedsprings up in the attic and tie it across the back of a jeep? We could strap him to that."

"Good idea."

I hate to think of it.

"We really ought to do it soon, Wont. If we need to get out fast, we won't have much time."

"OK, Vance, we'll rig it when I come down."

I hang up. It looks as if it's going to snow for a while. There's a low fog and with the snow I can't even see the château twenty yards in front of me. For some reason I'm beginning to feel scared again. I guess something in me is wanting to live.

It's about nine-thirty when I see someone coming through the thick snow. It's Mother. He slides down in the hole beside me.

"Gosh, Wont. It's crazy sitting out here. There's nothing you can do; you can't see anything."

"I know, Mother. I just have to be alone some."

"You want me to go back?"

"No. Thanks for coming out."

We sit quiet. I light up a cigarette. Vance doesn't smoke at all.

"Mother, I asked Ware to put you in for a citation. I hope you don't mind; I didn't have time to ask."

"Gosh, Wont, Mundy or Shutzer should get it."

"No, Mother. You're the one who saved our asses; the Germans had us pinned down."

I'm glad it's snowing so hard. I'm not looking at Wilkins.
I'm talking out into the floating snow. I didn't realize how
hard it would be lying to Mother. How does Gordon know
these things?

"Wont, I still can't figure why Mundy ran out that way. It
didn't make any sense."

"Maybe he panicked. It could only be that."

"Yeah, maybe, but it's not really like Paul. I can see him
forgetting to do something, or losing his rifle or sleeping with
grenades, but this was different."

"Let's not think about it, Vance. Love'll probably try to
horn in on the deal but I'm sure Ware will keep you in there.
We'll all swear on what happened."

"But I only shot twice. After Mundy went down, I didn't
shoot anymore. My glasses were fogged up from running and
I still don't know if I even hit anybody. I was shooting with
my gloves on, too."

"It doesn't matter, Mother. Just stick to the story. You shot
them all; that's the way we'll tell it. That's what I told Ware.
Maybe you can get pulled out of here if you get decorated.
After all this mess Ware's been talking about, they'll be looking for heroes to build up morale. Ride along with it."

"I'm just about ready to try for an honest Section Eight,
Wont. I hardly sleep anymore and when I do, it's nightmares
mixed up with Linda, the baby, Max and Jim. I think Jim
was the first real man friend I ever had. He never laughed at
me and he understood how I feel about things.

"God, Wont, when you think about it, we don't have a
chance. Two-thirds of the squad's gone now; I don't see how
any of us is going to make it."

I need to lie again. He's saying what I'm thinking, but you
can't make it that way. I guess this is what sergeants are paid
for, lying.

"It's not so bad, Vance. We've only had rotten luck. Maybe

I can get Ware to work a deal for you; something like security guard with the motor pool or working in the kitchen. When the new replacements come in, we'll figure something. With the citation and everything, I'll bet I can arrange it with Ware."

"God, I hope so."

"Make you a bet, Mother. In six months, you'll be back with Linda. She'll be pregnant and all this will be something you'll hardly remember."

"I doubt it. I'll never forget."

"We forget everything, Vance. But I'll bet a hundred dollars."

"A hundred dollars? Who has a hundred dollars?"

"You can pay me off a bit at a time, starting New Year's Day, 1946."

"OK, it's a bet."

We shake hands in our gloves. I'm hoping to hell Ware will help out. The snow keeps getting thicker. There's no sense staying out here in it anymore; talking with Mother has helped. We work our way back downhill. The new snow is wetter and slippery packed over the old.

For ten years, from January 1, 1946, to January 1, 1956, I got Christmas cards from Vance with a new ten-dollar bill each time. No return address, not a word, no interest. Then I never heard from him again.

At the château, Vance and I go up into the attic. We maneuver a single-bed spring down the two sets of steps, then outside. We choose our jeep without the fifty caliber and tie the spring on with more torn-up strips of satin. It's the jeep with the missing chains now. When we go out, we'll put this one in front so the jeep with chains can push if it gets stuck. In this snow it's going to be one tough trip.

"What do you think, Wont; should we tie Mundy up there now?"

"Mother, I'd hate that."

"But he could start stinking and we might not have enough time to tie him on later."

"I just can't, Vance. If he starts to stink, we'll bring him out, OK? We'll leave the strips here so we'll have everything ready. We can tie them to the springs now so all we need do is slip them over Father and fasten them when the time comes."

"OK. I know what you mean; it's hard thinking of Father out here in the cold, alone."

I'm asleep and it's almost five in the morning when the barrage starts. Everybody's running around, jamming on boots, grabbing up rifles, grenades. I try once more getting through to regiment. There's absolutely nothing. I try different frequencies but it's all blank.

This is serious stuff going over: screaming meemies, eighty-eights and something bigger. But nothing's landing in the forest; not near us, anyway. I get my boots laced and run to our post up on the hill. Miller's there; I've already sent Gordon and Wilkins down by the bridge. I send Miller back to the radio; if anybody can get through, he's the one. At least, maybe he can get a rise from some other outfit, tell them what's happening here, find out what's going on.

It's still snowing; the artillery sounds like fast freight trains going over us in the dull white, dark sky, a heavy displacement of air and a shrill diminishing whistle. There's no light, nothing to see, only that sound; on our left, the sharp, distant muttering whomp of guns firing and now the muffled crump of shells landing to our right. There's also the weird, sirenlike shrieking of rocket batteries going off. I have no idea what the range of those things is, but even if they're aimed at Eisenhower, there are always "shorts."

After five minutes, I know this isn't a casual barrage; troops will be moving through here. I phone to hustle Wilkins and Gordon back into the château. This looks like time for us to move out.

When I get to the château, Miller's still hanging over the radio, searching frequencies. I look at him but he shakes his head. I tell Gordon to pull wire and phones in from both posts. Wilkins and I carry Father on our shoulders. He's stiff, hard, but still doesn't smell. We tie him to the bedspring on back of our jeep. Then we go inside and pack the rest of our stuff, including whitening, camouflage suits, leftover wire; we throw it in back under Mundy. We stuff the fart sacks under there, too. We're all scared and running around like hell but panic hasn't struck yet.

We're just about loaded when the first mortar hits. The trouble with mortar is it hits before you hear it coming in. Then there's another, then eighty-eight. There are three bursts. That eighty-eight seems almost like direct fire. These are no shorts; somebody sees us and is calling it in. We're under observation.

Gordon and I jump in our jeep with Mundy; the one without chains, without the fifty caliber. I'm driving. The motor turns right over and I hear Miller start behind me. There's no time for fooling around. I roll over the edge and downhill toward the bridge. It's going to be mean without chains; just going down that little hill I'm slipping all over the road. It's dark as hell but the snow's let up some. Mel looks back.

"They're with us OK, Wont. Most of the stuff is landing uphill behind the château, above the upper post."

I nod. I'm concentrating on driving and keeping my mind in control. I stay in low-low with four-wheel drive and start uphill on the other side of the bridge, up and away from the château. I'm just about keeping traction, and at the same time losing speed. I can hear the slap-slap of chains on Miller's jeep. Mel's looking back, half standing up on his seat to see over Mundy.

"My God! They put one beside the bridge and blew the scarecrow to bits."

I hunch my shoulders a little tighter and peer over the hood. Miller's already dropped both windshields because snow piles on them and hand wipers don't keep ahead. So snow blows in my eyes unless I keep them squinted. I can hardly see a thing through the dark and snow. Also, the damned jeep's top-heavy with Mundy up high; the back wheels swing right or left with every rut. I'm not sure Miller can push us out if we get stuck on this hill.

Then, suddenly, the barrage lets up. I'm crawling along at less than ten miles an hour. Mel stands on the seat and leans back over Mundy.

"Holy Christ! Here they come! It's a weapons carrier with an eighty-eight and a packed personnel carrier. They're rolling past the bridge now! Jesus, there's another one! The whole road's swarming Krauts; some of them are running up to the château. Let's get the fuck out of here!"

Mel scrunches down, squatting, peering under Mundy now. I don't look back. I need to concentrate or we'll stall or slip. I want to get around the ridge and out of sight. I don't think they can see us much through the snow, but they can hear us and there are tracks. If they come on after us, we've had it.

I keep aiming on the road, using the angle-iron wire cutter we have welded to the bumper. The Germans were supposed to be using piano wire stretched across roads to cut off

American heads, so our motor pool put these cutters on every jeep, like masts on sailing ships. Miller almost had a fistfight with the warrant officer about it. I don't know if the Germans actually did such a thing or if those bits of angle iron would do any good, but right now it helps me aim. The only visual cue I have to go by is a slight opening of white ahead of me where the road winds through the woods. The pitch of the road has leveled off some and now we're going along a cut in the mountain. There's a steep drop on the right side; I hug the left as much as I can without going in the ditch.

I keep telling myself if it's really an attack they won't veer off the main road to come chasing us. We only have to get out of sight and away.

Just then a mortar explodes in front of us; it's close enough so clods of dirt hit the jeep with loud clunking sounds. Then another hits downhill on our right, fragments burying in the hill. I keep bearing down. When the next one hits behind us, between our jeep and Miller's, my first instinct is to stop; then I realize we're bracketed, our only chance is to keep moving. Mel stands up and looks back.

"They're OK, I think! Miller's hunched over the wheel and I can't see Mother, but Miller isn't signaling or anything. Just keep on rolling."

He slides down below the hood again, his knees on the floor of the jeep. I try shifting up one gear and holding to it. We're going about fifteen miles an hour; in the dark and snow it's all I can handle and stay on the road.

The next mortar explodes up on our left; it's close. Fragments ricochet and sing off the jeep. One piece somehow shatters the windshield flat on the hood. There are clangs against metal and a dull thump.

"You hit, Mel?"

"No; Mundy."

"Damn!"

Mel lifts his head again.

"I think they're still OK back there. Another hundred yards and we'll be out of range."

Two more come close but we've passed the place where they can lay one in directly; the ridge is between us. Either they'll chase now or we're out of it. There's a long downhill stretch coming up. I try holding it in second. The road's still only a cut into the side of a hill and I know it's a long drop on the right. I should downshift to low-low again but the panic's strong. We start picking up speed, and when I try braking, we slide. Snow's jammed in the treads and the damned jeep's like a toboggan. I hold her on around the first curve but by the second, we're going too fast.

"I can't make it, Mel! Jump!"

We're going too fast to jump. I keep pumping the brakes and I'm shifted down now but still sliding. I lose control completely. We go off the downhill side and hit sideways against a tree. We spin, bounce against the bank, twist and end up teetering off the deep edge, front first, over a drop of at least forty-five degrees. From our tilted-forward place in the front seat it looks like a cliff. All four wheels are free from the ground and spinning. I turn off the motor. Gordon moves to sit on his seat and the jeep tips farther forward, down.

"Hold it, Mel! We'll go over if we move."

I turn my head; Mundy hasn't budged. As I look, the other jeep pulls up behind us. Miller carefully brakes and comes to a stop. Wilkins jumps out of their jeep, runs toward us.

"You guys all right?"

"We're fine, Mother; but our jeep's about to slide over! Hold us down!"

Miller pulls the emergency on his jeep and leaves the motor running, gets out and comes over. He goes around and looks under our jeep.

"Christ, you guys are on a regular seesaw! Don't move! I'll get the towrope and see if I can pull you off."

We sit still while Miller and Wilkins hook the rope onto our back bumper and their front one. We all keep looking back up that hill, expecting hordes of Huns to charge down at us. Mundy's weight in back is keeping us from tipping over the edge. When the rope's secure, Miller runs to his jeep and begins backing uphill, but all he does is slip, even with the four-wheel drive and chains. He jumps out and runs back again.

"I could go downhill and tie to my back bumper. We'd have the hill in our favor then, but the angles are all wrong; you might go on over the edge. I'll tell you what; I'm going to back up and pull with the rope while you two climb out over Mundy. It should hold."

Before we can say anything, he runs to his jeep, backs up and pulls tight on the slack rope. Mel and I crawl over Mundy and off the back of the jeep. After we're both out, Miller unties the rope from his jeep and rolls downhill past ours. Without us in the front seat our jeep's more secure. Mother ties the rope to Miller's back bumper; Miller begins pulling again. He swings our jeep around but it slips farther over the edge. There's no way to pull it off now.

"Won't and Mother, you get Mundy out of the jeep while I hold it here."

Mother and I cut the satin strips holding the bedspring with Mundy to the jeep. Mel helps lift the whole thing off and lower it to the road. We take out the whitener, the camouflage suits and the 506, stuff them into Miller's jeep. There's no room for the fart sacks. Miller gives another pull but it only gets worse; our jeep's over the edge.

"Won't, cut the rope with your bayonet and stand away so you won't get caught in the whiplash when the rope breaks loose."

I hack away at the rope with my bayonet. The last few strands unravel and break themselves. The jeep twists slowly, then turns around and begins rolling, sliding, down. It hits a few trees but rebounds and disappears in the dark, crashing and picking up momentum. It doesn't explode and finally there's silence. One U.S. jeep at the bottom of a ravine in the Ardennes Forest. Miller puts his brake on again, comes back and stares down the hill.

"That was the best of them, too."

Together we lift Mundy and jam him, feet first, under the mount of our fifty caliber. His head is up at least two feet higher than the top of the gun; he's practically standing up. We all climb in. With the radio, the phones, the rations and all the other crap, there's not much room. I get in front beside Miller and stash the 506 at my feet. Mel and Mother are in back, half under Mundy's bedspring. Miller starts the jeep rolling. Chains sure make a difference.

When we get to where regiment was, there's no one. The snow has covered everything, even the bare spots where our squad tents were. Only the kitchen tent space is still warm enough so there's mud and grass showing. They've been gone for more than twenty hours. We drive in a circle around that regimental area, looking for the jeep, looking for some sign, but there's nothing. Miller stops and turns to me.

"Well, Sergeant Knott, what the fuck do we do now?"

"Christ, I don't know, Bud. What's your idea, Mel?"

"Look for tracks, probably. They couldn't move a whole regimental headquarters without tearing things up."

Mother is staring from behind Mundy out the back of the jeep.

"There could be Germans anywhere around here."

Miller shoves the jeep in gear.

"The best thing is, get moving. The most tracks go off on that road; it's the way out of here, so we go that way. Go west, young men! At least I think it's west."

I'm thinking if we run into any Germans, a squad or more, we give up. We keep looking for tracks but it's practically impossible. The road goes under trees and there, without lights, it's pitch dark. And the snow's coming down harder. We roll along in the dark, jammed together, each of us alone, not talking much. We've all put ourselves in Miller's hands.

Then we come out of the forest and into more or less open farm country. We only know we're on a road from the fence posts along both sides. The snow blows from every direction in gusts and we're miserably cold. Miller slows, stops and turns to me again.

"I don't know where I'm going anymore. I could be driving us straight to Berlin."

Not one of us has a compass. At Shelby we did maybe five hundred field exercises, shooting azimuths, all the rest of it, but we've never used a compass since. I think mine's in my duffel bag somewhere in the kitchen truck. My whole full field pack's in that truck; my whole life, practically.

It's bitching cold. My feet are numb, the fronts of my legs iced to my pants. We're covered with snow except where Mother and Mel are jammed under Mundy. Father Mundy looks like a statue; the snow's stuck to his face and packed in his eye sockets.

I don't know what to do. If we stop, we'll freeze. We can't build a fire; it'd attract any Germans in the vicinity. Also, all the wood's wet and I don't want to waste gasoline just burning it for heat. At the same time, riding along, going nowhere, isn't helping either. But what else?

I climb onto the hood and stretch out holding onto that vertical piece of angle iron. This way I can see better. Miller starts up again. The hood's warm from the motor. As we go along, I give hand signals to keep us on the road but twice we slip into ditches. We use the entrenching tool on the back of our jeep to dig out.

We've gone maybe five more miles when it happens. I'm out in front but I don't see anything. Everything's white against white, but set in darkness. I've lost any ability to separate close from near, up from down. Suddenly the right side drops. Our whole jeep rolls on its side and slowly turns over with the motor still running!

Without even knowing it, we were going over a small unrailed bridge. The drifts are so high it was invisible. It happens slowly so nobody's hurt; even Mel and Mother wiggle out from under Mundy. Miller leaps back to the jeep and turns off the motor.

The jeep's settled upside down, with Father and the fifty caliber jammed into and through the ice of a small running stream.

Together, we slip and struggle in the snow till we've pushed the jeep back onto its wheels. Mundy seems all right. I brush the snow and mud off his face. It's wet from the water and starts to freeze almost immediately.

We're all puffing. Even with four, it's tough righting a jeep in the snow. By the time we're finished, I'm sweaty but my hands and feet are wet and cold. Miller is going around checking. He reaches under the jeep and comes up, his hands smelling of gasoline. He looks at me, then points under the rear end. I get down on my knees. There's a puncture slash in the gas tank and gasoline is coming out in a steady stream at about the same speed and trajectory as horsepiss. Miller shakes his head.

"Must've scraped something going over the edge. There's a gash the length of my hand."

He slides under and packs one of his gloves into the hole,

stoppering it somewhat. We kick snow over the leaked gasoline, then Bud tries turning the motor over but no response. He checks everything under the hood and tries again. Nothing. All four of us push to get her back on the road; but the embankment's too steep. By the time we give up, we're all sweaty and pooped out. The falling snow seems to get thicker, heavier.

We pull Father Mundy from under the fifty caliber. Mother and I carry him up a slight hill to the edge of a wood overlooking the bridge. Miller and Gordon detach the fifty caliber, haul it up, too. The only thing I can see for us to do is dig in, wait for some light and try to find out what's happening. We have enough rations for a few days.

After the fifty's off, we swing back the mount and bend down that wire cutter on the bumper. We shove the jeep as best we can under the bridge. This is a low stone arch and we just clear. We push upstream till it's tucked away. In the process, we get totally soaked in ice water. We've taken off both jerry cans of gasoline. One's full, the other's three-quarters empty from the flambeaux.

Up under the trees it isn't snowing so hard. We take turns digging. First we scrape away the snow and leaves, then work our way through the first few inches of frozen ground with our entrenching tools locked at an angle. After that the digging's easy, dark loamy soil with strings of small roots easily cut. We dig two holes, slit-type trenches, only deeper, with fire steps for sitting at each end. We string our shelter halves as low lean-tos over the holes. Our fart sacks were in that first jeep down the ravine, so we're going to be cold.

We use gas from the jerry cans to soak sticks and brush. That way we get small fires going in our helmets in the holes. Mother and I are together in one hole; Gordon and Miller in the other; Father Mundy is behind and between us. Wilkins and I take off our boots and socks, wring out the socks and try drying them over the fires. There's nothing to be done with our boots. We have a shelter half tucked under us. The top shelter half is stretched so we have a six-inch slit looking down toward the bridge. The smoke goes out the slit but we begin to get warmer. I gnaw on a piece of K lunch cheese and try to forget where we are. Wilkins seems fine, better than I am. The snow's settling on the shelter half, so, except for the smoke, gray against white, we're practically invisible from the road.

At about seven-thirty, before it's even light, but when you can just tell it'll be light soon, I slip on my damp socks and frozen shoes. I slither out of our slit. Miller hears me and crawls out from the other hole. We have the same thing in mind and discuss how to do it. We're being very warlike.

We go down to the jeep. Miller unhitches the fifty-caliber mount and together we carry it uphill. Then the two of us, taking turns, dig a hole outside Miller's slit and set the mount into it, jamming rocks from the streambed around the sides. We haul up an ammo box, lock the fifty into its swivel and feed one end of an ammo belt into the chamber. We'll probably be surrendering within the hour if things're bad as we think, but at least we've carried through. If anyone can hold that damned gun down while it's firing and still hit anything, it's Miller. We go gather more sticks, dip them in the jerry can and scurry back to our holes. We've finished playing soldier. I don't think we exchange more than thirty words through the entire operation, and most of those Father Mundy wouldn't approve. While we're down at the jeep, I also pull our 506 from the front seat. I lower it into the hole with Mother.

The sky's beginning to lighten and it looks as if east is in exactly the opposite direction I thought it would be. From the light, it seems we *were* driving straight to Berlin before we were intercepted by an edgeless bridge. It's one bridge game I wish I could replay; not duplicate, replay.

I warm up the radio and fool around with different frequencies. All I'm picking up is what sounds like German; there are background tank noises. I get two bands of this, surrounded by static; not very encouraging. I'm wishing Shutzer were here; he might have some idea. This kind of "off the cuff" war is his specialty.

Wilkins and I take turns every fifteen minutes keeping an eye on the road. While I'm sitting up, I try to figure out what day it is, the day of the week and the date. I'm completely confused. What's the difference? I also try bearing down on what to do next. I know we can't stay here, and there's no way to get the jeep going. What do we do with Mundy? We could bury him in one of these slit trenches, like a roll of drawings, but I don't want to.

It's almost eight o'clock by Mundy's watch when we begin hearing sounds. There's no mistaking the noise of tanks; it's clanking and metal rumbling, a loud diesel roar like heavy construction machinery. They seem to be coming along the road we're on; only, according to the sun, they're headed east. Maybe they're retreating. Maybe a mob of GIs will come charging behind them, cavalry chasing the redskins back to the reservation. Then we see the real thing!

These are Mark V panthers, with German infantry in black hanging on to the back and top! Automatically I count; eighteen tanks, nine weapons carriers. Our fifty caliber looks like a peashooter. I only hope to hell they don't see the jeep, our tracks or the fifty. Thank God they're going so fast. Please, Miller, don't do it! When they're past and the rattling, ear-pounding din dies down, I look over at Miller and Gordon in the other hole. Bud's behind the fifty; Mel, closer to me, beside him, looks across.

"Did you see those uniforms, those markings. That was honest-to-shit SS!"

Wilkins's face is's white, drained as I know mine must be. God, they looked so hard, so professional, so unbeatable.

"What do you think we should do, Wont? What'll we do?"

"One thing I know, Mother. We'll stay's far away as possible from that bunch; they're *not* the ones we're looking for."

"There really were white skulls and crossbones painted on the sides of the tanks. Did you see that?"

"I saw it, Mother. I saw it. Maybe they're only trying to scare us, but it worked. I'm scared! Anybody have any ideas?"

The silence is sure and deep as the snow in front of us. There's nothing we can do but burrow deeper. I lower myself into the hole and drop enough gasoline-soaked sticks into my helmet to keep a fire going. It's time to think. If there's any wartime use for a creative-artistic-type imagination, this must be it.

Half an hour later I go down to the jeep again. It's definitely light now. East is still in the wrong direction. I find the whitening. I drag up the camouflage suits. I wonder what the squad will think; maybe this will convince them I'm over the edge. We'll have a mutiny. I'll join it. But I can't think of anything else. I signal Mother to come with me and we climb into Miller and Gordon's hole. I explain my idea as best I can. There's something of plotting a trick chess strategy about it: the "play dead" opening. I finish and wait.

"How about the radio?"

"Bury it."

"And the fifty caliber?"

"Bury it."

"Bury the rifles, too?"

"No other way."

Gordon, as usual, asks the hard one.

"If we actually pull this off and get back, what're we going to say?"

"We were captured. They took our weapons. We escaped. They'll have to send us back and clear us then; a few days of luxury. But we stick to our story. I'm betting things are so confused nobody will ask anybody any questions anyway."

Wilkins looks at me as if I'm past all understanding.

"Holy cow!"

"As I said, we do this together or nothing. There's no other way. If anybody has any objections, any at all, you don't have to explain; just speak up now."

There's a long silence. It takes some thinking. It's so typically ASTPR it stinks even worse than the German capture deal. Miller's first.

"I'm for it."

Gordon looks at him, at me.

"Me too. The whole idea's so wild I'd be sorry the rest of my life if we didn't try it. Then again, the rest of my life might just be today."

I turn to Wilkins. He's in a terrible spot.

"Don't let us pressure you, Mother. Make up your own mind."

"Oh, I've already done that. I was only waiting for the other guys so I wouldn't be putting pressure on them. This could be the deepest finesse in squad history."

Wilkins smiles, chalk-faced, but I don't remember if I've ever seen a better smile. It's the smile I needed to make myself do what we're going to do.

. . .

First we paint white circles on our helmets with the
whitener. We slip on the snowsuits. Then I draw a stencil of
a cross on one of my K ration boxes. I cut it out with a
bayonet. Next comes the hardest part. We turn Mundy over.
When we press down on him, blood comes out of his mouth
from his lungs. I soak some of it up on a pad from Wilkins's
aid kit, the last one we have, and I use it to stipple red crosses
on the helmets and on the sleeves of the snowsuits. The blood
is thick, viscous, dark, but mixed with whitening it comes out
red. I almost vomit twice in the process but convince myself
Father wouldn't mind. Maybe we're violating the temple of
the Holy Ghost but it's in a good cause, us. With the white
circles and the blood, there's almost something of a mass going
on, too.

We also paint huge white circles on the shelter halfs. I
dab red crosses, two inches wide and a foot high, in the
middles of these circles. We fold the shelter half corner to
corner and stick the double corner between our helmets and
helmet liners. It makes a kind of cape. When we're finished,
we look like a strange mixture of bridesmaids and extras for
The Three Musketeers.

It's midmorning when we bury the hardware. We put the
506, the fifty caliber, the rifles, the fifty-caliber ammo boxes
and ammo, all the grenades in the trench Wilkins and I dug.
We cover it all with a shelter half pressed down around, then
start kicking dirt over the whole pile. We kick until there's a
mound like a grave. Then we stomp it down and spread snow
over it. When we finish, we're all panting. Mundy's on the
ground beside us. I look around.

"Well, if any of us wants to start a private war someday

after this one's over, we know where to come. This is a burial place I'm not even going to mark."

We muscle Father up and onto our shoulders. We have him covered with our last shelter half, Shutzer's. I've painted a white circle and a red cross on that, too, for airplanes. We're two on a side and the weight isn't impossible but it's heavy. We walk straight down the center of the road.

We've decided the tanks are just as confused as we are, so we walk in the direction they've come from, what looks to us, from the light of dawn at our back, like the west. It doesn't matter all that much.

The walk becomes automatic. We change sides every ten minutes, lowering Mundy to the ground between us and walking around him. There's not much talking. Each stop, we take just enough time to stretch our cramped muscles or take a piss. None of us moves more than a step from Mundy; he's our passport out of this hell.

We walk for hours. We walk past other overturned jeeps, wrecked tanks, bodies. We hardly look. Finally, we walk straight into the outpost of an American engineering company. They've got a bridge all set to blow. We tell them about the tanks we saw going the wrong way. The sergeant on post take us to a lieutenant. We carry Mundy with us.

"What outfit you soldiers with?"

I tell him our regimental number and how we're an I and R observation post that got overrun. He can't keep his eyes off our weird getups.

"What the hell's with the costumes; you guys medics?"

I tell him something of how we got here.

"You soldiers are taking one hell of a chance, you know. Some cute buck ass brass's liable to pull a Geneva Convention on this one."

Then he laughs.

"I'll be damned. The whole fucking war's gone to hell."

"Yes, sir."

"OK, get on with it. Have my men at the other post lead you past our mines. We have anti-tank mines in the road back there. You probably couldn't trigger one just stepping on it, but no sense taking chances."

"Yes, sir."

The GIs on the other post give us cigarettes and breakfast K rations. We eat the rations before we set out again. Nothing matters much except not getting killed. These guys are sure they're surrounded, so we aren't home free by a long shot.

It's about five, almost dark, when we're challenged again. They yell out the first part of a password.

"We don't know the counter. We're coming from another sector."

"Stay just where you are."

"We're Americans."

"Says you!"

A sergeant comes walking out to us in a crouch with his carbine at the ready. When he sees us, he puts it down.

"All right. I believe you. My God, where'd you get those crazy outfits? Is that blood?"

As we go back, we give him our "escape" story. This is a division I never even heard of. They've come up from the Saar, part of Patton's army. He advises us to wipe the crosses off before we go any farther. We leave the shelter halfs.

He has a PFC lead us back to battalion headquarters where we jump in a truck that'll take us to our own outfit. They're a bit pissed when we insist on hauling Father with us.

We get driven all the way to division headquarters. When we get there, we tell them we were captured and escaped. After that, Wilkins and I take Mundy over to the grave registrar. There's a tent filled with bodies. The T4 who's in charge says none of these are from our division; they're all strays.

"Some of them have been on the ground since before the snow."

I wonder if anyone's found the bodies back by our château yet, both the ones from before we came and the ones we left.

We watch while the T4 snips off Mundy's dog tags. He forces one between Father's teeth and puts the other in a dark green string sack. He asks me Mundy's outfit. I tell him. He pulls out a wired tag and prints Mundy's name out on it, serial number and C for Catholic, reading from the dog tag between Mundy's teeth. He opens the mummy bag and wires it around Father's wrist. He stares at the golden satin quilt we wrapped Mundy in, then spreads a GI blanket over his whole body, covering his face. Mundy's so tall his bare feet stick out. We walk away before the T4 can ask any questions.

Two days later, we're taken in jeeps about ten miles forward to our regimental headquarters. I'm called straight in to Ware. I tell our "escape" story again. He buys it. I want to get away. Inside I seem to be melting; the shakes are grabbing me. But Ware can keep me there talking as long as he wants. I'm trying not to cry in front of him.

"Did the rest of the squad get out?"

"Yes, sir."

"How about the jeeps and the radio?"

"We had to abandon them, sir."

"Even the fifty caliber, your rifles?"

"Germans took the rifles, sir."

"Jesus Christ!"

"We got Mundy out, sir."

I don't know why I tell him. It's none of his business; he doesn't care. But it seems important.

"You escaped and you took Mundy?"

"Yes, sir. We went back and got him. We carried him out as if we were medics."

"Shit! Don't tell Love that!"

"Yes, sir."

"You let *me* report this. Don't say anything about bringing Mundy out. My God, how the hell far did you carry him?"

"Don't know, sir."

"God damn!"

"Any news about the first squad, sir?"

"Nothing.

"By the way, I did my best to leave you a radio and jeep when we pulled out, but every vehicle was needed for regimental supplies. There was nothing I could do."

I want to ask right then about Shutzer but my throat's stuck. If I open my mouth, I'll cry, scream or attack a commissioned officer. I just salute, turn around and walk away as if he's dismissed me.

I wander into the kitchen tent and crawl behind big pots full of hot water for washing mess kits. I'm between them and the wall of the tent. I don't know where Wilkins, Miller and Gordon are. I hope they've found shelter halfs and fart sacks; I'm too tired, too washed out to check. I curl up there on a shelter half where it's warm. I'm to a place where only sleep will do.

I wake. Ware is standing over me kicking my feet. I have a hard time struggling up, groggy, like a drunk.

"You don't have to get up, Knott. I only wanted to tell you I got it all worked out."

I steady myself onto my feet, brushing my knees.

"I saw Major Love. It's all settled. He says since you weren't in a POW compound you won't need to go through the whole shitload of clearance."

He pauses.

"We're going to fill out the I and R platoon with the old anti-tank group they broke up. Who do you suggest for non-coms?"

I can't think. Nothing makes sense.

"I don't know, sir."

"I thought Gordon for sergeant of the other squad and Miller as your assistant. There's one pissass corporal coming in; he can work with Gordon."

"Yes, sir."

"I've put in a Bronze Star for Wilkins. Love's signed the citation but he's not happy. I also got Wilkins reassigned to the security squad."

"Thank you, sir."

I'm ready to try it.

"Sir, how's Shutzer doing?"

"Real TS. Dead before we even got back. There wasn't much we could do on the trip out. That Kraut was dead, too; no chance to interrogate him."

I don't say anything. I only want Ware to go away. I want to be alone on the ground again.

"I almost forgot, Sergeant. You'll need to make out Statements of Charges for the jeeps, the radio and phones. I don't know about the rifles and fifty caliber. Since you were captured, I don't think there'll be any trouble."

He reaches into his breast pocket and hands the forms to me. I'm beginning to feel cool, not cold, only cool, not part of things.

"We lost a twenty-power scope, too, sir."

"Don't worry about it; just take your time and rest up. We'll be pulling out of here soon; going to push those fucking Krauts all the way back to Berlin."

He smiles and we salute. I can see so clearly. Everything's in very clear focus but I don't have clear vision.

I see the edge around the insignia on Ware's helmet liner where it used to be gold before he made first. I see bits of yellow sleep in the corners of his eyes.

I look down and see the dark green of winter grass on the floor of the kitchen tent where it's been smashed into the mud.

I see the steaming and hear the sizzling of dirty, galvanized fifty-gallon cans of water being heated to wash mess kits.

I smell grease in the hot water.

I hear drippings from snow melting off the top of this warm tent.

A NOTE ON THE TYPE

This book was set on the Linotype in Janson, a recutting
made directly from type cast from matrices long thought
to have been made by the Dutchman Anton Janson,
who was a practicing type founder in Leipzig during
the years 1668–87. However, it has been conclusively
demonstrated that these types are actually the work of
Nicholas Kis (1650–1702), a Hungarian, who most
probably learned his trade from the master Dutch type
founder Dirk Voskens. The type is an excellent example
of the influential and sturdy Dutch types that prevailed
in England up to the time William Caslon developed
his own incomparable designs from them.

Composed by Maryland Linotype Composition
Company, Baltimore, Maryland. Printed and bound
by Haddon Craftsmen, Scranton, Pennsylvania.

Designed by Judith Henry.